Kate Lawson was born on the edge of the Fens and is perfectly placed to write about the vagaries of life in East Anglia. In between moving house, raising a family, singing in a choir, walking the dog, working in the garden, taking endless photos and cooking, Kate is also a scriptwriter, originating and developing a soap opera for local radio, along with a pantomime for the town in which she lives.

Writing as Gemma Fox, Kate was short-listed for the Melissa Nathan Comedy Romance Award in 2006.

In various other guises Kate has had 12 erotic novels published, and as Sue Welfare published six romantic comedies, two of which are currently under development for TV. Her comedy 'Write Back Home' was part of the 1999 Channel Four Sitcom Festival. Most recently Kate has been working with BBC Voices on a variety of ongoing writing projects.

Please visit www.katelawson.co.uk for more information about Kate Lawson.

Visit www.AuthorTracker.co.uk for exclusive updates on Kate Lawson.

KATE LAWSON

Mum's the Word

AVON

AVON

A division of HarperCollins*Publishers*
77–85 Fulham Palace Road,
London W6 8JB

www.harpercollins.co.uk

A Paperback Original 2008

First published in Great Britain by
HarperCollins*Publishers* 2008

Copyright © Kate Lawson 2008

Kate Lawson asserts the moral right to
be identified as the author of this work

Extract from Kate Lawson's new novel © Kate Lawson 2008.
This is taken from uncorrected material and does not necessarily reflect the final book.

A catalogue record for this book is
available from the British Library

ISBN-13: 978-1-84756-052-0

Set in Minion by Palimpsest Book Production Ltd,
Grangemouth, Stirlingshire

Printed and bound in Great Britain by
Clays Ltd, St Ives plc

Mixed Sources
Product group from well-managed
forests and other controlled sources
www.fsc.org Cert no. SW-COC-1806
© 1996 Forest Stewardship Council

FSC

FSC is a non-profit international organisation established to promote the
responsible management of the world's forests. Products carrying the FSC
label are independently certified to assure consumers that they come
from forests that are managed to meet the social, economic and
ecological needs of present and future generations.

Find out more about HarperCollins and the environment at
www.harpercollins.co.uk/green

With special thanks to Maggie Phillips at Ed Victor, Max and the team at HC and Phil, who had no idea when we got together what sharing life with a writer would be like. He has now . . .

To Phil, and my family and friends – you know who you are. Oh and my sister Angela, who keeps complaining that she never has anything dedicated to her.
With love, K x

Chapter 1

'Candles, corkscrew, wine . . .' Susie's gaze moved slowly across the table, which was standing in the bay window of the sitting room, overlooking the garden. It was early summer and still warm, the long day just beginning to soften into evening. A breeze, gently strumming the leaves on next door's laburnum, brought the heat down to a gentle purr.

Through the open windows, a string of fairy lights strung between the branches of the trees, bright as glow worms, twinkled and shimmered, picking out the shrubs and pots on the terrace, while the honeysuckle and glittering dark green climbers rambled nonchalantly up over the wicker trellis, perfuming the air – the whole thing set off by the golden glow of the sun sinking in the west.

'Serving spoons, salt and pepper.' Susie glanced up at the clock; another ten minutes and Robert ought to be arriving, always assuming he wasn't late. Time, as Robert had once pointed out, wasn't really his strong suit. Although actually it wasn't time that was Robert's problem, it was punctuality that gave him the slip.

1

He seemed to think people had nothing better to do than wait for him, which was why Susie had cooked a casserole – although her instincts told her that tonight he would be on time. Tonight was special. Memorable. Important.

She smiled and tweaked the curtains straight. The sitting room looked wonderful, like something out of the Sunday supplements. *Susie Reed entertains at home in her stylish Norfolk country cottage.*

There was a vase of pink peonies in the centre of the table and acres of lighted candles arranged on various shelves and side tables close by, reflecting and glittering in the only two crystal glasses to have survived marriage, children, divorce and now singledom in the cottage on the edge of Sheldon Common. There were French-blue cotton napkins, casually folded and dropped onto the side plates – Susie didn't want to look as if she was trying too hard; spotless matching cutlery – Robert had a whole thing about smears and the odd bit of broccoli welded on by the dishwasher; alongside a little dish of pitted olives and some breadsticks.

In the oven the main course – chicken breasts, tiny button mushrooms, roast garlic, spring onions, ginger, cashew nuts and strips of red pepper – was doing interesting things in a clear stock.

While Susie patted and fluffed and tweaked, Milo, her mongrel, watched her from the rag rug in front of the hearth, wondering about chicken division vis-à-vis faithful hounds and long-standing lovers.

'*Susie, there is something I really need to talk to you*

about,' Robert had said when he'd popped by on Tuesday evening on his way home from work. He had looked very earnest. '*I think that we really need to talk about the future.*'

The future. Susie smiled, and then huffed on a serving spoon before giving it a brisk once-over with a tea towel.

They had been going out for the best part of three years. Robert wasn't exactly the kind of man she had ever imagined herself settling down and growing old with, but he was a nice guy. He could sometimes be a bit overbearing – pompous and snobby was how her sister had once described him, but then she was married to a man who thought anything you didn't grow, catch or shoot yourself was fast food, so she was hardly in a position to talk about peculiar male habits.

Robert was bright and reliable, intelligent, and even though he didn't do fun very often, he was presentable. Presentable, and tall, and well-dressed, and forty-six; he liked dogs and was a bit public school and, okay, yes, he was just a teensy-weensy bit on the bald side, but nothing that couldn't be coped with – after all, we all have faults – and he was rather endearing, and she loved him.

Susie glanced up at her reflection, caught in the mirror above the fireplace. Candlelight was a good choice, she thought, screwing up her eyes to focus. She looked fabulous, or perhaps it was just that she wasn't wearing her glasses.

'*There is something important that I want to discuss,*' he'd said. '*To be honest I don't feel I can leave it any longer.*'

Something important that couldn't wait any longer. She set the spoon back down on the table. Moving in together? Maybe marriage? Maybe both?

Would she change her name? Mrs Robert Harrison ... Mrs Susie Reed, wife of Mr Robert Harrison ... Or would they be hyphenated? Mr and Mrs Reed-Harrison; or did Harrison-Reed sound better? *The Reed-Harrisons entertain at home in their stylish Norfolk country home.*

Susie was wearing a long, elegant cream linen dress, with low-heeled brown leather sandals and some chunky wooden jewellery, although not too much because Robert wasn't keen on frills and had a 'strictly no fluff, feathers or sequins' policy, since he'd been rushed to casualty with a bugle bead up his nose after a particularly raucous scout-gang show. Not that she had many of those kind of things in her wardrobe, but she might have a mad moment, a show-tune, corset, kitten-heeled mule and fishtail frock afternoon.

If pressed, Robert said that he preferred white cotton underwear from Marks and Sparks. Unlike her ex-husband, Robert had never bought Susie anything black and red with suspenders for Christmas that needed taking back. Obviously Robert just didn't see her as that kind of woman, and Susie wasn't sure if she should be pleased by that or not ...

'Dessert spoons,' Susie murmured thoughtfully, touching them with her fingertips. She'd made this thing from the cookery page of the local paper for dessert, with summer fruits, double cream and Muscovado – it was currently chilling in the fridge. She planned to serve it with Florentines from Waitrose, after garnishing the top with a couple of fat raspberries and a mint leaf, all dusted down with a quick flick of icing sugar. It looked great in the photo.

Robert worked in the Environment Agency, doing something which mostly seemed to involve wearing a dark suit, sending memos, having meetings and getting really grumpy by Wednesday afternoon. They'd met at Sheldon Common's annual midsummer's dinner dance in the village tithe barn. He'd looked very good in black tie.

He'd said, 'Are you the woman with the long-eared hairy mongrel who's bought Isaac's Cottage?'

Hardly a chat-up line to make a woman go weak at the knees, but she'd never seen herself as high maintenance and didn't trust flash, so it wasn't a bad opening. Apparently he had always loved the cottage, seen it every day for years as he drove home from work – and before she knew it Susie was inviting him round to take a look at what she'd done by way of renovations. He'd arrived the next day with a decent bottle of red – a good sign – she'd cooked a spag bol and they'd been seeing each other ever since.

Robert was a little more staid and sensible than she would prefer in a perfect world, but Susie was getting to the point of thinking that maybe staid and sensible might be a good thing. She'd done her share of unreliable, lying, two-timing bastards. She'd been married to one for the best part of fifteen years, and once really was enough. Maybe staid and reliable was the new rock and roll.

And besides, Robert was good with power tools and

he'd got a pension plan and a good income and was always on about the future and financial security. It wasn't that Susie couldn't manage on her own – she could manage very well indeed and had done for years – it was just that she preferred life when there was someone to share it with, and when she considered it long and hard, Robert Harrison, if not exactly Mr Right, came out very high on the Mr Could-Do-a-Lot-Worse index.

In the kitchen the timer went ping, and while Susie wondered how she would say yes, she practised gliding effortlessly across the floor like a nun she had once seen in a film, and reconsidered the possibilities. Should she smile and say, 'Oh Robert, of course,' or should she make him wait, explain that she needed time to think. Or maybe she should just smile winsomely and nod, all bright-eyed and overcome by emotion.

She bobbed down to open the oven door, the heat hitting her like a slap before Susie carefully manoeuvred the cast-iron pot up onto the worktop, imagining she was Delia.

'And here we are, piping hot and ready to serve – smells absolutely wonderful, doesn't it? Let's have a little look, shall we?'

Susie lifted the lid; the chicken casserole was done to a turn, perfect. There were tiny new potatoes, sugar-snap peas and baby carrots in the steamer to go with it. She dipped a spoon in the sauce – maybe it needed just a tiny bit more pepper. Susie had brought a handful of chives in from the garden to chop up and sprinkle on top just before serving, hoping Robert wouldn't be late. *'And now, having adjusted the seasoning, just a few chives on the top to garnish – if you haven't got chives you can always use a little freshly chopped parsley.'*

Susie had had to stop being Delia out loud since dating Robert; nor was he keen on her being the woman on *Gardeners' Question Time*, or Linda Barker when she was decorating either. She'd made a conscious decision to spare him the full Nigella. He'd said very early on in their relationship that he found it unnerving to hear people talking to themselves.

She looked round at the cosy kitchen and let her mind wander. Would they sell up and buy somewhere together? And what happened if Robert wanted a bungalow and she fell in love with a place with blackened beams and an ingle nook? What if he had always hankered to live on that horrible little housing estate near his fat, miserable sister and Susie couldn't resist the lure of a narrowboat? Maybe renting somewhere together first was a better idea. Would he go down on one knee? More to the point, would he be able to get back up again, given the state of his back?

Susie sighed. None of this was straightforward at all, and it hadn't got any easier since she'd got older. Still the same questions, still the same hopes and fears – nothing any simpler just because you were over forty.

You wait three years for someone to pop the question and when the moment finally arrives, all your brain can do is come up with excuses, obstacles, shortcomings and an internal commentary that wouldn't be out of place on a daytime TV phone-in. Bloody thing. Worse still, it had been doing it all week; she was exhausted from weighing and reweighing the possibilities, the pros and cons.

Susie opened the fridge door and peered inside. They were going to have a little roule of salmon pâté for starters, whizzed in the blender, rolled up in a smoked-salmon sleeve and then cut into slices and served with melba toast – all of which was busy chilling inside a mould at the moment. She had thought about doing big meaty prawns on mixed salad leaves, trickled with chilli dressing and served with wedges of lime, but realistically, who wanted to kiss a hand that had been peeling prawns all afternoon?

Would they get married at the local registry office? she wondered.

First time around she'd been nineteen and living with Andy in a bedsit in Cambridge. He'd rolled in at three o'clock in the morning, drunk as a skunk, and before she could ask him where the hell he'd been, he'd said, 'I was thinking, babe, maybe we ought to get hitched – what d'ya reckon?'

But second marriages were different, they were about knowing what you wanted, and knowing that it was totally unreasonable to expect someone else to provide it for you. Second marriages were not about children or convention or being able to share a bed when you stayed at your parents' house, they were about wanting to be together, about wanting to say that this is it. Second marriages were about who you are, not what you planned to be.

Maybe they'd jet off to somewhere hot and foreign? Get married under a palm tree, barefoot and suntanned on the white coral sands of a tropical beach. Mind you, Robert was careful with his money so that wasn't likely, and besides he was prone to heat stroke and sweat rash, so maybe they should think about one of those new wedding venues: a quaint, out-of-the-way hotel in the Cotswolds, an old railway station in Gwent or a castle in the Scottish highlands. Much simpler when you just bought a white meringue of a dress and hotfooted it to the local church like she'd done the first time. God, marriage was a minefield – and then there would be the question of the frock, and who to invite . . .

Just then the doorbell rang. Smiling, Susie whipped off her apron, took one last glance in the mirror, added a deep breath and hurried down the hallway towards the front door.

She was considering the guest list as she reached the door; there was her dad, his parents, her brother and sister, his brother and sister, her kids, her friends, the guys from work . . .

'I've told you before just to come straight in,' Susie said, wiping her hands and pulling the door open. 'It's silly to ring the bell after all this ti—'

'Hi Mum, thank god you're in, I was going to ring only I haven't got any credit on my phone. Have you got some money for the cab?'

'Jack?' Susie stared at her son. 'What on earth are you doing here? You're supposed to be in Italy.'

Jack shuffled uncomfortably under her scrutiny, moving his weight from foot to foot. He was wearing long khaki shorts, battered army boots, a tour tee shirt that had, once upon a time in a universe far, far away, been black, and he smelt as if he needed a shower, badly.

'I am. Well, technically I am. We got a call out of the blue, we've got some big presentation to do and the budget won't run to flying the funders out there – they're not the kind of guys who do bargain bucket and buses. It's all gone a bit belly-up really.' He grinned and leant in a little closer, kissing her on the cheek, a couple of days' stubble catching her like a rasp. 'I've only just got back; the flight was delayed. I went round to the flat –' His voice cracked a little. 'Ellie's gone. I mean, I'm not surprised really, things have been a bit flaky over the last couple of months. Although I thought at least she would have waited till I got back home before buggering off.'

Susie stared at him. 'Gone? Oh, I'm so sorry, Jack, I hadn't realised things were that bad between you two – but I don't understand, why didn't you stay there?'

'Apparently she's sublet the bloody flat while I was away. I mean, how mean is that? They're in there till September – two guys from the university. They did say I could crash on the floor if I wanted to, till I got myself sorted out, but it didn't seem right. So I came here, I didn't think you'd mind.'

Susie didn't move. God, did you *never* get time off from being a mother? Given the circumstances, how could she tell him that she *did* mind, that in fact she minded quite a lot? That today, any minute now in fact, Mr Could-do-a-lot-Worse was popping round to change her life forever.

Jack lifted his nose like a hungry whippet and sniffed the air. 'Something smells good. Nice frock, by the way. Going out somewhere, are you? Oh, and have you got that money, only I think the guy in the taxi's still got his meter running?'

There was a little pause and then Susie picked up her bag from the hallstand, handed Jack two twenty-pound notes and watched him bound back down the path towards the waiting cab. She distinctly heard him say, 'You're all right, keep the change, mate – yeah, no sweat, thanks. Have a good un.' And then he jogged back towards the door and moseyed on past her into the hallway, shimmying his rucksack off one shoulder as he went and dropping it at the bottom of the stairs where it landed with a damp thud.

'Cottage looks really great, Mum. I'll stick my stuff upstairs, shall I?' He bent down and started to unfasten the straps on his bag.

'What exactly are you doing?' asked Susie.

'Just getting a few bits out. Where do you want the washing? Down here or upstairs? I thought I'd stick a load in straight away – you know.'

The smell from the open rucksack would have blistered paint.

'Whoa, Jack, can you just hang on a minute? You can't just barge in here expecting –' She stopped for a moment as he pulled that hurt, unloved puppy face he'd perfected as a toddler. '– expecting to be welcomed with open arms. First of all I haven't finished doing up the spare room yet, it's all flat packs, bare plaster and floorboards at the moment, and secondly

11

I'm expecting a friend round for supper any minute now.'

'Not a problem,' said Jack cheerfully, scooping out his dirty washing onto the hall floor. 'I don't mind camping out, I'm not fussy, I've got my sleeping bag – and I'll watch TV in the kitchen while your friend's here. Don't mind me, I'll keep the noise down. God, I'm famished, is it all right if I whip myself up a sandwich? You've got it really nice in here. And I love what you've done with the garden.'

Susie stared at him. 'Actually, Jack, I'm really sorry but at the moment I don't think staying here is a ver—' she began, just as Robert stepped in through the front door.

'Susie,' Robert said, taken by surprise. If anything he looked even more earnest than normal, not to mention a little balder, paler and very, very tense. For a few moments he didn't appear to notice Jack squatting down beside the rucksack.

'How are you?' he said.

Susie looked up at him, trying to work out whether it was nerves or if he was sickening for something. 'Are you okay?'

'Yes, I'm fine,' he said dismissively. 'I've been thinking over what I want to say to you for some time – the thing is, Susie –' He paused, nose wrinkling. 'Good god, what on earth is that terrible smell?'

Jack, who was sitting on the bottom of the stairs, looked up and grinned. 'Hi there, Robert. How's it going?' He was holding a bundle of rancid socks which he dropped casually onto the floor before getting up and holding out a hand.

12

Susie saw Robert stiffen; Jack wiped his hands on his shorts and tried again. Robert ignored him and turned his attention back to Susie.

'Look, I'm most terribly sorry but I really can't stay,' said Robert.

'What do you mean, you can't stay? I've cooked supper,' Susie said, completely wrong-footed. 'Salmon roule and summer chicken; it's free-range. And I've done a pudding.'

Robert glanced back over his shoulder as if checking that he could still find the way out. 'Oh, I didn't realise,' he said. 'I wasn't expecting you to go to any trouble. You know, not cook or anything.'

Susie stared at him. 'What do you mean, *not go to any trouble*, Robert? I always cook when you come over. You know I do, I just thought tonight I'd do us something special . . .'

For the last three years they'd spent almost every weekend together, taking it in turns to stay at each other's houses, cooking for one other. What was so different about tonight of all nights?

Robert glanced down at Jack and then said, 'Look, is there any chance that your mother and I can have this conversation privately?' He felt around for a name and when none came continued, 'The thing is, I really need to get going.' And before either Jack or Susie had time to react, he said, 'Actually, there is no good time to tell you this; the thing is, I've been thinking a lot recently, Susie, and I want you to understand that I've not come to this decision lightly.' The words all tumbled out on one long breath as if

13

there was some chance he might run out of air or resolve.

'Jack, will you please go?' snapped Susie. Whatever Robert was going to say, the last thing she wanted was for it to be in front of her twenty-four-year-old son.

Jack pulled a face. 'What?'

'Please, Jack. Just go, will you?'

'Sure,' he said, looking hard done by. He started to get up. Slowly. Susie quelled a throwback impulse to smack his legs; couldn't he see that he should make himself scarce? And quickly. Frustration and bewilderment bubbled up inside her. This wasn't how she had anticipated this evening going *at all*.

'And can you take all this with you?' she said, waving at the heaving mass of washing.

'I was going to put it in the machine,' he protested.

'*Now*, please, Jack,' she growled.

Reluctantly and still at a glacial speed, Jack picked the backpack up. As she turned her attention back to Robert, he sloped off towards the kitchen grumbling to himself.

He'd barely closed the kitchen door when Robert said, 'Look, I'm sorry, Susie, there's really no easy way to say this. The thing is – I've been thinking about this for some time now. What I really want is a family.'

'What?' It felt like the floor had fallen away. She re-ran the words in her head, trying to grasp what they meant, while Robert pressed on.

'I've been mulling the idea over for a long time now, thinking that these feelings, my needs, would go away, but they haven't. If anything they've got more intense. To be honest, I've been so depressed over the last few months, Susie. When we've been together I keep thinking to myself: Is this all there is, is this all there is to look forward to – *is this my life?*' he said glumly, lifting his hands to encompass him, her, her life, her home, her dog. 'Susie, the truth is that what I really want is to settle down and have a family. I want to have a baby.'

She stared at him, struggling for breath, not sure whether to burst into tears or punch his lights out.

'What do you mean "have a baby"?' she said, finding her voice. 'I'm forty-five, Robert, I've got a baby, I've got two grown-up babies.' She waved towards the kitchen door where, by the sound of it, one of them was raiding the larder. 'I've already done that, I'm too –'

And then the penny dropped. 'You don't mean with me, do you?' she whispered. 'You don't want *us* to have a baby, do you?'

'I have thought about it, but as you say, Susie, you've already done it. You don't want to go back to that place – even if you could. And I mean, it isn't that likely, is it? Not at your age – not that you're that old but, you know, babies, all that falling fertility and everything.'

Susie stared at him, wondering if he had any idea what he was saying or how it made her feel.

Robert sighed. 'I didn't want it to be like this, Susie, really I didn't – I thought it would go away.'

'Robert, you're nearly forty-seven.'

'I know, that's the whole point. I keep thinking that if I don't have children soon I'm never going to have them. And I'd like more than one, probably two, possibly even three, and I'd really like to start having them before I'm fifty – I mean, after that I think you're *too* old, don't you?'

Please god he was being rhetorical, thought Susie, as she carried on staring, not certain what to say, all the words and thoughts and pain and anger and hurt and indignation and the downright ridiculousness of it all snarled like a motorway pile-up in the back of her throat.

And then, against all the odds, Susie started to laugh. It was a close-run thing as to who was more surprised, she or Robert, but as she laughed some more he stared at her in horror.

'I don't see why on earth you're laughing, Susie. This isn't funny, this is my future we're talking about,' he said indignantly.

She was laughing so hard now that she could barely breathe. 'You're right, Robert, this isn't funny, it's crazy. It's madness. For a start you can't just summon up a family, you need to find the right person,' she said, struggling with a giggle.

'I have to take the chance, Susie. This may be my last shot,' he said, his colour rising rapidly.

Susie shook her head, not picking up on the cheap joke, the laughter not abating. If anything she was laughing harder, tears rolling down her face. 'Oh, Robert,' she said, opening the front door for him. 'Best you go and have a baby then. Take care.'

Robert stood for a second or two, looking bemused. 'Look, Susie – you have to understand. It's just that we want different things.'

She stared at him. 'How was I supposed to know that?' she said.

As he moved she noticed the last of the sunlight glinting on his bald patch. He looked uncomfortable and pained. 'I'm sorry, Susie. I didn't want to hurt you,' he said, as if that made it all right.

'Too late,' Susie said, guiding him back towards the door.

'I'll ring, maybe we could talk, maybe I could pop over later in the week?'

'Please don't bother on my account,' she said, closing the door behind him. There was a fragile silence and then the tears that had come with the laughter turned into great, wailing, miserable sobs; sobs that consumed her whole; sobs so huge that she could barely breathe. Bastard. *The bastard.*

Jesus Christ, how could she have been so totally stupid, so totally blind? Susie sat down on the bottom of the stairs feeling so many things, some of which she hadn't got a name for – and then, very slowly, the kitchen door opened.

'Mum? You okay?' asked Jack, peering round the door.

'No, not really, but I will be, just give me a minute or two,' she said, backhanding the tears away.

He sat down beside her and put his arm around her, gently. 'You want to tell me about it?' he said, handing her half a dozen squares of kitchen roll.

Susie shook her head, infinitely touched by his gentleness and concern. 'This isn't how it works, I'm the grown-up here. I'm supposed to look after you,' she said, between sobs.

He leant closer. 'In that case, is it all right if I have some of that casserole, only it smells wonderful? And the veggies are done. The pinger just went – I've switched them off. Do you want to come in here and Delia or shall I?'

Chapter 2

It was a horrible, long, long night. Susie slept fitfully, and when she slept she dreamt she had been jilted by a grumpy bald taxi driver who had driven over from Italy. He left the meter running. Delia was there. She'd brought along a large box of homemade biscuits and a twice-baked lemon soufflé; they ate it over coffee, sitting on the flat-pack boxes in the spare bedroom. The great secret for a successful soufflé, apparently, was to fold the ingredients into the egg whites, never beating them, and to use a spotlessly clean bowl. Susie had to pay the taxi driver with a cheque.

In the post the next morning was a catalogue full of really useful things for the more mature shopper, things to help pick your socks up off the floor with a clawed pincer on the end, an A4 plastic magnifying sheet for reading newspapers and one of those big single faux suede slippers, modelled by a blonde thirty-five-year-old in a bri-nylon floral housecoat. Jack was thumbing through it when Susie came downstairs to the kitchen, feeling like hell.

Outside in the back garden, the trellis, the terrace and

most of the bay hedge was festooned with socks, tee shirts and underpants. It looked like the bunting for an orgy.

'Someone's been busy,' said Susie, settling herself into a chair by the kitchen table. She felt tired and frail and headachy, as if she was sickening for something. Her eyes had puffed up like doughnuts from a combination of sleeplessness and crying. She made an effort to corral her thoughts, not letting them stray anywhere near the sore, turbulent wilderness that threatened to engulf her. 'Had you not thought of using the washing line?' she asked.

Jack looked up at her; he had a mouth full of breakfast cereal and was currently shovelling more out of a blue and white striped pudding basin. 'Uh?'

'The washing line? The rotary thing.'

'I couldn't fathom out how to work it.' He jabbed with his spoon towards the catalogue. 'You know, there is some really cool stuff in here, there are these things that hold bin bags open for garden rubbish, solar-powered rocks – and then there's this springy stainless-steel nipper for opening jars, looks like some sort of weapon from *Star Wars*. Cool.' He mimed frisbeeing the jar opener across the room with accompanying space noises before turning the page on to the insect-shaped boot scraper and shoe jack selection. 'How are you feeling this morning?'

'Probably best not to ask.' Optimistically, Susie leant over and picked up the teapot from the table. It was cold and empty; across the kitchen Jack's tea bag lay resplendent on the top of the cooker in a little venal bleed of tannin.

'And I couldn't find the pegs either.'

'Your father would be so proud. Now, would you like to tell me what your plans are?' she said, pointedly setting the little enamel bucket marked pegs onto the table alongside him.

'I have to have plans?' Jack asked, looking at her. 'The love of my life has given me the old heave-ho, sublet my home and sent all my stuff to Oxfam; I've just walked out of a job I loved, I've got nowhere to live and I'm supposed to have *plans*?'

'Uh-huh,' said Susie, while refilling the kettle and prising open the biscuit tin. 'Life's a bitch, and anyway you told me you'd come home to do a presentation.'

'Well, I have – walking out of my job was more of a metaphor for the general chaos and hopelessness in my life at the moment. Ellie's always saying how much pressure it puts on our relationship, what with me travelling, never being there for her, and money is always an issue. Her dad was the same when she was a kid, and she keeps saying she doesn't want to end up like her mum. I can see her point, although I haven't got a woman in every port like Simon. I was thinking maybe I ought to jack it in – get a proper job, there's plenty of work in Cambridge, maybe take up a career in telesales, or maybe I could stay around here for a while?'

Susie stared at him. 'In which reality would that be?'

'God, you're a hard woman,' he said. 'I thought you'd understand – you're my mother, you're supposed to love me unconditionally, help me out in times of need and not be offended or hurt that I only ring you when I want something.'

Susie shook her head. 'See, this is why I always tell people, read the small print,' she said, handing him the biscuit tin. 'And why on earth didn't you go to your dad's last night? He lives a lot closer to the university than coming all the way out here.'

There was a short, weighed pause as Jack sorted through the Rich Tea to find the last chocolate digestive. 'He's a hard man,' said Jack.

'He's a complete pussycat; he just won't take any crap. And he most certainly wouldn't have paid for your sodding taxi,' said Susie as she opened the fridge.

'He's on holiday,' said Jack.

Susie lifted an eyebrow.

'Well, I think he is – he didn't answer the doorbell.'

There was no milk left – although, thoughtfully, Jack had put the empty carton back in the fridge door.

She glanced up. Jack opened his mouth, still half-full of chocolate digestive, but before he could speak, Susie said, 'I suggest that if you know what's good for you, you'll abandon what remains of your cereal-a-thon, get your butt down to the post office and get me some milk. Or else.'

'Right you are,' Jack said, pushing himself to his feet. At the back door he hesitated and patted the pockets of his jeans, then turned to speak. 'I don't suppose –' he began.

Susie growled, 'Don't even think about it.'

'Fair enough. Oh, and by the way,' said Jack as he stepped outside, 'Alice rang, she said would you ring her back ASAP if not sooner.'

'Your sister?'

'Do you know anyone else called Alice who's that bossy?'

'Did she say what she wanted?'

'What makes you think she wanted anything?'

'I gave birth to her, why else would she ring?'

'You're really not a morning person, are you?' said Jack, and then, grinning, he ran down the path to avoid the empty milk carton winging its way towards him.

When he was gone Susie sat down at the table and rested her head on her hands. In the silence all she could think about was Robert, even though she tried very hard not to.

Robert. Robert Harrison, Robert David I-want-a-baby Harrison.

The idea of having another baby had played on her mind all night long. Even if it were possible would she want to do it? Would she want to go back to the beginning and start over? And would she really want to do it with Robert? It would be like going back in time, and she had no desire at all to go back there, not to the sleepless nights, the constant tiredness, the worry, the total responsibility. She realised that she had fondly imagined growing old with Robert, but long before senility set in, being carefree, eating out, travelling, going on long holidays, swapping Christmas with the family for Christmas in a beachside cabin in the Caribbean. Having a great time together, not sitting up half the night with a hot, miserable toddler in her arms as she soothed away measles or a sore throat.

It had been fine when she was in her twenties – she'd had years of being sensible and responsible, and the energy to do it – and although Andy hadn't been the greatest husband in the world he was a natural as a father. But she didn't want to do it now, not now when there were other fish to fry. On the other hand, the trouble was that not wanting another family, not being broody for Robert's children, made her feel old. The face in the mirror that looked back at her was full of laughter lines, rich with experience and life and wry knowing smiles – but no, it didn't matter how much she wanted to be with Robert, she'd had her fill of labour pains, teething and toddlers.

But because of Robert, far from giving her the sense of peace that knowing all this had given her for the last few years, it gave her a sense of time passing. Up until now Susie had been happy getting older if not wiser, had looked forward to more freedom, new adventures, new experiences; but now, thanks to Robert, she was slammed hard up against the fact that whether she liked it or not, realistically pregnancy and motherhood were behind her, that chapter of her life over – and while on one hand that was a wonderful relief there was also a sense of poignancy and loss. As the tears started to fall all over again they were for the children that she and Robert had never had, and now never would have.

God, surely she should be able to handle it better than this? Surely as you get older things ought to hurt less? At seventeen a broken heart feels like it might kill you, a missed phone call the end of the world, but now? Susie sniffed. Surely you should know more, you should be able to rationalise and understand and realise that even though it hurt now it would get better – some-time, eventually. Trouble was the way she felt at the moment the voice of reason wasn't helping one iota, instead she felt sick.

Amongst the raw, bleeding stumps of rejection and hurt, humiliation twinkled and crackled like lightning; and there she was thinking Robert was about to go down on one knee, that he was her happy ever after. Susie felt her face redden. How the hell could she have got it so wrong? How come she hadn't seen it coming?

Why hadn't Robert mentioned the baby thing before? She had listened to his opinions on everything else; on foreigners, the government, education, immigration, the economy, Botox, cheap wine and middle-aged women wearing leather trousers. When she had mentioned going on holiday together in the autumn, he'd picked up a whole pile of brochures from town. If he'd gone broody why hadn't he said, 'Actually I was thinking more Mothercare than Montenegro.' Bastard.

Susie reran memories of the last three years, trying to come up with anything, any conversation or comment that had brought them anywhere close to fatherhood, but came up dry. Although there was the time he'd said that if he had his time over again there were things he would have done differently. Susie remembered topping up their glasses and saying she was certain everyone felt the same; there was always stuff that you would like to change if you had the chance.

And he'd nodded and gone on to moan about the state of bread in this country, before moving on to include food generally, gastropubs and vegetarians, and especially the man who ran the corner shop in the village who had had an out-of-date vegetarian lasagne in the freezer. Susie sighed; in three years she'd never caught Robert peering longingly into prams, or cooing over commercials for Pampers. Three bloody years wasted.

She really needed a cup of tea. The cure for everything. Susie glanced at her reflection in the toaster – surely this was the time she should be having a life, having missed out on one first time around because she was bringing up Jack and Alice. She wanted to travel now and *do* things, stay up late, see the world, buy a sports car, wear wonderful, sophisticated clothes and swan around looking impossibly elegant with nicely cut hair, not be negotiating buggies up kerbs and in and out of shops, with a bottle, baby wipes and spare nappies in her handbag.

She'd already been there, done that. Susie squared her shoulders. She'd had Jack when she was barely twenty and Alice when she was twenty-one, stayed home, tended a garden and a dog, a cat, goldfish, various hamsters and a rabbit and regretted none of it. But that didn't mean she wanted to do it all over again, especially not now.

How would she have felt if, when they first met, Robert had said, 'Susie, I think you're lovely. I want to have a family with you.' Truth be told, if Robert had said that she would have said 'thanks but no thanks', and run away as fast as she could, safe in the knowledge that he had picked the wrong woman. She certainly wouldn't have wasted the last three years of her life listening to him whine on about the state of Britain today, global warming, young people, refugees, dole scroungers and education. The more Susie thought about it the angrier she got. Robert had totally misled her. She'd spent all this time thinking they had some kind of future together, while all along he'd been busy thinking about raising a family with someone else.

When they had first met, Robert had told her that he liked gardening, foreign travel, long nights in and good nights out . . . There was nothing at all about wanting to burp small incontinent people and scrape puddles of puréed carrot off the front of his nicely pressed Boden rugby shirt – not a hint, not a bloody clue.

At which point the phone rang. Susie hesitated, wondering if she could really face talking to the big wide world without having had a mug of tea, if it was Robert, and why she hadn't signed up for caller display to take the guesswork out of whether to answer the damned thing or not. While still debating, she found herself picking up the handset.

'Mum?'

'Alice –'

'Oh, you *are* there. I spoke to Jack earlier, what's he doing home?' Alice snapped. 'And why weren't you up when I rang? Are you ill? I *told* him to tell you to call me back.'

'Alice, I –'

'Did he tell you that I'd rung?'

'Yes, but –'

'Did he tell you to ring back as soon as you got the message?'

'Yes – but –'

'Did he tell you that it was important?'

'Yes, but –'

'The thing is, Mum –' and all at once the voice of the modern-day Spanish Inquisition softened and Alice giggled. 'The thing is, Mum . . . I'm pregnant.' Her voice rose to a full-throated chuckle at the end of the sentence. 'You're going to be a granny.'

Chapter 3

Susie stared at the phone, not quite able to catch her breath. Granny? *Granny?* Caller display really was the only option; from now on she'd just pick up crank calls, heavy breathers and people who wanted to sell her double-glazing. She'd ring and organise it as soon as she'd had a cup of tea.

'Well, what do you think? Aren't you going to say anything?' said Alice, who still had an odd, whoopy, slightly hysterical tone to her voice.

What was there to say? 'Well yes, of course – I'm – I'm –' said Susie. *What the hell was she?* 'I'm shocked.'

There was a little snarl at the far end of the line. Shocked was apparently not the right response.

'I mean, I'm shocked and *delighted*, and very pleased too – obviously. Thrilled but surprised, I mean. I didn't know that you and Adam were – well, I mean . . .' What exactly did she mean? *Granny*, what sort of word was that to spring on anyone? 'I knew you were, you know, but not . . .' The pit Susie was digging for herself was steadily getting deeper and deeper. 'You know,' she said weakly.

'I thought you would be pleased for me, Mum,' said Alice, now sounding weepy and grumpy and hurt; it seemed as if the hormones had already kicked in.

'I am, darling, I am, really. It's just a bit of a surprise, that's all,' Susie said, not quite sure whether she was lying. 'I'm delighted, absolutely thrilled,' she continued, wondering if she was laying it on too thick. What was it she was supposed to ask?

'When is it due? I mean, are you still going to work? How is work going and how *is* Adam? Is he pleased? Have you thought of any names yet?'

Did that cover everything?

'January, and of course he's pleased, Mum, why wouldn't he be pleased? To be honest, we're both a bit surprised but we both wanted a family at some point so . . . Obviously it wasn't exactly planned, but these things happen, and we were thinking maybe next year anyway, so this just brings things forward a little bit. And once we've had the scan and we know what it is we'll choose the baby's name. Hardly seems an efficient use of my time to pick two sets of names.'

Well, obviously. 'Right. I mean, congratulations, well done – it's wonderful, wonderful news. I'm delighted for you. Really.'

'Things are going to be a bit tight, obviously, for a while, but then again you and Dad managed. I was saying to Adam this morning that you didn't work at all while we were little. I know things were different back then and you weren't qualified for anything in those days so it wasn't like you were losing a proper salary or anything –'

30

Back in the dark ages, thought Susie grimly. Maybe she would just give up answering the phone altogether.

'I said to Adam that if you and Dad could manage it then I know we can.' Alice made it sound like a done deal, her unborn child sorted out and organised from being an embryo up to and including university. After all, if back in the dark ages people like her feckless parents could manage it, without degrees and with an inability to understand the mysteries of predictive text, just how hard could it be?

None of which helped Susie work out what to say to Alice. For a start she hadn't just bought a flat the size of a garden shed for more money than Susie could imagine without tranquillisers, nor had she ever assumed foreign holidays were a right not a privilege, and never in all her born days had she thought £199.99 was a reasonable price to pay for a pair of raffia wedges.

'I'm sure it will be fine,' was all Susie could come up with.

'You know, I knew you'd say that,' snapped Alice.

'Mum, can I move now please? I'm getting cramp. My leg is absolutely killing me.'

Susie looked past the easel to where Jack was sitting. He was at her workbench surrounded by the weekend papers, a mug of coffee and half a packet of biscuits. Late-morning sunshine caught his fringe and the beginnings of a beard, so that he appeared to be surrounded by a great corona of golden light, although her gaze was slightly abstracted so it wasn't exactly Jack she saw but the painting he might become – if only he would just sit still.

'No.'

He groaned.

Susie had had nothing planned for the weekend – if you discounted the bottle of champagne chilling in the fridge, the fresh strawberries and the Belgian chocolates that she had bought in anticipation of a long, lingering celebration breakfast in bed with Robert – which was why she needed to keep her mind firmly occupied with work.

She closed her eyes, trying very hard to clear her head. Her throat was locked solid and a heavy pain hovered above her heart. Bloody man.

Susie let her eyes move slowly across the canvas. It was blank and creamy white, the surface very slightly raised and rough to the touch so that as she drew a stick of charcoal across it, it bit, giving a satisfying, almost mouth-watering, sensation.

'Please, Mum? I'll wash up the breakfast things,' whined Jack.

'I've got a dishwasher.'

The studio – once the washhouse adjoining Susie's cottage – smelt of linseed oil, turps and oil paints, mixed today with the smell of hot wood, baked tin and stone where the sun burned in through the open French windows and drank up the spilt water from the profusion of herbs and geraniums in pots and window boxes. The cottage and the little studio formed an L shape, with a flagstone terrace set with tubs and planters, and cane furniture framed in the crook of the right angle.

Outside, Milo, the hairy hound, had found his spot in the sunshine and was snoring softly.

Susie taught art three days a week at the local college in Fenborough, and worked on her own projects in the time left over. Not that there had been that much time since she'd been going out with Robert; he found the whole art thing completely unfathomable.

The charcoal rasped softly under her fingertips. Susie had drawn and painted for as long as she could remember, long before she knew what art was, discovering very early in life that, somehow, laying her feelings and thoughts down on canvas or board or paper made more sense of them. When it was going well she felt as if she painted right from the core of herself, totally connected to the painting and yet at the same time almost an observer, as if the hands working across the canvas weren't her own.

Not that she told many people that, having come from a family who were about as creative as tin tacks. Susie was altogether more pragmatic when she talked about her work, realising that people had enough preconceived notions about artists without being told that when it was going well she felt she was possessed by the spirit of Elvis. Worse still, Susie really did paint at the top of her game when she was unhappy. This morning the lines were flowing onto the blank canvas effortlessly, like melted chocolate.

'I don't mind unloading it. Or I could walk the dog – oh, how about I water the garden?'

'For god's sake, Jack, I've only just started. And you chose the pose: young man reads newspaper.'

Jack shifted his weight without breaking position. 'I

hate doing this. My leg's gone numb now. I should have done young man sleeps peacefully in hammock.'

'Bear in mind that you could have very easily been doing young man emulsions spare room. And besides, you didn't used to hate it.'

'Only because you bribed me and Alice with sweets and money and trips to the zoo.'

'You could always go and stay with your father.'

Jack sniffed and flicked the page over. 'Did I tell you you're a cruel and heartless woman?'

'I thought we'd already established that. Now, do you want me to put the radio on?' Susie said, glancing back at the canvas and then back at Jack, her eyes darting quickly between the two, trying to catch him in the cross-hairs of her imagination.

'Radio Four?'

'Yup.'

'Not really.' There was a second's pause and then he said, 'So, are you going to ring what's-his-face, try to kiss and make up?'

'You know the rules, Jack,' said Susie, without taking her mind's eye off Jack's silhouette. 'At least ten minutes at a time without talking, now stay still. And no, I don't think I'll be ringing Robert, we've got nothing to say to each other as far as I can see. He wants a baby and, let's be frank, I'm all babied out.'

She smudged the charcoal with her thumb and then paused to gauge the effect.

Jack sniffed. 'Radio Four then?'

'If you want, the afternoon play will be on soon. It's always good on a Saturday.'

'Says you. Are you feeling okay?'

Susie nodded. 'Bit battered but I'll be fine, now sit still.' She had made a habit of never discussing her emotional life in depth with her children and she wasn't going to start now. All the way through the death throes of her marriage, the hand-to-hand combat of divorce, and the new men, broken hearts and false starts since, she'd always kept the gory details to herself, never expecting her children to take sides or, worse still, dispense advice. Besides, she wasn't the only one nursing a broken heart. It couldn't have been easy for Jack to come home and find that Ellie had upped sticks and gone. Ironic really that they were in the same boat, and that while she kept encouraging Jack to talk about it, saying it could really help, she kept her own pain neatly tidied away.

Susie let the charcoal sweep down the page, catching the line of Jack's back, working down over his shoulders, her eye and fingertips guiding the charcoal, trying to capture the subtle thing that was him, wondering as she always did if there was any way to truly capture the shadows and the texture and the vitality, so that someone would look at the finished work and see Jack as she did.

Jack had broad shoulders but was still rangy like a colt; he had his father's jaw line and her long neck, blue-green eyes deep set under heavy brows, a good tan, and taut skin that reflected the light so he seemed to glow. She smiled; her baby had grown up to be a rugged outdoorsy man, with strong, gentle features.

She had painted and drawn Jack and Alice and their father hundreds of times, but never Robert. Robert had objected, saying it felt invasive, and that he didn't like the way she looked at him. It felt, he said, one day when she got him to sit for half an hour, almost as if she could see right through him. Shame she hadn't really, thought Susie miserably as she added another line, it would have saved everyone a lot of trouble.

'He seemed like a bit of a no-hoper to me,' said Jack, without moving.

'Really? And how could you tell?' said Susie, eyes working back and forth, back and forth. When Susie was certain she'd got the right line, she'd look less often, for reference, but at the moment Jack's pose was the only thing she had to hold the image. At the moment there was no dense safety net of lines or shapes or shading, just an idea caught by the most fragile gossamer of charcoal marks.

'I was being polite,' he said. 'If I'm honest, I don't really know what you ever saw in Robert, Mum, he didn't seem like he was your sort at all – came across like a real stuffed shirt. Selfish, a bit spoilt. How long did you say you'd been going out with him?'

'Jack, instead of picking over my love life, why don't you go and ring Ellie when we've done here and try to sort things out with her,' she said. 'You can use the house phone as you haven't got any credit.'

There was silence. He looked away. And then Susie noticed that there was the merest vibration, a tiny shudder in Jack's shoulder and then another, and as she watched a single tear rolled down his cheek and

believe it?' And to her horror, Susie heard her voice crack and then break.

'Really? A granny? Wow. Congratulations,' Matt said with a grin, looking across just as she started to cry. 'That's amazing. Oh no, don't,' he said, reaching out towards her. 'Don't cry, I think it's wonderful.'

Milo started to fret too; he hated women crying.

'Easy for you to say,' Susie snorted, brushing the tears away, stooping down to clip Milo's lead on. 'It's not you it's happening to. I'm really pleased for Alice but it makes me feel so – so –'

'Old?' suggested Matt helpfully.

Susie glared at him furiously, struggling with the temptation to punch him as well as Robert. 'No, not old,' she snapped. 'It feels kind of responsible. Granny sounds like a really big thing to be, and I'm not sure I'm ready. I'm really pleased about it for Alice's sake, but the word doesn't fit me, it doesn't go with how I see myself at all. I can't be a granny. I'm just getting my own life together,' she said, blowing her nose. 'I'm not grown-up enough to be a granny.'

Matt looked at her, his expression softening. 'Granny, eh? I really loved my granny, she used to knit me woolly hats and buy me jelly babies – how are you with Fair Isle?'

Susie slapped his arm. 'It's not funny,' she snorted. 'And I'm not going to be that sort of granny.'

'Shame,' Matt said with a grin. 'I really miss her.'

Despite the early-morning confessional and having to deal with puffy eyes and heavy-duty bags, Susie got to college on time, not really wanting to share any more girly heart-to-heart time with Matt, despite his offer to make her tea and fix her a full English breakfast. He was officially perfect, and at that time of the morning a bit bloody irritating.

'How're you feeling?' asked Nina, her expression all concern and empathy, as Susie bowled in through the door to the main studio. The aroma of fresh coffee and turpentine greeted her like an old friend.

'Why is everyone obsessed with how I feel?' she growled, taking the mug Nina had in her hand.

'Eyeliner and lippy first thing?' said Nina. 'Trust me, it speaks volumes.'

'Okay. Truth? I'm in bits, with a pain in my chest the size of a London bus, but I'll be fine. Just fine. Eventually. I just need to occupy my mind till then.'

'How long do you think that'll be?'

'Six months, a year, who knows.' Susie took a long pull on the coffee before handing it back. 'God, that's good. Any more in the pot? And besides, Robert was a shit.'

Nina nodded. 'Well, yes, we all knew that, but he was *your* shit. And yes, there's more coffee. Have you forgotten? Tuesday morning meeting? Posh coffee and good biscuits. We've got a budget for it.'

Susie laughed. That's what real friends were for – to support you when you made stupid choices and then help pick up the pieces when it all went horribly wrong. 'So, where are we with the master plan?'

'Follow me,' said Nina, beckoning her closer with a hooked finger.

Tuesday morning and the regular staff meeting – they were meant to be discussing progress for the arrangements for the departmental end-of-year exhibition, which was less than a month away. Truth was, as always, it fell squarely on the shoulders of those that did, the ones that talked a good game having long since vanished over the horizon – and that meant it always seemed to be the same faces gathered around the big art-room table.

'Where's everyone else?' asked Susie, sliding her bag under the desk.

'Traffic, bus strike, leaves on the line, dog ate their homework,' said Nina, counting the excuses off on paint-stained fingers. 'God only knows. I'm only on time because I walked here.' She glanced down at her watch. 'You should know by now. They're all artists, *darling*; time is not what they do best.'

'Robert used to say that, and he works for the Environment Agency.'

Nina pulled a face.

'So, how's it going then?' asked Susie.

Nina pulled a sheet of A1 paper out of a folder and slid it across the workbench towards Susie. On it were drawn a series of cubicles, bays, display boards and plinths, with numbered stickers on each one. Nina took a notebook out of the desk drawer and opened it up to the first page.

'It's filling up nicely,' she said, pointing to bay number one. 'Ceramics, mostly blue dishes and those great big garden pots. Bay two we've got slumped glassware and some lizards.'

Susie sipped her coffee. 'What I meant was, instead of talking about me, how's it going generally, you know, as in life?'

'Oh, that? Generally? Fine. Specifically? Not bad at all, just finished grouting the bathroom, cat had kittens, and as for how the end-of-year show looks, it will make everyone look fucking marvellous. Again. What else do you want to know?'

Susie decided to give up on the social niceties and get on with the job in hand. She pulled the sheet of paper nearer and cast a world-weary eye over the floor plan. 'Once we've put in god knows how many hours overtime, chased up the work, hung it, lit it, manned the bloody thing and resisted the temptation to strangle the sideline whiners, you mean?'

Nina grinned. 'Exactly. By the way, have you heard from Hill's Nurseries yet? You know, flowers, plants, ambiance, style?'

'Bugger me, I'd forgotten all about them. Good news is I have done a skeleton press release, though, we just need to add the names in. I'll chase the nursery up. I'm really hoping that they'll stump up some sort of floral display outside the main foyer. I mean, it's great advertising for them and we send enough slave labour their way from the floristry department.'

'The college prefer to call it work placement,' said a male voice from the back of the art room.

Susie looked up and grinned at Austin, their head of department, who was heading in through the glass doorway. He was a man who had made his way up through the ranks. An artist first and foremost, Austin wore his administrator's hat at as jaunty an angle as was possible to achieve while keeping the machinery oiled. He had the look of a rugged, earthier Melvyn Bragg and was not only a devoted Christian but seriously married, which made him a bit of a rarity in higher education.

'Maybe you should get the boss to ring?' said Nina with a grin.

'You mean grub around for sponsors and support – not really his style, is it?'

'I heard that. Taking my name in vain again, are we?' Austin said. 'Coffee smells good. Who do you want me to ring and where the heck is everybody else?' he asked, glancing around as he settled down at the table with the two of them.

Susie shrugged. Nina shrugged. He opened his briefcase and slid a piece of paper Nina's way. 'There we are. One of my minions managed to persuade Pettifers to sponsor the wine, and Browns have said they'll cover the cost of the catering again.'

The two women nodded appreciatively as the double doors swung open, and Colin, the ceramics studio technician, ambled in, pulling off his beanie hat. He was followed by a small plump woman from textiles called Eleanor, who always spent a lot of her time at meetings saying, 'I'm not sure I should be here, after all I'm only part time, and to be honest I feel I'm out of my depth. I mean, I don't really know how relevant my input is.'

'I thought we'd got all the sponsorship sorted out?' said Colin, sliding onto a stool alongside Nina.

Nina consulted her notebook. 'Basically we have now, thanks to Austin, although this year apparently we are supposed to refer to it as contributory partnership, not raffle snafflers or soft touches. So that's catering, wine.' She ticked things off on her list. 'We've got some great fabric for banners, printing costs are all covered – just the sourcing of the busy lizzies to go now.'

'Which is down to me,' said Susie, holding her hand up. 'I'm really hoping we can get the place brightened up a little more dramatically than last year. Robert –' saying his name made her feel as if she was crunching across glass shards in bare feet '– suggested that we try a company he's had dealings with to supply tubs and hanging baskets and stuff for the area around the main entrance. Hill's Nurseries? The college already have links with them in terms of work placement. Apparently they've just started doing a lot of corporate work and he thought they might be keen to get involved with something like this. I've got a name –' Susie pulled a notebook out of her bag. 'Usual stuff, from their point of view we'd give them publicity for their new venture, lots of people would see it, mention it in the press, etc., etc. And I thought we could maybe beef up their bit in the catalogue as they've also provided twice as many placements in their business this year as last.'

Austin nodded. 'Good plan. Front foyer and that grey bit outside, with the sliding glass doors and the prevailing sense of doom, always reminds me of an abattoir. Who's your contact there? I'll give them a ring if you like, no point in having a fancy title if you don't get to flaunt it once in a while.'

'Do you mind?'

Austin shook his head. 'Not at all.'

Susie flicked through the pages of her notebook till she got to one with a slim, winding, detailed doodle of a rambling rose that made its way up the side of the page, winding its way through a shopping list and a dental appointment till it got to, 'Saskia Hill, events and conference coordinator, Hill's Nurseries.'

Colin nodded appreciatively. 'Boss's daughter?'

'Or his wife, or maybe it's even, incredibly, her business,' Susie said coolly.

'And the number?' asked Austin.

Susie slid the pad over. 'There are two there.'

'Okay, well, I'll try and sort it out. Now – in terms of content, how are we doing?'

'Well,' said Nina, glancing down at her list. 'We've got some great paintings of Electric Mickey's arse.'

The rest of the meeting was done and dusted inside half an hour. Susie's first class rolled in at ten; she and Nina got down to working with the second-year childcare students, finishing off their project on printing. After lunch it was collage and calligraphy with some special-needs kids, and at three there was a life class with a group of mature students on the Arts Access course. In between times, students wandered in to pick things up, ask advice, work on their own projects or sit at the back, gossip and drink coffee. One thing about working in college was that life was never dull.

And the good thing for Susie about being so caught

up in what she was doing was that it pushed Robert out to the margins of her mind.

Just as she was leaving for the day, Austin appeared. 'Susie?'

She swung round.

'I managed to speak to the nursery this afternoon and Saskia Hill suggested you pop in to discuss what you have in mind. She sounds very up for getting involved with the college. Lots of noises about wanting to develop partnerships with education and local industry – anyway, I don't suppose there's any chance you could pop in on your way home, is there? She said she'd be there till around six thirty.'

'Okay.'

'Great.' He grinned and then added, 'So how are things?'

Susie pasted on a big cheery smile. 'Things? Things are not bad. How about you?'

Austin's expression softened. 'I've known you a lot of years, Susie, and you're a lousy liar. Neen said there was trouble at t'mill.'

'How very kind of her. Is there anyone who doesn't know about me and Robert splitting up?' Susie said crossly, and then paused and waved the words away. 'Sorry, that was horribly rude, Austin. Thanks for asking, but I'm okay and it's nothing I can't work my way through.'

'Well, if you need anything –' He left the sentence and the sentiment open.

'A bigger studio?' Susie picked up her bag and headed for the door. 'A pay rise?'

The girl waved the words away. 'Not at all. I've got another appointment this evening. No rest for the wicked.'

She exuded a cool confidence that Susie found disconcerting; it had to be business school and the effects of lots of cold hard cash.

Saskia directed Susie into a small office overlooking a paved area set with shrubs and a little pool, the perfect example of how to style a small town garden. 'Now, how can we help you?' she said as she slipped behind her desk and indicated a seat.

'It must be wonderful working with plants,' Susie said, looking out at the display. 'The terrace out there is very nice.'

Saskia smiled again, although Susie noticed it still didn't quite make it to her eyes. 'Thank you. We regularly remodel all the exhibition gardens on a rota basis. Some people prefer to buy a complete look – we can provide the whole thing as a kit. Plans, plants, hard landscaping. It's the kind of service busy people appreciate; it was one of my ideas to improve turnover, bring the family firm up-to-date – take the guesswork out of gardening.'

It wasn't quite the answer Susie had expected so she turned the conversation back to the exhibition. 'I'm not sure exactly what Austin told you, but what we're hoping for is a display in the main entrance of the college for our end-of-year art exhibition – something eye-catching.'

Saskia made a noise; it could almost have been a laugh. 'Something to cover the concrete?'

'You know Fenborough?'

Saskia coloured very slightly; the first time she had shown any genuine reaction. 'I did my first business qualifications there. So, concrete covering is a main requirement?'

Susie nodded. 'That would be wonderful.'

'Well, you may be in luck. We've got a range of planting that we hire out to dress shops, events, various shows –'

'We haven't got a budget for this,' Susie said uncomfortably.

'Austin did explain that, and it's fine.'

Susie smiled. 'In that case it sounds perfect.'

'We obviously have promotional material that we'd like on display – and . . .'

The next half hour was spent working out a site visit, and what Saskia might be prepared to offer, and what Susie had to offer in return. By six thirty Susie was on her way back to the car. She slipped in behind the wheel feeling like it was a job well done. Austin and Nina would be delighted, and for the first time in days she felt happy.

When Susie arrived back at the cottage, Milo was basking in the sunshine on the terrace, on his back, paws in the air, looking for all the world as if he was topping up his tan. He opened one eye to acknowledge her arrival and did a wag or two just to let her know that despite appearances he really was pleased to see her, and that he was absolutely on the ball, no one would get by unnoticed on his watch.

As she headed down the path, Susie noticed a peculiar smell in the air. The smell of cooking. She pushed open the back door to find Matt, with a tea towel tucked into the waistband of his jeans, busy doing something extraordinary with a paella pan and a whole mess of seafood.

The table was set, and Jack was opening a bottle of wine. There was a salad and fresh bread and what looked suspiciously like dessert spoons on a clean tablecloth. Susie looked at the two of them. 'So what did you break?' she asked, dropping her bag onto the chair.

'Mum,' said Jack. 'As if –'

'Did you set fire to something?'

'Hi,' said Matt, looking up from the cooker. 'How's your day been? Jack was just telling me about Deliaing. I was thinking more Rick Stein.' He swept his hand across the top of the pan with all the finesse of a magician's assistant. 'Here we have classic paella – really simple, local ingredients – great served up with a classic green salad and lots of warm, new, crisp bread to sop up all those delectable juices, garnished with lemon wedges and just a sprinkling of chopped parsley.'

'Fantastic,' said Susie, unable to keep the merest hint of suspicion out of her voice.

'You hungry?'

She nodded.

'Good, should be ready in about five minutes.'

Susie slipped off her jacket and accepted the glass of wine Jack handed her.

'So?' she asked.

'What?' said Jack.

'Did you spill varnish on the landing carpet? Break a window?'

'None of the above. We're waiting for the floor and until that's ready –'

'*Nada, niente*,' concluded Matt. 'We've just got to sit it out. So, you want to come join us watch paint dry?'

Who could possibly resist an offer like that?

Chapter 6

After supper, while Matt helped clear away and Jack filled the dishwasher, Susie picked up Milo's lead. Milo and Susie went back a long way. He predated Robert and the cottage and had outlasted by several years the boyfriend who'd bought him as a present for Susie because he thought Milo was cute and Susie was cuter. It seemed a lifetime ago now, but Milo had been there for her through thick and thin, a gentle, amiable, non-judgemental companion who loved her exactly the way she was. He knew the score and without a word padded over to her, eager for an amble round the common. Tail wagging, he sat down at her feet ready for the off.

Matt too, although obviously not the sitting or the wagging bit.

'Fancy some company?' he asked, sliding the last of the dirty dishes onto the countertop. 'It's a lovely evening for a walk.'

'Perfect if you're into sniffing and weeing up trees,' added Susie on Milo's behalf.

'Whatever floats your boat,' said Matt, scratching the

mongrel behind the ears. Milo wagged appreciatively. The dog was *such* a tart.

'I thought you were going to get on with the floor?'

'*Mañana.*'

Susie laughed. 'I thought you were working in Italy not Spain.'

'I think you'll find the *mañana* principle is pretty much universal.'

On the other side of the kitchen, Jack groaned. 'Oh that's right, bloody typical, the three of you bugger off and leave me with all the clearing up.'

Susie smiled and slipped on her walking shoes. 'See, there is a god. I knew that one day all those years of running around after you would pay off and there would be a break-even point. You should have cleaned your room up, come home on time and not bitten your sister. It's karma.'

'Where are we going?' asked Matt, rolling down his shirtsleeves.

She turned her attention to him. 'You can only come with me if you promise not to give me a lecture on the nature of relationships, ask how I am or try to counsel me. Oh, or mention getting in touch with your inner woman.'

Matt mimed pain. 'Owwwww.'

'I'm serious. The paella was wonderful; I really appreciate your cooking. I've had an excellent day after a difficult start and if at all possible I'd like to keep it that way.'

Matt mimed lip-zipping.

It was tempting fate.

Susie had barely snapped Milo's lead on when the phone rang. She decided to ignore it and continued on her way outside, Milo dancing behind her, Matt meandering.

'Phone,' called Jack, as if she might have missed it.

'It's okay – the machine will get it, and if it's important they'll ring back,' said Susie, over one shoulder. And if it was Robert she didn't want him to think she was sitting at home pining, waiting for him to call.

Jack didn't listen. When she was halfway down the garden path, he appeared, hurrying after her, phone clutched tight against his chest. 'Mum?'

'Take a message, I'll ring them later.'

'It's Alice.'

'I'll be half an hour.'

'She said it was urgent.'

'Is it ever anything else?' said Susie, turning on her heel and grabbing the phone out of his hand. 'Alice,' she snapped. 'I don't know what it is you want, darling, but I'm just going out, I won't be long. I'll ring you back in half an hour. All right?'

'No, no, it's not all right,' snuffled Alice. And then there was a split second's pause, followed by a great wailing sob. Susie winced. Trust Alice to turn the tables on her. The one time in her life that she was being as assertive and as grumpy as her only daughter and Alice had to trump her ace.

Jack was right, it had to be something serious. Since she'd been a little girl Alice had hardly ever cried unless there was a furry animal involved. As a teenager she'd been banned from watching *Animal Hospital* in order to save Scandinavian pine forests from being pulped into tissue, not to mention going to school the next day with eyes so swollen that the school nurse had suggested she might be suffering from some sort of nasty allergy.

At the far end of the line the wailing was slowly easing down to a snotty miserable sob.

'Oh Alice – is it the baby?'

'No, no –' sobbed Alice. 'The baby's fine.'

'It's not Mr Tiddles, is it?' asked Susie gently.

Matt peered at her; Susie covered the receiver. 'Next door's cat,' she mouthed.

At the far end of the line the wail rose by an octave.

'Oh honey, I'm so very sorry, I know how much you loved him,' said Susie, 'but you said yourself he was old and frail and a bit smelly.'

'That's Harry.'

'Harry?'

'Mr Tiddles' owner, and besides it's not the cat, Mum, and anyway I'm not letting him in the flat now that I'm pregnant. I'm feeding him on the landing wearing Marigolds.'

'Are we talking about Mr Tiddles or Harry?'

'It's not funny. They carry something nasty.'

'In Mr Tiddles' case he's carrying about a stone and a half of tinned pilchards and way too much full-cream milk. I've told you before it's not good for him.'

'I don't mean fat, Mother, I mean toxoplasmosis. It can be dangerous for pregnant women. It's just not worth taking the risk. You never take *anything* I say seriously, do you?' Alice growled.

'Alice, of course I do. Now please tell me, what's the matter?' she asked gently. 'It's not like you to get upset.'

At which point Alice started to sob again.

'Oh come on, darling, please,' murmured Susie. 'What is it? It's all right, you can tell me.'

Alice sniffed. 'It's Adam.'

Susie felt her heart lurch. 'Adam? Oh no, oh, Alice, why didn't you say so to begin with – what happened? Is he all right?'

'No,' Alice sobbed. 'No, he's not all right, not all right at all. Oh Mum, it's awful. What on earth am I going to do?'

'Oh my god, has there been an accident?' Susie asked anxiously, while her imagination ran amuck with chainsaws, knitting needles, sharp scissors, elderly cats, stairwells, motorways and uncovered manholes in a graphic collage of carnage. 'What's the matter with him, Alice?'

'He's a moron, Mum, a complete moron and an insensitive, stupid pig and I hate him.'

Susie stopped mid-panic, her imagination scuttering to a halt clutching a badly wired plug and a huge screwdriver. 'What?'

'Adam. He's a complete bastard.'

'He's not had an accident?'

'No,' said Alice derisively, 'of course he hasn't had an accident. What on earth made you think that? No, but the thing is, since I've been pregnant he's just being so unreasonable. I never realised what a totally insensitive person he is.'

Milo sighed, lay down on the flagstones and closed

his eyes. Matt took the hint and made his way back towards the house. Susie sat down on the garden bench and repositioned the phone to get herself comfortable. 'As long as he's all right, that's the main thing.'

'It's not the main thing *at all* – I *knew* you'd take his side,' growled Alice. 'He's driving me mad, Mum.'

'I'm not taking his side, Alice. The thing is, a lot of men feel threatened when their partner gets pregnant. It's a well-known phenomenon; it's a big thing to take responsibility for someone so tiny, for the two of you –'

'I'm not asking him to take responsibility, I can do that myself.'

Susie sighed and waded back into the fray. 'The thing is, Alice, some men get terribly worried about how having a family is going to change their lives, they are worried that they'll get left out – they –'

'Please, Mum,' Alice said testily, 'I have read the books.'

'Well, then you should understand how he's feeling, try and reassure him – try –'

'Mum, this is not about Adam's ego or him feeling left out, all right?'

'Then what is it about, Alice? I can't remember you being this upset since Rolf said they'd have to put Honey the three-legged golden Labrador to sleep.'

'Sunny View Nursery.'

'What?'

'Sunny View Nursery. The thing is, it's *the* place to go and we're right on the edge of the catchment area here, and all I said to Adam the other morning was that we really ought to get the baby's name down now. I mean. it's only sensible, and once we've got a place they automatically take siblings, even if we moved. It's just perfect, I could walk if I wanted to, not that I would of course, but I could – I want to be certain of getting the baby in there as soon as possible. It's a feeder nursery for the best primary school in this area. I've been looking at the league tables. Surely you of all people can understand the value of a good education?'

Susie wasn't sure exactly what to say, but apparently Alice wasn't expecting a reply.

'And then he insisted on having Brie when we went out to supper – insisted! What does that say about the man? I said have you got any idea about the dangers of listeria? A few crumbs, a microbe carried home on that peculiar sweater he likes that his mum gave him for Christmas. Designer my arse. I mean, what does it take to make him understand? This is our child's life we're talking about, for god's sake. And then he brought me over a glass of red wine, said it would do me good, help me relax. He said I was getting myself in a bit of a tizz. A *tizz*? How patronising is that? Well, honestly, Mum, I can tell you now I was livid. Anyway, when we got home I went straight upstairs and Googled the latest reports about foetal alcoholic abuse for him to take a look at, and he said I was overreacting, that they meant binge-drinking not one glass, and I said it was a slippery slope. And then this morning I was just saying that I thought two years was a nice gap and maybe he should think about giving up his guitar lessons – I mean, Adam's never going to be an Arctic Monkey. And maybe the money would be better used elsewhere – I mean, I was just saying. In conversation.'

There was a short pause, presumably while Alice took on more oxygen, and then she said, 'So what do you think?'

'What do I think about what, Alice?' Susie asked cautiously.

'Do you think he's being unreasonable?'

'Well –' Susie began.

'You see, as far as Adam is concerned it's all me, all my fault apparently. He can't see that he's done anything wrong. He said just before he went off to his guitar lesson – he said – he said –' Alice paused, struggling to spit it out.

'What did he say, love?'

'He said that I was being silly and irrational and completely self-obsessed and he was sure it was probably just the hormones and that he loved me very much.' Alice sniffed back the tears. 'And then he hugged me and kissed me on the top of the head. The patronising son of a bitch. I want to come home, Mum.'

'What?'

'Just for a few days. I can't stand it here with him.'

'But what about work?' spluttered Susie. 'I mean, you've got a mortgage to pay, and sandals to buy, and Mr Tiddles to keep in pilchards and Jersey gold top.'

'It'll be fine. I've got some leave due and I've been working from home for part of the week anyway – I can just as well work from your house as mine – and

Chapter 7

'So who exactly is this Matt Peters then? He seems to have got his feet under the table pretty damn quick, if you ask me,' said Alice the following morning.

Although her tone was light and teasing, Susie could hear the steel core running through the question, and wondered, not for the first time, exactly what had happened in the genetic mix at Alice's conception to have thrown up a twenty-first-century version of Lucrezia Borgia from two relatively laidback parents.

It was barely eight o'clock, and outside Matt and Jack were climbing into Matt's battered Discovery, heading back to the university for their big meeting. Matt was dressed in a sharp black suit, while Jack looked like an extra from an Indiana Jones film.

Susie had been waving them off and was just heading back inside to tidy the kitchen before starting work in the studio, when Alice ambushed her. Susie had hoped that Alice would take the opportunity to have a lie-in, but apparently not. Resplendent in her teddy bear PJs and matching fluffy dressing gown, Alice looked deceptively benign with her hair caught up in a pink slide.

Freshly showered and without a shred of make-up on, she looked about twelve.

'He's Jack's boss. But he's really sweet and it's been brilliant having the two of them here, you saw how they've sorted out the spare room.'

Alice didn't look convinced. 'He seems very comfortable here for someone that you've only just met.'

'You're right,' said Susie casually. 'But Matt strikes me as the kind of guy who fits in more or less anywhere. He's just split up from his partner, Alex.'

Alice did a little double take. '*Alex*?'

'That's what I said.'

'Oh my god, you don't think he's got his eye on Jack, do you? I mean all that chummy *"why don't you come and stay at my place?"* stuff.'

Susie didn't like to say that the thought had crossed her mind. 'Alice, I have no idea, but Jack's a big boy now and can take care of himself. Seems to me Matt's a really nice guy –'

'Yes, but Jack's in a vulnerable state,' Alice pressed.

Susie stared at her. 'There is a huge difference between vulnerable and gay. Now do you mind if I get on, only I've got quite a lot to get done today?'

'Maybe I ought to have a word with him.'

'Honey, I think Jack's got other things on his mind at the moment. Anyway, I'll be back later.'

Alice frowned. 'But we've barely had time to catch up at all yet, Mum. I'd really like to discuss the situation with Adam and the baby and what's going on between Jack and Ellie. That whole situation sounds like a complete mess to me.' Alice paused and beaded Susie with her big blue eyes. 'It almost feels as if you are deliberately trying to avoid me.'

Susie shrugged. 'Don't be silly, of course I'm not,' she lied. 'You're here, aren't you? You can always come and sit in the studio.'

'What, and end up having to sit still for hours?' Alice pulled a face. 'No thanks.'

'I did tell you that if you came to stay I'd be busy. I was thinking maybe we could go and see Granddad while you're here. It's ages since you've been to see him. Does he know about the baby?'

'His phone is always engaged, I mean he could be dead – who would ever know? And I'm certainly not leaving a message telling him about his great-grandchild on an answering machine.'

'So that's a no then – in which case we could pop round over the weekend if you like.'

Alice pouted. Obviously visiting relatives wasn't high on her agenda. 'I just need to talk,' she said.

'And we will. Now come on, I really need to get on. I've got work to do and you said you had too.' Susie tried to make it all sound jolly and bustling. As she spoke she started to bundle dirty washing into the machine. 'I need to get out to the studio and I've arranged to meet someone at two o'clock.'

'Oh that's typical.' Alice's eyes narrowed. 'Arranged to meet who?'

Susie was beginning to get annoyed with the constant game of twenty questions. 'Alice, honey, who I meet and why I meet them is entirely up to me. I should be back here at around four thirty at the latest – how about we catch up then?' She didn't add that far from being some wild romantic assignation, her meeting was actually Saskia Hill's rescheduled site visit for the college's art exhibition – apparently Saskia had had an unexpected window in her diary.

'What do you fancy for supper? I was thinking, how about I invite Granddad over, that way we could kill two birds with one stone?'

But it wasn't that easy to throw Alice off the scent. 'That's a good idea. Maybe Robert would like to come round as well?' Alice said, watching Susie's every move. When Susie didn't answer, Alice continued, 'Mum, are you going to tell me what exactly *is* going on between you two? Jack was saying that you've had some sort of a *thing*.' She paused; still Susie said nothing.

'You know, to be perfectly honest, by your age, Mum, I really thought you'd have got all this stuff sorted out.'

Alice wasn't alone in that, Susie thought grimly.

'If I were you, I'd be thinking about settling down, enjoying life. There is that whole companionship, growing old together, retirement thing – and Robert has always been very sensible when it comes to money and planning for the future.'

And mean as charity, thought Susie furiously, trying hard to bite her tongue. 'Alice, darling, I'm forty-five not ninety-five.'

'Exactly,' said Alice, as if forty-five was the end of life by anyone's standards. 'To be honest, at your age

I really wouldn't be playing hard to get,' Alice said, with what Susie hoped was a stab at humour. 'I think you should be thinking about long-term plans.'

'So did Robert,' said Susie, setting the dial on the washing machine to stun.

'Well, there we are then,' said Alice briskly. 'I don't see what the problem is.'

'The problem, Alice,' said Susie, swinging round to face her, finally unable to take any more, 'is that Robert's long-terms plans include a baby – well, actually, more than one. Two or three if he can manage it.'

Alice's mouth dropped open.

'Presumably,' Susie continued, as she started clearing away the breakfast things, 'your plans for my dotage don't involve a baby brother or sister, do they?'

Alice's mouth worked up and down like a ventriloquist's dummy. Finally, she sat down and said nothing – which under the circumstances was a blessing for both of them.

Saskia Hill was wearing an immaculately pressed white linen shirt, discreet silver jewellery and jeans with creases so precise that you could probably have used them for something complex and mathematical had you wanted to. Her long blonde hair was twisted up into an elegant knot and held in place by a hinged flower-shaped clip.

Nice touch, thought Susie as Saskia sashayed her way across the tarmac at the front of the college, from her spotless, shiny brand-new black 4x4. She was carrying a clipboard and as she approached she held out a hand in greeting in a way that reminded Susie of a politician on a walkabout greeting the great unwashed.

'Hello, Susie, so sorry about the change of plans, but you know how it is,' she said, gaze working backwards and forwards across Susie to Neen and then back again.

'Not a problem. We're very grateful for your support.' Susie made the introductions. 'This is my colleague, Nina Freeman. We work together in the art department and Nina is responsible for coordinating this year's end-of-year show. Nina, this is Saskia Hill from Hill's Nurseries.'

Nina snorted. 'This year's, last year's – pleased to meet you – I can't think of one I haven't arranged since I took the job. I like your hairclip.'

Saskia's cold, empty little smile held as she took in Nina's dreadlocks, old-fashioned brown shop coat, purple leggings and open-toed sandals, then she nodded coolly, pulled her hand away after the briefest of touches and murmured something unintelligible, apparently not in the mood for any girly chit-chat. As Saskia's attention and gaze moved on, Nina pulled a snooty-bitch face. It certainly wasn't a meeting of hearts and minds.

Oblivious, Saskia consulted her clipboard and then turned her attention to the front of the college building, which from the main road looked a little like an oversized World War II gun emplacement, something that wouldn't have looked out of place in a remake of *The Guns of Navarone*, with its tiny slit windows set deep into the heavy concrete façade to make returning fire tricky. Only the ground floor had windows of any reasonable size, and they were feature-less brown-framed panes, set flush with the concrete façade. There was an attempt at a portico – a slab of reinforced concrete with two narrow red poles giving an illusion of supporting the far edge. Beautiful it wasn't.

'So, this is the main entrance,' Saskia said rather unnecessarily.

'Yes. We were really hoping for something here,' said Susie, indicating the broad steps that fronted the foyer. 'I appreciate it's not exactly an inspiring spot, but it is the point of entry for everyone and it would be really nice to do something with it.'

Saskia nodded. 'Realistically, I don't think we can do anything to soften the front without it looking ridiculous, so we go for impact. Something big and bold. Reds, hot colours – something striking. We've got all kinds of things that would work here. Palms, big cannas, cordylines, banana trees, lots of lush green foliage and big architectural shapes.'

Susie nodded. 'Sounds wonderful,' she said, trying to work out how they'd stop students from stubbing out their dog-ends in the planters.

'Is this area secure at night?' asked Saskia, glancing around. On the far side of the road, beyond the bollards and the skip and the little corner shop, was a row of dingy terraces, a lot of them rented out to students, the rest occupied by low-income families. Secure wasn't a word Susie would have used.

The three women looked at each other. 'Realistically? No, not very,' said Susie finally. 'The main gates are closed after evening classes finish and the last of the students leave, which is probably around ten at the latest, but I'm sure some enterprising soul with a set of bolt cutters, a forklift and a flat-bed truck could be in here having stuff away in the wee small hours if it was worth his while.'

Saskia nodded and scribbled something down on her clipboard before whipping out a digital camera and taking half a dozen pictures. 'Let's go and take a look inside, shall we?' she said.

The atrium – a large two-storey space – and the main reception area were basically grey, although both had recently had a half-hearted makeover in a kind of dark wine-red that reminded Susie of a cheap hotel chain.

As Saskia made notes and took photos, Nina talked them through the layout for the exhibition and handed out a plan, along with a list of the different exhibits and their themes. By three o'clock Saskia had seen all she needed to see and was climbing back into her 4x4 and heading for home.

'Wow,' said Nina, watching her drive away. 'Scary or what?'

Susie turned Saskia's business card over in her fingers. It was tasteful, crisp and quite obviously expensive. 'If her plants and displays are as impressive and spiky as she is then the whole thing will look fabulous and it's a great link for the college to develop. She'll get lots of publicity in the local press and if it works well maybe we can convince her to have a permanent ongoing display here. Let's face it, this whole forecourt area could do with a bit of colour. Maybe we could think about getting some sculpture out here.' She pointed towards the sad concrete tubs full of weeds and dog-ends and the desert of tarmac that led down towards the road. 'I mean, I do appreciate it would take a lot of work.'

'It would take a fucking miracle,' Nina said. 'Throwing ourselves into our work, are we?'

Susie sighed. 'And then some. It's been a rough week. What with Ellie and Jack splitting up and now Alice has come home because she and Adam have had a row about the baby; I haven't seen Robert since he came round with a bunch of cheap flowers and a gleam in his eye; and Matt, Jack's boss, has been staying too – '

'Really? And what's he like?' said Nina with a grin.

Susie sighed. 'Drop-dead gorgeous and bent as a box of frogs, not to mention nursing a broken heart of his own. To be honest, I feel as if I've woken up in the middle of an episode of *Hollyoaks*.'

Nina stuffed her hands in her pockets and looked thoughtful. 'Better than staying home by the fire with your cat.'

'Depends on where you're standing. I could murder a cup of tea.'

'Follow me to the art room,' said Nina. 'I've got a couple of emergency bags on standby.'

At which point Susie's mobile rang.

They both looked at each other. 'Robert?' Nina

mouthed. Susie shrugged and then scrambled to get the damn thing out of her handbag before it went to voicemail.

'Nope,' she said, glancing down at the screen and then pressing the call button. 'Hi, Jack, how's it going, love?'

'God only knows. We've been in there for hours. They were a seriously weird bunch. Anyway, I've done my bit. Matt is still in there doing his. I was just wondering –' He paused.

'Wondering what?'

'Well, I've kind of painted myself into a corner. Matt's invited me to stay over at his for a couple of days because of Alice being at yours, only I've just found out he's arranged to see someone this weekend. Last thing I want to do is be there on the sofa playing gooseberry.'

Given the conversation Susie had had with Alice earlier, it was a graphic image. 'I can see that,' said Susie. 'So are you saying you want to come home? You're more than welcome to the couch.'

'And the third degree from Alice.'

'I didn't say it was a perfect solution. You're the one in the corner.'

Across the path, Nina was miming tea. Susie nodded and mumbled 'And a biscuit.'

'Sorry, am I interrupting something?' asked Jack.

'No, no, you're fine, honey. I'd just popped into college to sort some stuff out for the end-of-year show. You're very welcome to come back to the cottage if you want to, but surely you must have some friends

116

in Cambridge you could stay with? Or Dad?' She paused. 'Or how about you ring Ellie?'

'Ellie?' he said flatly. 'Why would I ring Ellie?'

'Why not? You're in town, it makes sense to ring up and talk to her. You said yourself the pair of you need to talk.'

'Uh-huh, right, so we talk and then I try and bum a night on her floor. Or, worse still, in her bed. How's that going to look? She's always saying I'm just like her father, unreliable, no good with money.'

'It wasn't you who sublet the flat.'

'True. I suppose you could argue that the only reason I've got nowhere to stay is down to her. Not that that'll cut much ice. You know that she's staying with her dad at the moment, don't you? Bit ironic given that he's the idle good-for-nothing fuck she's always saying I'll turn into if I don't get my act together.'

Susie sighed. 'Simon's okay, he's just a bit of a –'

'Of a what, Mum? He looks and acts like an ageing eighties rock star. What man in his right mind still has a mullet and pushes the sleeves of his suit up to his elbows?'

'I was going to say a complete flirt and a good-looking waste of space, and Ellie's wrong about you turning into him. I'd give her a ring if I were you. You never know, she may well be thinking that you're not anything like her dad now that she's back under his roof. He's probably borrowing fifty quid off her even as we speak.'

There was a long pause and then Jack said, 'I suppose

I could always ring Eddy – you remember Eddy? Ginger guy, used to play in a band. Tall – got a tattoo.'

'Jack, just ring Ellie.'

He sniffed. 'I don't suppose it would do any harm. She's already left me, flogged all my gear and rented my flat out, how much worse can it get? And I can always ring Eddy later if she says no. Or sleep under a bridge in a cardboard box.'

'Sounds like a plan.'

The silence opened up again, as wide and deep as the ocean. 'What if she says no, Mum?' he asked quietly.

Susie's heart ached for him as she heard the pain in his voice. Why did no one ever tell you that being a mother just never stopped? It was obvious when they were little, but even when they grew up, just one word, one look, would have you back there at ground zero.

'Do you want her back?'

Jack said nothing.

'Then it's a chance you have to take, love,' said Susie. 'Just ring her up and see what happens.'

As she was about to close her phone the text alert beeped twice. One message was from Alice saying she had tried to ring Susie's father again and it still went straight through to his answering machine, and the other was from Robert, not that he'd signed it:

Hi, just wondered if you'd like to come over for supper on Saturday evening at 8.00 p.m.?

He despised text-speak, so he always spelt everything correctly and used the appropriate punctuation, which kind of gave the game away as to the sender, although she did check the number, just in case.

'You're not going to go, are you?' said Nina, in the art room a few minutes later as she handed Susie a large mug of tea.

Susie wasn't altogether sure what to say. Obviously, 'Over my dead body' would have been a good response but she didn't think she'd be able to carry it off with any conviction. She was also conscious of Nina watching every facial expression.

'He told me that he wanted to be friends,' said Susie lamely.

Nina lifted an eyebrow. 'Really? He's got a pretty funny idea of how friends treat each other. Obviously whoever he's thinking of breeding with is playing hard to get,' she said.

Susie was stunned. 'You think he's already found someone?'

Nina pulled a face.

'I don't think he's got anyone else yet. And "breeding with"? That sounds awful. Makes him sound like a farm animal,' said Susie.

'Uh-huh. Let's face it, Robert isn't the kind of man who can cope on his own. He likes a woman in his life to boss around and moan to.'

'And your reasoning for that is?'

'Listening to you and years of experience. The guy is like Tarzan, genetically incapable of letting go of one vine before he's got another one to grab hold of. I bet he's been lining this one up for months, he's just mistimed the changeover.'

Susie stared at the text, feeling a little kick of pain in her heart. 'Really?'

'Or maybe she's busy on Saturday night.'

'Neen, you are such a cow. You don't think there is any chance that he genuinely misses me and that he wants to talk?'

Nina considered the idea for a few seconds. 'Nah, not a chance. The man is a complete prat. If he had any sense at all he would have known when he was on to something great and have hung on to you with both hands. In my opinion, Robert wouldn't recognise something special if it came up and bit him on the arse. Anyway, it's his loss and your gain. He wouldn't have made you happy and you don't need me to tell you that, do you?'

Before Susie had time to think about an answer, Nina said, 'Tell you what, how about me, you and Cruella de Vil go to the pictures on Saturday night instead? They've got that new thing with what's-her-face in it on at the Majestic – you know, the one with the big nose – won an Oscar. Tall, blonde.'

Susie laughed. 'You should be writing reviews for the *Telegraph* with a mind like that.'

So Alice couldn't accuse her of not taking notice of what she said, on the drive home Susie went the long way round and called in on her father to see if he was dead, and if not if he wanted to come over for supper. That way, they had a full social calendar booked – supper with Granddad, a film with Nina – and it also meant that she wouldn't be tempted to

120

call Robert, even if she wanted to, because she was busy. Very busy.

Sitting in the driveway to her dad's house, Susie scrolled down to his number on her mobile and rang him, just in case Alice had caught him at a bad moment. She waited to be connected; the number was still engaged.

Susie had to admit that Alice was right, his phone was almost always either engaged or on voicemail, but Susie had put this down to lengthy conversations with the council complaining about the things his council tax was being wasted on, and a long-held desire to be left the hell alone. Her mum had died when Susie was in her twenties and – as well as mourning her passing – her father had managed to make it sound as though her mum had died out of spite. For years he'd begun sentences with, 'Of course this wouldn't have happened if your mother was still alive . . .'

Another few years and Susie planned to play the grumpy old person card herself, something her father had been trumping her with for years. As she got out of the car it crossed her mind that maybe this was where Alice got it from. It wasn't a blip in the family DNA, just early-onset curmudgeonliness.

Susie's father's house was a large, rather handsome Edwardian semi in one of the better parts of Fenborough. Although it was only about ten minutes' walk from the town centre, here the street was lined with lime trees that smelt divine when they were in blossom. Today they offered an oasis of dappled shade under their leafy canopies.

121

Susie headed up the front steps, rang the bell and waited. Nothing. She rang again and waited some more, and fleetingly thought about Alice's comment that her dad could be dead and no one would know. Maybe he was out. Maybe he was asleep. Maybe he really was dead . . . She waited a few more seconds and then hurried round to the back gate.

While the front garden was always neat and tidy, the back garden was like a jungle. It took a little while to force the gate open over a pile of rotting leaves and gnarled tree roots. Her heart started to thump a little harder.

Picking her way along the path between the creepers and the overgrown shrubs, Susie headed for the conservatory and knocked, and as she did so the door very slowly swung open with an unpleasant creak, making the hairs on the back of her neck rise.

'Dad?' she called out.

Surely if her father was dead she would know, she would feel it, wouldn't she? Surely a neighbour would have called round and seen him slumped over the dining table, or a friend would have suspected that something was wrong and forced their way in.

'Dad? Dad, are you in here?' Susie called again, feeling more worried and guilty by turns. Beyond the heat of the conservatory the kitchen was cool and dark and there was a tap dripping into a sink full of dirty dishes. As she stepped inside Susie felt sick and nervous.

'Dad?' she called again into the gloom. 'Are you in there? Are you all right?' She tried hard to keep the slight edge of hysteria out of her voice. How long was it since she'd seen him or talked to him? Three weeks? Four?

'Dad? Are you all right?'

'Of course I'm bloody all right,' growled a voice from somewhere far off, deep inside the house. She could hear somethng stirring from upstairs and then the re-assuring thump, thump, thump of footfalls on the staircase as he made his way down, wrapping a dressing gown around himself as he came into the kitchen. 'Or at least I was till you showed up. What the hell are you doing here?' He was red-faced and his hair was all mussed up like Jack's, and for an instant she caught a glimpse of the family similarity.

'Oh thank god you're alive!' she said, not quite under her breath.

'What did you say?' he asked. 'You know my hearing's never been very good. I blame your mother and all that bloody hoovering.'

'I said I was worried about you. Your phone's been engaged for hours.'

'I know. It's the only way I can get some bloody peace,' he grumbled, jerking open the fridge door and peering inside.

'Sorry, I did ring, and then when it was constantly engaged I thought I'd drop by. See if you were okay. You know, Alice is home at the moment and I was wondering if you'd maybe like to come round for supper this evening? I'm sorry, were you having a nap?' she asked.

'No,' he said. And then grudgingly nodded in her

direction. 'Nice to see you. I meant to ring or pop round. I suppose you want a cup of tea now that you're here?'

Susie was about to answer when she heard a noise upstairs and then a disembodied voice called down, 'Nicky, sweetie, are you all right? Who is it?'

Her father looked across at Susie, totally unfazed. 'I don't suppose your invitation extends to Adele, does it?'

Chapter 8

Susie struggled to regain her composure. 'Adele?' Her mind was racing. Who the hell was Adele and what was her father doing in bed with her at four o'clock on a Friday afternoon? Not that she actually needed an answer; you didn't have to be a genius to work it out. Good god, the man was seventy if he was a day. What on earth was he thinking of?

'Why not?' Susie heard herself say. 'The more the merrier. I mean, of course she's welcome. Obviously. Lovely.' It all sounded way too bright and bouncy, like a scout mistress on drugs.

As Susie spoke, her father wedged the kettle up under the taps and started sorting through the washing-up for some cups. 'Adele brought me a cake round somewhere. Cherry, I'm very partial to cherry cake.' As the kettle filled, his gaze wandered around the kitchen, trying to track down the cake, quite oblivious to Susie's embarrassment. 'So, tea then?'

'That would be lovely,' she said lamely. 'How have you been?'

'What do you mean how have I been? I've been fine.

I was going to invite you round and introduce you to Adele,' he said. 'Lovely girl. I have to say that this isn't quite how I hoped you'd meet, but hey-ho it's as good as any other. Now where's that bloody cake?' Abandoning the kettle, he started rooting furiously through piles of newspapers on the dresser, lifting up bags and trays.

Meanwhile, from across the landing came the sound of bare feet on boards and then the tap, tap, tap of heels. As Susie looked through into the hallway she could see the hem of a short blue robe and a pair of shapely brown legs ending in matching fluffy feather-trimmed mules teetering down the stairs. Susie waited for the rest. It didn't take long.

Adele was around five feet tall, small-framed but curvy in all the right places, with blood-red toenails, bleach-blonde hair tortured into some sort of curly top-knot, a spray-on tan and lots of heavy-duty eye make-up. Beyond that she didn't appear to be much older than Susie. She posed for a split second in the open doorway, making a show of pulling her robe tight around voluptuous curves, and then said, 'Hello, nice to meet you,' warmly but in a kind of breathy high-pitched squeak, offering Susie her tiny little hand as she did.

Adele's fingernails were painted to match her toes; some nails had tiny diamanté stars glued to them. 'You must be Susie, you know I've heard so much about you,' she said, still smiling. 'He is so proud of you, you know.' Her attention wandered. 'Nicky, baby, what are you looking for now, sweetheart?'

Susie's father threw up his hands in despair. 'I'm looking for the cake. What happened to the fucking cake?'

'Come here, let me look, baby, while you make the tea,' she said, pulling a shared girly, what-can-you-do-with-them face at Susie. Susie didn't know where to look as Adele gave him a peck on the cheek and he slapped her bum. God, and there was Susie thinking the old boy was dead.

'Adele and I have been discussing the future,' said Susie's dad as they drank tea and ate the cake, which had been in a Tesco's bag in the middle of the table all the time. 'We've been thinking Spain.'

'Spain? You're going on holiday? That's lovely, whereabouts are you thinking of going?'

'We're thinking of moving there,' said Adele. 'Weather's nicer and your money goes further.'

Susie looked at her, wondering exactly *whose* money she meant.

'We've been surfing the Net,' said her dad.

'Really?' Susie asked, trying to hide her surprise. This from the man who couldn't set a radio alarm clock.

'Oh yes,' he said all manfully, chest puffed out. 'Nothing to it really. Went on Google, found exactly the kind of thing we've been looking for. Sent off a couple of emails. Anyway, we thought we'd go on an extended holiday and take a little look around. Didn't we, Adele?'

Susie was very conscious of the heavy-duty '*we*' element in all this chat.

'We found two independent companies who specialise

in English people retiring out there, they'll meet you from the airport, sort out a hotel and everything if you want them to, and then show you around various properties they've got on their books.'

Susie was about to jump in with dire warnings about timeshare scams, sharks and old people being relieved of their life savings when her dad said, 'We've checked them out, obviously, hired a solicitor used to dealing with property in Spain and been in contact with a couple of people who've already bought with them – nice, they were, weren't they, Del?'

'Very helpful, lots of really practical advice. We're looking forward to having a little nosy round, aren't we, Nicky? We thought we'd go at the end of the month, before it gets too hot,' said Adele, cuddling up to him. 'You know your dad is a wonderful man – amazing for his age,' she said, and then, addressing Susie's father, eyes all bright and teasing, said, 'And a very naughty boy as well.'

At which point Susie's father pulled Adele down onto his knee, and Susie rapidly made her excuses and left.

'You said you'd be back by four thirty,' said Alice. She was sitting on the sofa surrounded by books, folders, her laptop and the remains of various healthy snacks. 'I was getting worried about you.'

Susie sighed. Trapped between one generation and the next was hardly a comfortable place to be, although she hoped she'd still have the capacity to shock at seventy.

'So is Granddad coming round then?'

'Yes, and he's bringing his new girlfriend.'

Alice smiled. 'Isn't that sweet? Fancy calling her his girlfriend at that age.' She started to gather her things into a heap. 'You see, that's how you ought to be thinking, finding someone to share the autumn of your life with. Companionship is very important when you get to a certain age. What are you cooking for them?'

'I was thinking either risotto or maybe a spag bol. Nice bread, salad . . .'

Alice considered the menu for a few seconds. 'I suppose they're both nice and soft, aren't they.'

'What?'

Alice nodded. 'Soft. You know, easy for them to manage, not too much to chew, easy to digest. Probably the risotto would be best, being mostly rice – I'd have thought your spaghetti bolognaise would be a bit rich, probably a bit too spicy for the elderly.'

Susie, heading into the kitchen, decided not to spoil the surprise.

'So what do you do?' asked Adele, handing Alice a bowl of green salad. It was later that evening and they were eating outside on the terrace under the pergola. The fairy lights strung between the wooden slats and the honey-suckle were just beginning to come into their own as the daylight faded into evening.

The risotto looked and smelt wonderful, in fact the whole meal was crying out for a Delia moment, but Susie held back, sipping her wine instead, while her father piled his plate high with rice and chicken, and commandeered the entire contents of the bread basket.

Adele, meanwhile, who was seated alongside him, so close that she was almost in his lap, was talking nineteen to the dozen about how lovely the cottage was, how beautiful the garden, how easy the drive over, how green and picturesque the common. She was lovely, bright, funny and obviously seriously in love with Susie's father, who, after god knows how many years in cavalry twills and sensible cardigans from Marks, had come dressed as something out of *The Great Gatsby*, complete with fedora and a paisley cravat.

Adele had been a hairdresser all her life, apparently. 'Always loved doing hair and dressing up, me – you know, girly things. Nails, make-up. And my dad said, when I was about fourteen – I'd just set me mum's hair and dyed it Nouveau Chestnut, which was warm but not brassy – he said, "You know, you could make a good living out of that, Adele." And he was right.'

Thirty-five years on and she'd got herself three shops, a tanning parlour and nail salon, but was now seriously considering selling up and joining Nicky in a villa in the Costa del Somewhere.

'I mean, we've both worked bloody hard all our lives; we reckon it's time to enjoy life a bit, don't we, Nicky? We've booked a nice apartment so's we can take a good look round. We're not going to rush into it though, take our time, find the right place – and we should be all right financially,' she said. 'Shouldn't we, babe? I've always been canny with my money. I thought I'd rent me house out here, sell the business, you get managers in and they always let things slide and get greedy if you know what I mean – 'specially if you're not there to chase 'em up. And Nicky's got his pension. Although I was saying to Nicky, if we can't make ends meet I can always whip out me scissors.' She giggled. 'Maybe I could drag your dad out of retirement, teach him to do nails or something. Anyway, tickets are booked and paid for now – I mean if we don't like it we haven't lost anything, just had a damned good holiday.'

Next to her, Susie's dad laughed. 'Good risotto,' he said, holding a forkful out towards Susie.

Since meeting Adele earlier in the afternoon, Susie was rapidly warming to the bleached-blonde pocket Venus. Alice, meanwhile, was surveying the scene like a puritan schoolmarm, lips tightly pursed, disapproval written in capital letters right across her face. True, Adele was noisy and demonstrative and deliciously indiscreet – she was all over Alice's granddad like smallpox – and, okay, so maybe the red polka-dot halter-neck sundress she was wearing was twenty years too young for her and a size or two too small, but Granddad was obviously as happy as Larry and who could blame him? Adele oozed vitality and clearly thought the sun shone out of his every orifice. She'd worked wonders for him.

'So are you going to sell your house, Dad?' asked Susie lightly, rescuing the last of the wine. 'You know, even if you don't go to Spain that might be worth considering – it's way too big for you on your own, or even for two of you, it's a lot to look after.'

Alice glared at Susie. 'I don't think selling it is a good idea at all. What about renting it out? I mean, it's the family home.'

'Who have all left and got homes and families of their own,' Susie pointed out.

'Grandma loved that house,' growled Alice, presumably seeing the family nest egg trickling away.

It was a low punch but Susie's dad nodded. 'That's right, she did, 'specially when Robert and Gill and your mum were little, but when they had grown up she was always saying how it would be nice if we could sell up and get somewhere smaller and less draughty. The garden used to drive her mad. She always wanted a bungalow. A bloody bungalow.'

'What do Uncle Bob and Aunty Gill think of the idea?' Alice pressed.

Susie's younger brother and sister lived in Gloucester and Manchester and were both married with children. Other than occasionally nipping home at Christmas or dropping in on the way to or from somewhere else, Susie couldn't think of a time when any of them had stayed at the family house for years.

Susie spoke to them a couple of times a year. It wasn't that they weren't close – they always had been – it was just that time and life galloped by, and no sooner was she sending off a Christmas card with a note in to wish them and theirs well and ask how life was than it seemed time to do it again.

Across the table, Susie's dad shrugged. 'They're fine with the idea, not that we've talked about it in any great detail. What's not to be fine about? It's my bloody house, and I'm not stupid or senile, I'm just thinking of retiring to somewhere where the climate is a bit kinder and my money will go further. Seems sensible to me.'

'Exactly,' said Adele, scooping some more risotto onto Susie's dad's plate. 'And I'm not planning to waltz off with your inheritance if that's what you're worried about.'

Alice had the decency to blush. 'That wasn't what I was thinking at all,' she mumbled.

Susie made a mental note to ring Bob and Gill sometime soon to see how things were. Last time they'd spoken Bob had mentioned something about Dad having a new girlfriend but it was fairly obvious that he couldn't have met her.

Meanwhile, Adele carried on chatting. Apparently they'd met when Nicky had popped in to have a bit of a trim, and had been seeing each other for nearly six months now. Adele grinned as she took Nicky's hand and said, 'It's early days yet and no one's got a crystal ball, but you know whether it's something special or not, don't you?'

Susie smiled, her eyes unexpectedly filling with tears as she saw the expression of pure delight on her father's face as he looked across at Adele. God, if her grumpy old dad could find someone to love him then there was hope for her after all.

'Yes,' she said. 'You do, and I'm really pleased for both of you.'

'So are you two thinking of getting married?' asked Alice coolly.

Adele waved the words away. 'Who knows, we might – we might not.' She was all giggling and embarrassed. 'And besides, Nicky hasn't asked me yet, have you, baby?'

Susie's father beamed. 'Don't worry, you'll be amongst the first to know when we do, probably get a call from the ambulance service when they come round to try and get me up off my knees.' Which made Adele giggle some more.

It was obvious that it wasn't quite the answer Alice had been expecting. 'What on earth would Grandma say?' she snapped, as if unable to hold herself back any longer.

Susie's dad lifted an eyebrow. 'Grandma?' His expression softened. 'She'd say there's no fool like an old fool. And she would be right, but we're a long time dead, chicken. And your grandma loved me far too much to want me to spend the rest of my life on my own. If the shoe had been on the other foot, I would have hated to think of her being lonely.'

Alice stared at him, while Susie, with a great lump in her throat, nodded. Her dad was right. Her mum had loved her dad very much, and even though she'd have shaken her head and rolled her eyes, she would have seen the good heart in Adele, seen beyond the red spotty sundress and the matching red nails, and known her precious Nicholas would be safe with this woman.

Alice opened her mouth to say something else, but Susie, anxious to lighten the mood, jumped in. 'Actually, Dad, Alice has got some news as well, haven't you, darling?'

Alice looked daggers at her.

'Don't tell me,' said Adele, all smiles and expectation. 'Let me guess? You're getting married as well? Is that why you asked?'

134

Alice glared at her. 'No, no, actually, I'm not getting married. Actually, I'm pregnant.' She managed to make it sound like a threat.

There was a moment's silence and then, to Susie's surprise, a tear rolled down her father's face. 'Oh sweetheart,' he said, voice all quivering and emotional. 'Oh, Alice. That's the best news I've had in a long time, how wonderful. God, I'm so pleased for you. Isn't that great?'

The depth of his reaction totally threw Alice, and Susie too.

'Oh that's so sweet,' Adele whooped, clapping her hands together with genuine delight. 'When is it due; how far gone are you? Do you know what it is yet – I bet you're so excited, aren't you? I love babies. Have you thought of any names? What does your boyfriend think? Oh, isn't that lovely, Nicky? You clever, clever girl.' Adele managed, in under thirty seconds, to say all the things that Susie had struggled to think of, and to say them with genuine delight and enthusiasm.

'Oh, isn't that perfect, Nicky, you're going to be a great-granddad.' And then to Alice, 'No wonder you look so well. You'll have to bring the baby out to Spain to see us when it's a bit older – sun, sea, the beach – the flights aren't very long, we could meet you from the airport, couldn't we, Nicky? Oh, isn't it exciting? Isn't it lovely . . .'

Susie could see that Alice was totally wrong-footed.

The rest of the evening was a gush fest of enthusiasm from Adele. If she was conscious of Alice's frostiness she was doing a sterling job of working round it and by nine o'clock had managed to wheedle a due date and half a dozen names out of Ms Icicle. And when Alice, totally bemused by Adele's rapt attention, started to moan about Adam, to Susie's amazement Adele nodded in sympathy and encouraged her to talk about nursery-school places, carrying heavy shopping, the unknown side-effects of inhaling the fumes from pine car-fresheners, support stockings, next door's cat and the dangers of contracting listeria at buffet suppers.

Come ten o'clock, the unlikely allies were back indoors making more camomile tea, while Susie and her dad sat in the long shadows, watching the stars appear in the midnight-blue sky. They sat for a long time in silence, the voices and laughter from the house sounding like the cackle of ducks on a lake.

'Before you say anything,' said her dad finally, 'I know what you're thinking, and I wanted to tell you that Adele's not a gold-digger, and all right she can be a little bit loud and a bit –'

Susie put her hand on his arm. 'Dad, don't – I wasn't going to say anything bad about Adele. I think she's lovely, and all right so I admit I was a bit shocked when I caught the pair of you this afternoon, and no, she isn't exactly the kind of woman I imagined you spending the autumn of your life with, but she is great – really – and I hope the pair of you are very, very happy together.'

Her dad looked up at her. 'You mean that?'

Susie nodded. 'Uh-huh – cross my heart.'

Her dad grinned. 'I love her. And she loves me.'

Susie smiled. 'I know, and it shows.'

'And isn't it good news about Alice?' said her dad, helping himself to the last slice of raspberry and mango cheesecake. 'It'll settle her down, maybe take the starch out of her. Where's Robert by the way? I thought he'd have been round this evening. Not like him to miss a free supper.'

'Robert and I have decided to call it a day,' Susie said, not quite meeting his eye.

Her dad nodded. 'Good, I'm pleased about that. I always thought you could do better than him. To be honest, Robert struck me as a bit of a wanker. So what else is going on?' he said, moving on without a backward glance.

Alice miraculously wasn't up when Susie rolled out of bed at eight o'clock the next morning, which gave her time to clear up the kitchen, load the dishwasher, walk the dog, and think about whether she had been too hasty turning down Robert's supper invitation. Maybe, on reflection, she ought to have said yes. Casually, of course, it wouldn't do to look too eager.

After all, Susie and Robert had been through a lot together, maybe they could be friends, and even if they couldn't, she missed him. And whatever Nina said, Robert undoubtedly missed her. Why else would he ring her up and ask her to come over for supper? No one had forced him to ring. What was the harm in getting together for a meal?

Even at eight in the morning the day was hot and heavy. Out on the far side of the common, Susie unfastened Milo's lead and let him womble off through the bushes, wishing, not for the first time, that her brain had an off switch. The trouble was that, left to its own devices, it could try and convince her of anything. The truth was, once you cut to the chase, Robert wanted a family, a baby. And if she'd got an ounce of common sense she should move on, not pine, get to grips with the fact that it was over, join a dating agency, go speed dating, take up a new hobby, take the veil.

Certainly *not* hang around waiting for Robert to come to his senses or change his mind, and definitely *not* go round for supper.

And even if he did say he'd made a mistake, how awful would it be to be with someone you knew wanted something that you couldn't give them? It wasn't exactly a recipe for peace of mind whichever way you looked at it. How long would it be before he started looking wistfully at younger women with child-bearing hips?

In the back pocket of her jeans, Susie's phone went off. She pulled it out and checked the screen. '*Tonight, 7.00 p.m., no excuses*' the text read.

Susie's heart leapt – no text-speak, proper punctuation, maybe Robert wouldn't take no for an answer after all. It gave her an odd little frisson of excitement and throttled the sensible voice into frustrated silence. She rather liked the idea of Robert coming over all forceful after all this time. Maybe this had been the wake-up call they both needed. Maybe he realised he'd made a mistake. Perhaps they had got too cosy. Maybe the baby thing was just a blip, a mad moment. Maybe they needed to get together, reignite the spark? Susie scrolled down to check the sender's number when the alert beep went off again.

It didn't take long for Susie's bubble to burst. Apparently the first text had come from Nina, and the second text was from her too. It read:

I know what you're thinking. Don't weaken, the man is a complete moron. Meet me outside the Majestic at 7.00 p.m. sharp. The popcorn is on me.

Which didn't stop Susie looking longingly at Robert's gable end, framed by trees, and wondering what the odds were on Milo being drawn instinctively to the back gate, a homing mongrel, if she took the path down beside Robert's drive, just for old times' sake. Up until now, she had avoided going that way, but what could Susie do if Milo just happened to slip inside? Or happened to run up to the front door and bark to be let in, wagging his tail with joy as the door swung slowly open to reveal Robert in a silk bathrobe, a completely unexpected all-over tan and nothing vaguely bald in sight?

'*Sorry, Robert, didn't mean to disturb you but you know what Milo's like, all fluff and no brain, cute though . . .*' she'd say, and then she'd shrug and Robert would notice just how much cuter she looked this morning with her hair all windswept and make-up all done, and he'd invite her in for coffee and – and at that point Susie very quickly made a sharp right turn and headed down to the river.

When she finally got back to the cottage, about an

hour later, Alice was up and, despite the heat, wrapped in her fluffy dressing gown, pale as milk and grumpy as hell. 'You might have told me that you were going out,' she growled, stomping around the kitchen.

'I thought I'd leave you sleeping, I thought you might enjoy a lie-in while you're here. Oh, and a good morning to you too.'

Alice snuffled. 'The phone woke me up. Apparently the boy wonder has got himself into trouble again and needs rescuing. Again.'

'Jack?'

'Who else?' Alice said. 'Bloody typical.'

Susie decided not to point out that Jack wasn't the only one who had come running home when the going got rough.

'Did he say what he wanted?'

'Oh, he won't talk to me,' said Alice peevishly. 'He says I only ever find fault with him, but let's be honest, Jack's a walking disaster area – he just doesn't like the truth, that's all. I can see why Ellie got fed up with him, always expecting people to bail him out. He is a total liability.'

'Alice, what did Jack want?'

Alice glared at her. 'Don't snap at me, just because you're up early. You're really not a morning person at all, are you? Oh, and while I think about it, Robert rang as well. Something about him inviting you to supper this evening?'

Totally frustrated, Susie stared at Alice, trying to decide who to ring first and what to say to Alice that would make her realise just how infuriating she was without provoking another tirade.

'It must be hard for you,' continued Alice, 'you know, with this stuff with Robert. Although it's lovely that he wants to stay friends. I mean, that is nice, isn't it? Despite the whole baby thing. Anyway, I was thinking that maybe we ought to go shopping while I'm here. It must be a bit of a knock to your ego and it's so easy to just let yourself go, isn't it? So a bit of retail therapy, give yourself a bit of a lift, a bit of a makeover. You really don't make the best of yourself, you know, and I'll be there to make sure you don't make any real howlers. There's nothing worse than that whole mutton-dressed-as-lamb look. I mean, look at Adele . . .' She rolled her eyes heavenwards as she helped herself to a glass of skimmed milk. 'Caught in a time warp or what? Those clothes – maybe we should all go out together. I mean, you could both do with the help.'

Susie couldn't think of an answer as Alice coolly appraised her and then laughed. 'Don't look so worried, Mum, I was only joking about Adele, maybe we could do her online?'

Eager to get away, Susie headed for the phone and tapped in Robert's number from memory.

'Hi, Alice said you called?' she said all bright and breezy as he picked up.

'Oh yes, nothing really very important, just wanted to say – well – maybe another time. You know, it would be good to catch up. Have a coffee. You okay?'

He sounded odd and awkward as if she had caught him off guard.

'Is this a bad time?'

'Oh no,' he blustered, all breathy and with all kinds of forced joviality. 'No, not at all. How are you doing?'

'Oh, I'm fine. You rang me earlier?'

'Yes, yes, I did, but you know –' There was someone there. Susie would have staked her life on it. 'I was just checking in, seeing how things were. You know,' he said. 'Anyway, tell you what, how about I ring you later, mate, or maybe we could catch up in the week?'

'Sure,' said Susie, wondering who was there, and who had managed to rattle Robert so thoroughly.

After they hung up, before she could have time to really think about what Robert had said, the phone rang in her hand. It was Jack. And he wasn't full of bluster.

'Hi honey, how's it going?'

'I don't know, Mum – it's – it's not exactly easy.'

'What do you mean, love?'

'It's like Ellie's a completely different person to the person I lived with, she's all kind of spiky and defensive. And I don't know what to say to make her the Ellie I know.'

'Don't rush it. It's going to take time. Where did you stay last night?'

'At Eddy's, and he said that I can stay there tonight if I need to – but I'm not sure what the hell I want. Except for things to be back like they were with Ellie and me.'

'Darling, she wasn't happy or she wouldn't have left.'

He sighed. 'We could have sorted it out if she hadn't just upped and gone. We need time to talk.'

Susie stayed quiet and then Jack said, 'Anyway, she's

invited me round tonight. Her dad's going out, so she said I could come round and eat supper – probably be a takeaway – I don't suppose she's planning to cook.'

He laughed, but even so Susie could still hear the hurt. 'Just take it one step at a time. Tell her the things you want to say, but most important of all listen to what she has to say.'

'Wise words, Mother.'

This time it was Susie who laughed. 'Which are easy to say when it's someone else. Put it down to a lifetime of experience, a lot of misery and way too many trashy magazines. If you need me you know where I am.'

'You're a star, Mum. What are you up to today?'

'Just pottering around at the moment. I thought Alice and I might nip into town and then we're all going to the pictures later.'

'Uh-huh, and how is the Witchfinder General this morning?'

Susie glanced through into the kitchen where Alice, wearing marigolds and a determined expression, appeared to be going through the contents of Susie's fridge. 'Don't ask.'

Saturday went very slowly. The day was oppressively hot, not a breath of wind even with all the windows open. Milo lay on the flags in the kitchen, panting miserably.

Over a very late no-wheat, no-dairy breakfast, Alice explained the importance of an appropriate diet for the perimenopausal woman and suggested a singles Saga holiday, Pilates and soya milk as ways Susie could get her life back on track. Apparently she had seen an article in the *Independent* – she would email it as soon as she got back to the flat.

'Have you spoken to Adam?' said Susie, as Alice sipped mint tea.

'I've already explained to him that we need time apart to reflect – I told him not to ring so he's been texting me instead, it's so annoying – he doesn't seem to have any grasp of how unreasonable he's being.'

'And have you considered that it might be you?'

Alice's expression hardened. 'I'm assuming that's a rhetorical question, Mum? All I'm doing is looking after your grandchild's future welfare –'

'I do understand that, Alice, but I wonder if perhaps you're overreacting. Adam cares about you and the baby – all this forward planning is all very well but having a family changes things. You may need to be less rigid –'

Alice sighed, her expression suggesting that Susie had finally shuffled off into the land of those who need humouring. 'Mum, you have to understand that things move on – pregnancy and childbirth have totally changed since you had me and Jack. It's all completely different now.'

Somehow Susie doubted the basics had changed that much, but said nothing.

Because it was so hot, the promised shopping trip didn't materialise, which was a relief. Come mid-afternoon, Alice went upstairs for a little nap with some uplifting literature, an eye mask and a Baby Mozart CD designed to improve the intellect of the unborn child, which some woman in the Sunday broadsheets swore had had her son reading the *Iliad* by the time he was two.

While Attila dozed, Susie went into the studio to carry on working on the portrait of Jack that she had started the previous weekend. At least it was cool, the old washhouse sheltering under the shade of the cottage. She loved it out here.

Susie pulled back the dust-sheet on her easel. Jack was still there waiting for her on the canvas, sitting at the bench reading the newspapers, steaming mug within reach, hair backlit by morning sunshine. For an instant, Susie stared at the image and then looked up, almost expecting to see him sitting there – and then, smiling, picked up her palette and a favourite brush and started to work. Maybe she should ask Alice to sit too – maybe do a portrait of them both while they were both so close to home – and as she worked, Susie fought the temptation to think about Robert or ring him or consider whether Alice had been switched at birth by goblins, and slipped slowly into the peaceful, all-engulfing place where there was just the canvas and the paint, her skill and her imagination.

Susie and Alice left the cottage at six fifteen. Alice insisted they ate before they left so that her blood sugar levels didn't drop, as recent studies conducted by somebody in Cardiff, or maybe it was Manchester, had shown there was a link between something and something else that wasn't good for the unborn child, which Susie didn't bother listening to as she reversed out of her drive and into the lane. It was still so hot.

She'd overheard Alice talking to Adam on the phone just before they left. Alice had said, 'I think *miss* is a rather emotive word, Adam, don't you? I've only been away since Friday . . .'

Susie drove down past Robert's, trying not to look. His car was parked in the drive.

The film went on for far too long and was about a beautiful middle-aged spinster, a hot-shot lawyer who had murdered her cheating lover – eventually – but only after she had stalked him for weeks, sent his ageing mother mad, destroyed his children's lives and set up his vapid wife with a man from the Foreign Office, as she watched him day after day from the window of a top-floor flat opposite his office, eating sushi that she had delivered and sent him the bill for.

It was meant to be a black comedy, apparently, and according to Nina and Alice was very likely to be nominated for several Oscars, a Palme d'Or and possibly a silver bullet.

All Susie could think of as they dragged the demented blonde woman away in handcuffs, wearing a black evening dress and a triumphant smile, was that she had the same curtains in her bedroom as the murderess. Her heart really wasn't in it.

'Do you want to eat?' asked Nina as they piled out of the cinema into the heavy, almost tropical, warmth. 'It's early yet, we could go to Manolitos in Tower Street, grab a bowl of chilli, sour cream and –'

Alice shook her head. 'I'm afraid I can't do chilli at the moment. Or sour cream –'

'Italian then, Benito's in King's Street, seafood linguine and –'

'No seafood,' said Alice, holding up her hands like a clerk in a bank raid.

'Well, you could always have something else,' said Nina. 'It's just that seafood is their speciality.'

'I'm not sure I could cope with the smell,' said Alice. Nina pulled a face.

'And actually, although it's a great idea, to be honest I'm completely knackered,' said Susie.

Nina looked from one to the other. 'Oh, that's great. It's Saturday night, folks – it isn't even ten o'clock yet and you want to go home?'

'It's been a long week,' said Susie.

'I know, which is exactly why we need a little R and R. How about going to the chippy round the corner, we could have sit-down cod and chips, mushy peas and curry sauce?'

'Oh, too greasy,' said Alice, wrinkling up her nose.

'I give up,' said Nina, slumping onto one of the benches outside the Majestic. 'Here was me thinking that we could make an evening of it. Good film, dinner with friends, catch up on the baby news, the goss, and take turns at pointing out weird people in the restaurant. I didn't realise I was already out with the weird people.'

Nina sounded genuinely disappointed, and Susie, overcome by a sense of guilt, said, 'Okay, actually I am a bit peckish, maybe I'll perk up once I've eaten something.'

And then, turning to her daughter, said, 'So, Alice, what do you fancy for supper then?'

Which was how they ended up in a funny little whole-food vegetarian noodle bar in Norfolk Street, with Susie and Nina struggling to find anything on the menu that didn't have tofu as the protein of choice.

It was around eleven when they finally arrived back home. Alice, replete after a wheatgrass and soya milk smoothie, went straight up to bed, so Susie sat outside for a while in the garden, star-gazing, cradling a glass of Baileys, with Milo curled happily at her feet. Her treat after what seemed like a long day. After the second glass she started to think about Robert. Halfway down the third glass he was all she could think about.

He was there all on his own, and she was here all on her own, and after all hadn't he invited her round to supper? Maybe she should just wander over there with the bottle of Baileys and the dog? After all, it wasn't that late and it was the weekend.

The common was all lit up in the moonlight, and it wasn't far to Robert's cottage. Susie would have known the way even in the dark. And if she needed any other reason to be out, Milo usually had one last wee before bedtime. The two of them headed across the night-black grass. There were still lights on in the cottage windows, and as she reached the back gate Susie stopped. With hindsight maybe this wasn't such a good idea after all.

She hesitated, gate half open, torn between good sense, instinct and habit. Maybe she should come back in the morning. Things looked different in daylight. Nina was right, she shouldn't weaken.

Unfortunately, Milo had other ideas. Programmed by three solid years of cottage hopping, when she opened the side gate he slipped between her legs and the gate and scuttled cheerfully down the path, tail wagging. Without thinking, Susie hurried after him, under the covered pergola where the roses they had planted a couple of summers ago were heady with perfume, and made her way round towards the conservatory and terrace.

Maybe the wind was blowing in the wrong direction, which would explain why she didn't hear the sound of voices. Maybe they weren't talking. Maybe the Baileys had anaesthetised the part of her brain that spotted little signs or picked up the subtle clues, but a few seconds later Susie rounded the corner and found herself clutching half a bottle of Baileys and Milo's lead as he bounded off across the herringbone-weave terrace to where Robert was sitting with his arm draped round another woman's slim, suntanned shoulders, his tongue halfway down her throat.

The extraordinary thing was that the girl didn't notice Susie at all. She was turned towards Robert. Held tight against him, she was completely oblivious, while Robert, eyes wide open – the old romantic – looked as if he might choke when he spotted Susie heading towards them.

In that moment Susie took it all in: the girl curled up against him, her white peasant blouse unbuttoned and just slipping low enough to reveal a couple of acres of firm golden flesh, her hair brushing Robert's finger-tips, the empty bottle of wine on the table, the brandy balloons, the glowing embers in the fire pit – and yet it was all over, done and dusted in a split second.

Before Robert could so much as move, let alone pull away or say anything, Susie caught up with Milo, bent down, snapped on his lead, turned, and was out of the gate in barely a single breath, except in her head where it all took a lifetime, an eternity, moving through air as thick as treacle with limbs of lead, and then time got real and she was back out in the lane, unable to breathe, raw with hurt, stunned numb.

As she ran across the common, Milo running with her, she was vaguely aware of something or someone close behind her but didn't look back, didn't break her stride, didn't stop until she was back safely in the kitchen of her cottage, breathing hard, barely able to see for tears.

Saskia Hill. Why the hell hadn't she seen that one coming? How come she hadn't realised, how come with all that insight and intuition she credited herself with she hadn't twigged? How dumb was that.

'We've been having some landscaping work done by Hill's Nurseries, they've got this consultant there, she's very interested in getting involved in the wider community, you ought to ring her – I've got her number if you're interested . . .' and on and on – this really nice girl this, this consultant that. Susie had just thought that finally Robert had found something he really enjoyed doing; but now that Susie knew, the clues lit up like an airport runway.

'Susie?' Barely ten seconds behind her, Robert burst into the kitchen, red-faced and if anything more breathless than she was. 'Why didn't you stop? Are you all right?'

What a stupid thing to ask. 'What the hell do you think?'

As she struggled to get her breath, she couldn't help but wonder what Saskia was thinking at this precise moment – presumably Robert hadn't hung around to explain what he was doing before tearing himself away from her and haring across the common after Susie.

'I didn't mean for you to find out that way, Susie,' he said. 'I'm so sorry – really. I want you two to meet, to be friends. Saskia is great – I mean, you've met her. The thing is, she prefers older men. She needs a steady hand to guide her, someone who can take care of her. She's perfect for me.'

Susie slumped into a chair. She couldn't speak; tears and misery and rejection and sheer fury had closed her throat down.

'Look, can I ring you tomorrow?' Robert asked, glancing back over his shoulder almost as if he expected to be caught.

Susie looked up at him. 'Is there any point?'

He nodded. 'I think so – I want to explain.'

'You don't need to explain, Robert, there's nothing to explain, it's all perfectly obvious. What you want is for me to approve, say it'll be all right, say that I'll be all right, and I will, but not now,' she said thickly. 'Maybe not for a while, and no thanks to you. Now go away.'

He stared at her, swallowing hard. 'Please, I want

you to understand – Saskia's lovely. I mean – I really think she's *it*, Susie, I really, truly think she is.'

Susie stared at him. Had the man got no idea what his words were doing to her? She blinked. 'It?' she repeated. The tall, blonde ice queen with her chilly eyes and that imperious, patronising little smile. Was that *it*?

Robert nodded. 'I think so. She's lovely, isn't she? Perfect.'

'Please, just go,' Susie said, although her voice sounded a very long, long way away and like someone else's, someone she didn't know and probably wouldn't like.

'Are you sure?' Robert said, and then looked at Susie and knew that she was positive, and then he turned and went, and for an instant he was caught in sharp relief in the moonlight and Susie could see what Nina meant about his ears. Strange how some thoughts come at totally inappropriate moments.

Robert left the back door wide open, which seemed odd, almost as if he was inviting her to follow him, to observe his moonlit courtship of Ms Perfect.

Chapter 9

When Susie woke up on Sunday morning she lay for a long time looking up at the ceiling, thinking about Robert and babies and Saskia Hill and her perfectly suntanned shoulders. She thought about their future wedding and – what the chances were of her being invited. Robert was bound to think that was a good idea. What the hell did you wear to the church as the runner-up? And then she found herself imagining what their children might look like. It had been bad enough when the future Mrs Robert Harrison had been an abstract possibility, but now she could see them in glorious Technicolor.

They would have names like Camilla and Hugo, and if she concentrated hard enough she could picture them clearly – all blonde and beautiful with Robert's ears, or balding and plump and with florid skin like him, but with mummy's perfect white-blonde hair – it would be just Camilla's luck to get that combination. Susie could see them going off to prep school in the family 4x4 in their dinky little blazers and exquisitely pressed flannel skirts and shorts, driven by the family's Swedish au pair, who Saskia would watch like a hawk.

Susie could see it all: the Shetland pony in the paddock, Mrs Harrison-hyphenated-Hill leading little Camilla round the common on a Sunday morning while Robert taught Hugo how to spin-bowl.

Groaning miserably, Susie rolled over, covered her head with the pillow and closed her eyes as her mind carried on creating little Saskia–Robert combos, as she wished her imagination dead.

Just as Camilla and Hugo were moving on to bigger ponies and better schools and baby Archie had arrived, the phone rang. Susie pulled the duvet up over her head and ignored it – six rings and the machine would cut in. What she hadn't bargained for was Alice.

'Mum? Mum, the phone is ringing,' said a disembodied voice from somewhere across the landing.

'I know, just leave it,' said Susie.

'You can't just leave it.'

'Of course I can. I've got an answering machine. It's what they're for.'

'That's hardly very polite,' growled Alice.

'If I wanted to talk to people this early in the morning, Alice, I'd have a phone beside my bed. Now go back to sleep.'

Even as she was speaking she could hear scrabbling across the landing, and then the sound of Alice's one-way conversation.

'Oh, it's you. What do you want? It's Sunday morning,' snapped Alice. 'It's barely ten – no, of course we aren't up, we're having a lie-in.'

Susie suppressed a smile. She had rather naïvely assumed that answering the phone was an act of compassion on Alice's part, not another chance to tear a strip off some poor sod.

'No, she's not up yet. No, I'm not going to wake her up, you know what she's like in the mornings. It's like jump-starting Genghis Khan.'

'I resent that,' said Susie, giving in, clambering out of bed and dragging on her dressing gown. 'Who is it?' she asked once she was on the landing.

Alice put her hand over the mouthpiece. 'You said I should leave it to ring.'

'Alice, just give me the bloody phone, will you?'

For some reason Alice stepped away from Susie, holding the handset way above her head so that Susie couldn't reach it, which really didn't help Susie's mood.

'Now,' Susie snapped, feeling her temper rise, holding out her hand. Instead Alice held it a little higher. Susie went up onto tiptoes and still couldn't reach.

'Stop,' warned Susie. 'Give it to me now.'

'Here she is,' said Alice, turning fast and giggling into the phone. 'I'd be careful what you say if I were you, she is in a foul mood.'

Susie glared at her. 'I wasn't until you started buggering about.' And then into the receiver said, 'Hi', in a tone all calm and collected, hoping that she would be able to work out who was speaking in the first few words.

'Mum?'

That gave the game away.

'Jack, hello – are you all right, love?'

He sighed. 'Yes and no.'

'How did it go with Ellie?'

155

'Phuhhh.'

'Is that good or bad?'

'I don't know, we talked a lot, hours – most of the night, really – but I don't know if it changed anything very much.'

'Did you stay at Eddy's?'

'Uh-huh, I left Ellie's about two or three this morning, I didn't want to push my luck, you know.'

'Okay, well, that's good. So how have you left things between you?'

'She invited me to come round for lunch today.'

'Well, that's got to be good, Jack.'

'Yeah, that's what I thought.' He didn't sound altogether convinced.

'But?' asked Susie.

'Well, but nothing really. I called round there a little while ago and her dad, Simon, is there, and I think they've been talking. I was planning to take Ellie out for breakfast, croissants and coffee and stuff, you know. Anyway, before Ellie had even got downstairs, Simon was going on about how he couldn't bear to see her so upset, how since she'd been home all she did was cry all the time – how he'd got plenty of his own problems without seeing his little girl upset.'

'That's natural, Jack, he's worried about her. It's what parents do.'

'Anyway, we chatted for a while, and he said he was glad I was coming round for lunch, it would give us all a chance to talk things through and get things straightened out.'

'All?'

'Exactly. That's what he said.'

'Simon's going to be there?'

'He said he's going to cook.'

'Okay, well, maybe that isn't such a bad idea – he cares about her and sometimes it's easier to sort things out if there is someone else there.'

'You mean like a referee?'

'Not quite, Jack, but sometimes it keeps things calmer if there is someone else there. You can say things that you can't always say when you're on your own.'

'That's what I'm afraid of. Simon treats Ellie like she's still twelve and I'm the big bad wolf come to take her away. He's such a bloody hypocrite. I mean, his last girlfriend was younger than Ellie – Jesus, the man is a legend when it comes to women.'

'They're often the worst kind, Jack –'

'It just pissed me off. Anyway, I made a joke about needing moral support, and you and Alice being home at the moment . . .' He paused. 'And Simon said in that case why don't you come over too. The more the merrier. He's going to cook something special, said it's ages since he's seen you.'

'Jack, a family lunch hardly seems the ideal time or place to sort your relationship out, and I can't have met Simon more than half a dozen times.'

'Don't tell me, tell Simon. Trouble is, he'll be there whether you come over or not. I was thinking that at least if you're there too then you can distract him, maybe you could create some sort of a diversion.'

'What do you mean, create a diversion, Jack? Start a fight? Burn a barn down? I'm an art teacher not Sigourney Weaver.'

Jack laughed. 'Please, Mum, can you just come over? I know it's a pain in the arse, but at least it means you won't have to cook – and tomorrow me and Matt get to hear the fallout from Friday's meeting with the board. I could be back on a plane to Italy first thing Tuesday morning. Please.'

Thinking about Italy and Matt and Jack flying out gave Susie an odd and unexpected sense of loss. 'How is Matt?' she asked.

'Dunno. I haven't seen him all weekend, but he's a big boy, I'm sure he's just fine. He spent the weekend with Alex, apparently. So, will you come? Only I've said I'll let Simon know how many there'll be.'

Susie hesitated. 'I'm not sure it's such a good idea.'

'Please, Mum. For me?'

'Oh all right,' said Susie after a moment or two's consideration. At least refereeing and diversion creation might take her mind off Saskia, Robert and baby Archie. 'What time's lunch?'

'One thirty.'

'So what time would you like us to roll up?'

'Twelve thirty or one would be good – time for a chat and a sherry is what Simon said. Not that I think he's ever had a sherry in his life. Presumably gagging Alice is not an option?'

Susie glanced over her shoulder. Alice was sitting in the window seat at the top of the stairs eating a banana and watching the world go by. She looked as benign as a dozing piranha. 'You're the one who suggested inviting us.'

The traffic was kind; they arrived at Simon's a little before one.

'Great to see you again, come on in,' said Simon. 'Come in.' He was standing on the doorstep of his huge Victorian villa waving his arms around like someone directing Harriers on an aircraft carrier.

Simon Hammond was probably in his mid to late fifties, although it was hard to tell unless you were up close. He was well over six feet tall with shoulder-length bleached-blond hair, capped Californian teeth, a spray-on tan, cornflower-blue eyes – possibly contact lenses – the recipient of an unspecified amount of cosmetic surgery and slim as a garden cane.

Thirty years ago he wouldn't have looked out of place fronting a New Romantic band, except that he had been behind them, grafting away as a promoter and making a small fortune in the process, the first of many won and lost. At the moment he was winning.

Simon was wearing skinny-fit jeans, cowboy boots, a cream silk granddad shirt open at the neck to reveal a sprinkling of chest hair, and a single diamond-stud earring. He was still outrageously handsome if you liked the ageing rock-star look, and he knew it.

'Susie, my god, honey, you look absolutely gorgeous. Is that glow all natural?' he said, hugging and kissing her on both cheeks before holding her at arms' length to look her up and down. He smelt of something soft, subtle and very expensive. Close up she could just make out the slight scars of his facelift. 'God, I've always thought you were so hot.'

Susie laughed, feeling herself redden under Simon's undisguised interest. 'It's called vitality, Simon, you can't inject it, sniff it or buy it and nobody can ship it in from China for you.'

'Damn,' he said theatrically. 'Oh, and Alice, how nice to see you too. How are you, pigeon? My god, you look radiant too, absolutely radiant – maybe it's genetic. So how's it all going?' He glanced down at her non-existent bump. His gaze lingered far longer than could be considered polite. 'You know, Alice, I always think pregnant women are just so incredibly sexy,' he purred. 'All those hormones rushing through your bloodstream. You are positively glowing, sweetheart. Glowing.'

Alice didn't blush, instead she arched an eyebrow and held Simon's gaze. 'Leched by a man old enough to be my father – the perfect way to start a Sunday. I wouldn't have thought that too much excitement was good for you at your age.'

'Owww meow,' he said, miming great pain as he waved them both inside. 'I promise I'll get you back for that. You got here okay? Did you find somewhere to park? This road can be a bloody nightmare. Now what would you like to drink?'

As he spoke, Susie and Alice followed Simon through towards the back of the house and into the conservatory that adjoined the huge American-style kitchen, where Jack and Ellie were sitting. As they said their hellos, Susie noticed rather sadly that if Jack and Ellie sat any further apart one of them would have to move into next door's garden.

Meanwhile, Simon opened up a silver fridge the size of a Mini Cooper and peered inside. 'Presumably you're driving?' he asked, nodding towards Susie. 'And presumably you're not drinking for two?' he added, glancing at Alice.

'Actually I'm not drinking at all,' snapped Alice.

'Okay, well in that case how about I do you a really nice chilled fresh fruit cooler – strawberries, peaches, cranberries, lots of other healthy stuff – maybe a little sparkling mineral water. Or I've got some really great ginger beer if you'd prefer. Organic and all that stuff.'

Susie smiled. 'Doesn't sound like you, Simon?'

The first time she'd ever met Simon had been at a family barbecue, at which he and the six-foot-six, rake-thin model he was dating at the time had worked their way through a bottle of tequila. The time after that Susie had met him in the company of an ageing rock princess, when they had consumed an endless flow of Caipirinhas, and the most recent time was at some prestigious local social fundraiser that Jack and Ellie had been part of for the university – like her father, Ellie was good at organising events and had shame-lessly used his connections to get the great and good to support them, while Simon had sat under a sunshade and drunk champagne cocktails until Benny, his driver, and Jack had carried him back to his waiting car. Abstemious really wasn't Simon Hammond's middle name.

'I didn't say that I'd be joining you. Here –' he said,

tossing Susie a peach while he rescued some strawberries and a tray of plump raspberries. 'You can give me a hand.'

'What, no staff on today?'

'Benny is on his holidays, waterskiing on Windermere,' he said. 'How mad is that? The man's sixty if he's a day, five foot two in every direction. I've already told him if he breaks anything I'm going to have him deported. And Nika is upstairs, choosing outfits for when she goes to visit him in hospital, although she has said she'll come rescue me when it all goes horribly wrong.'

In the sun room Ellie said, 'Bit late for that, isn't it, Dad?'

'We're talking lunch here, honey, not life,' said Simon, as if he was returning a snappy volley.

Susie, saying nothing, followed Simon over to the countertop where there were lots of stainless-steel things hanging from racks and arranged on the surfaces, together with endless gadgets and an acre and a half of high-gloss granite work surface, all clinically clean and set with sinks and hobs and all manner of whizbang bits and pieces. The Filipino couple, Benny and Nika, had been with Simon for years and treated him like a cross between a god and a very badly behaved child. From what Jack had told Susie, normally this kitchen was Nika's jealously guarded domain.

'So how's life?' asked Susie.

Simon shrugged. 'Complicated. So no change there.'

He started dropping things into a super-size blender, ice and fruit and juice, while Alice wandered off to talk to Jack and Ellie. In the kitchen area any conversation was close to impossible over the noise of the whirring machinery.

'How about you?' Simon yelled above the roar.

'Well, I'm still here.'

He grinned, dropping strawberries one at a time through the mouth of the blender; for an instant they rode on a foaming sea of fruit pulp before being consumed, sucked down into the food abyss. 'So Jack was telling me. What is it with relationships? You know I'm the same – unlucky in love. God, sweetie, you've got no idea just how unlucky.' When he saw her expression, Simon continued, 'I thought you and what's-his-face were all set for happy ever after.'

'Shows that you're no judge of character – me neither, actually. But anyway, my private life isn't why we're here, is it?' hollered Susie at the top of her voice just as Simon switched the blender off and plunged them into echoing silence. Ellie, Jack and Alice turned round to stare at her from the conservatory.

Simon grinned. 'You can do better, we all can. Ellie says I shouldn't be let out on my own.' He took a couple of glasses down from a shelf then turned a tap on at the base of the blender, half-filling them before topping each up in turn with sparkling water, adding a thick stripy straw and dropping a mint leaf into the glass.

'*Voilà*,' he said, handing her the drink.

Susie sipped it cautiously. 'Ohhh wow, that's lovely.'

'Don't sound so surprised. I'm not a complete klutz. Better with a slug of vodka, though.' He took the second glass off to Alice and then headed back to Susie. 'I thought

I'd do fish for lunch. Grey mullet with blackberries – very underrated fish, the grey mullet, apparently – in season now and very tasty, according to Nika.'

As he spoke Simon poured himself a glass of wine and unpinned a sheet of paper from the noticeboard by the fridge.

'How do you fancy Fannying to my Johnny?' he asked, peering at what Susie could now see was a recipe, written on a postcard in bold block capitals.

Susie looked at him. 'I thought we were here to referee Jack and Ellie.'

'You did? Really? God, I was hoping you'd turned up to give me moral support. I can't be doing with all this mooching around the house crying and moping. Wailing and slamming doors. It's just like being married.' Simon took a slurp of wine. 'What can I say? You and I both know that Jack's a good chap, kind, conscientious, keen to settle down and make a go of it – not a bit like me at his age, actually at any age. Trouble with Ellie is that she just can't see beyond the fact that he travels a bit. She can't see that he loves her and that he's doing his best trying to put bread on the table. She's just like her bloody mother. Now how about joining me in some wine? We can't possibly play at being the Cradocks without a little drop of vino to oil the wheels. And besides, you look like you need a glass of something without pips in it. Here . . .' He pulled the bottle closer and took a wine glass down for her. 'Chenin blanc, from my friend Larry's vineyard in California. Don't look so bloody self-righteous. God, woman, you're footloose and fancy-free again – don't knock it – and besides, Alice can always drive you home. Now,' he said, sliding a pair of gold half-rims out of his top pocket and peering down at the list of ingredients. 'Apparently we need to get the fish out of the other fridge and then finely chop some onions, celery and – fuck – did I just liquidise the blackberries?'

Lunch was late, delicious, funny, loud and wine-fuelled, and all the way through it Simon flirted outrageously with Susie. She had to keep reminding herself that she wasn't there to have fun – a point brought home by Alice's steely expression and evident disapproval. Jack and Ellie talked a lot, but not to each other, and every time Susie picked up her glass it appeared to be full. It was the best time she'd had in weeks.

'You know,' said Simon, as they went into the kitchen to rustle up dessert. 'We really should do this more often.'

Susie looked at him. 'What, get drunk and embarrass our children?'

'Good god no, I can do that without your help, and besides, I'm not embarrassing Ellie, she's used to it by now. No, I meant get together, laugh – talk complete bollocks over a good meal. You know it's really nice to talk to someone ordinary for a change.'

'I'll take that as a compliment, shall I?' said Susie, getting the dishes down from a shelf above the countertop.

'Yes . . . no. Look, I meant it as a compliment not a putdown – in the business I'm in *ordinary* is at a premium. Most of the people I work with are either detoxing, rehabbing, coming out, going in or finding

God. And it never gets any better, every generation throws them up. The ones the press say, "Oh, so fresh-faced and so unspoilt, so nice" are usually the worst by a long way.'

Simon lifted his granddad shirt to show off a tanned, gym-toned midriff and what looked remarkably like the scar from a nasty stab wound. 'The evidence, m'lud: butter wouldn't melt in her cute little cupid's-bow mouth, she's so easy to work with, so emotionally stable, so sweet, so she tried to kill me with a fucking bread knife. She was twenty-one at the time, under five feet tall, household name – size six, worth a fortune, mad as a smoked haddock.'

Susie touched the scar, a shiny silver star on an other-wise washboard-tight belly. 'Was it something you said?'

'Ummm, what a nice touch you have. I've always thought you are a very attractive woman, Susie,' he purred.

She raised her eyebrows. 'With a line like that it's no wonder she stabbed you. Any more and *I'll* finish the job.'

He aped hurt. 'I'm serious. Look, why don't we go out for dinner sometime – and before you start bleating, no strings, no nothing, just a great dinner, good food, good company. Just the two of us rather than *en famille*.'

'Are you serious?'

'Didn't I just say I was? Look, cross my heart – really – tell you what, how about next weekend? Friday night. I'll come over and pick you up.'

Susie turned her attention to a pile of homemade meringues, the remains of the raspberries and a pot of double cream that needed assembling into dessert. Simon, meanwhile, poured them both yet another glass of wine and then smiled at her as he handed her one. 'You know I should have done this ages ago – you're absolutely wonderful. It's so good to be with someone sane.'

Susie shook her head and set about the raspberries. Every instinct told her that, however flattering, Simon would have forgotten all about asking her out when he'd sobered up. It was nice to be asked, though.

'I just can't believe the way you behaved, Mother,' Alice snapped, slamming the car into gear.

'It was just a bit of fun, and please don't talk to me like *I'm* the child here. To be honest I could use a little fun right now.'

'You're drunk.'

'Really?'

'I'm glad I came home now. Is this sort of thing happening a lot?'

Susie stared at her. 'What on earth is that supposed to mean?'

'This whole drink thing.' Alice sniffed. 'I was just wondering if maybe you had a problem. It would certainly explain lots of things.'

Susie stared at her. What exactly did Alice mean? That she couldn't keep Robert because she was a lush? Susie beaded her furiously. 'If you hadn't been a home delivery I would swear blind they swapped you at birth.'

Alice, stony-faced, hands gripping the steering wheel like she was strangling a whippet, eased the car into the narrow lane that ran round the common towards Susie's cottage. They had driven nearly all the way home in an icy silence that Susie had at first put down to Alice being unsure of the route, then being slightly nervous of driving an unfamiliar car, before finally twigging that Alice was just out-and-out livid with her.

'You're not really going out to dinner with that man, are you?' snapped Alice.

'Simon? I don't see why not, nor what it's got to do with you, although I think the chances are that when he sobers up he'll have completely forgotten about it. Mind those pot holes –'

'I can see them.' Alice slowed the car down to a crawl. 'I think it's disgusting.'

'I know, I've rung the council twice this year.'

'That's not what I mean and you know it, Mum,' growled Alice as they got to the cottage. 'You were supposed to be there for Jack and Ellie,' she continued, reversing slowly into the driveway.

'And I was. Jack asked me to cause a diversion so that he could get a chance to talk to Ellie.'

'He asked you to cause a diversion, not get off with his girlfriend's father. All that giggling and flirting stuff with Simon in the kitchen – I mean, what on earth did you think you were playing at? It was disgusting.'

'For god's sake, Alice, what do you want me to do? Become a nun? Spend the rest of my life on my own with Milo, knitting tea cosies to pass the time between visits from the library van?'

'No, no, of course I don't. Don't be ridiculous.' Something in her tone made Susie suspect that actually

Alice was lying. 'What you need to do is find someone more suitable. I've seen adverts for some very nice agencies, or you could go on a singles holiday for older people. I saw one to the Dordogne in the *Sunday Times*, by coach so you wouldn't have to drive. Going out with Simon would be – would –' Alice struggled to find the right words and finally, failing, said, 'The man is a – well, he's almost family, Mum – it's incest.'

Susie stared at her in astonishment. 'It's not incest, Alice, it's dinner. Now if you'll excuse me I'm just going inside for a little lie down. You need a little afternoon nap when you get to my age.'

It was dark when Susie woke up, and she had a headache that stretched from somewhere in sub-Saharan Africa up to the Urals – maybe further, it was hard to tell without moving, although opening her eyes was difficult enough. While resisting the temptation to move anything else, she tried to think about what she'd said at lunch, and what she'd done, and considered that against all the odds, unless of course she was still drunk, she'd had a great time, not made a complete tit of herself, and had a potential dinner date, although Susie had some doubt that Alice would agree with her about how well it had gone.

After another ten minutes or so, unable to stay stock still any longer, Susie very carefully rolled over onto her side and looked at the clock. It was almost midnight and from somewhere close by she could hear the sounds of the TV. Gingerly she eased herself towards the edge of the bed, moving with glacial slowness, and tried sitting up and then standing, until finally she felt able to make her way downstairs.

Alice was in the sitting room eating raw carrots and watching a black and white film. She looked up as Susie came in.

'Oh, you're alive then,' she said, muting the TV. 'I've been up a few times to check, just in case you had choked to death on your own vomit.'

'Well, thanks for that. Do you fancy a cup of tea?'

Alice shook her head. 'Not at this time of night, caffeine is bad for the baby. Did you know there is more caffeine in an average cup of tea than in a cup of coffee? Oh, and Jack rang, and Ellie. I think they were worried about you.'

'In case I had choked to death on my own vomit?'

'In case you took Simon's offer seriously.'

Susie felt a little sting of indignation. 'There's no reason on earth why Simon shouldn't invite me out, Alice. I'm not completely over the hill, you know.'

Alice rolled her eyes heavenwards. 'I never said you were over the hill, Mum. Get a grip, for god's sake. This isn't an age thing, this baby thing with Robert has really freaked you out, hasn't it? It's just that Simon is bad news. Ellie doesn't think you're too old for him. She thinks you're too *good* for him. And Jack's worried that he'll hurt you and that after Robert you need something nice to happen, not to be jerked around by Golden Boy.'

Susie struggled to regain her composure. She hadn't realised just how good it had made her feel to be asked out by Simon. They hadn't been that drunk, for god's sake. 'That's sweet, but I can take care of myself.'

'Said the woman who got hammered over lunch and needed driving home,' said Alice in an undertone. 'It was totally irresponsible. What would you have done if I hadn't been there to rescue you?'

Susie stared levelly at her. She really resented the idea that Alice saw her as someone who needed rescuing. Truth was, if Alice hadn't been there she would have stayed sensible, stayed sober, laughed at Simon, still probably have had a great time and been home by three p.m. 'Probably ended up in bed with him,' Susie said, not dropping her gaze. 'Isn't that what we irresponsible people do?'

Alice tutted. 'Good job I was there to bring you home in that case. Now would you like me to make you a cup of tea, or would you prefer a glass of water and a couple of soluble paracetamol?'

'Or a nice bath chair and a tartan rug?'

'I'm only thinking about your welfare, Mum. I was going to suggest a cup of tea and then I think you should pop upstairs to bed. Have you ever read anything about liver damage?'

For one terrible moment, Susie saw her future flash before her in glorious Technicolor. Coach trips and Sanatogen, sensible shoes, cream teas and Alice popping round to make sure she was eating properly. 'How long are you staying for?'

Alice switched the TV back on. 'I thought till the end of the week,' she said, snapping the end off a carrot.

Jack rang Susie at work on Monday morning. He sounded really despondent and for a few seconds Susie thought it was something to do with Ellie, but apparently not. The bad news was that the funding had been pulled on the Italian dig. Worse news was that Alice wasn't joking about staying. Apparently she'd emailed her office and had arranged to work from Susie's until Friday. God only knew what she'd told Adam. And the final straw was a note in Susie's pigeonhole asking if she could ring Saskia Hill ASAP. Something urgent, apparently. Susie didn't like to contemplate what that might be.

All in all it was proving to be a long morning. Electric Micky had taken his clothes off for the final time this term and there was a lot of finishing off planned generally across every class. Nina had been beavering away ticking lots of boxes on her end-of-term show list, and Susie still had the tenacious remnant of a hangover.

'So how was your weekend?' asked Nina when they finally settled down in the art room for the lunchtime lull. At which point Susie's mobile rang – Simon's name flashed up on caller ID, although she couldn't remember giving him her mobile number or vice versa.

'I'm just about to find out,' said Susie, taking the call. 'Hi, how's the head?' she asked, before he could get a word in edgeways.

'Fine, and how about yours?'

'Ummm, good question, fine as long as I don't try moving or thinking. I spent about fifteen hours in bed.'

'On your own? My god, woman, what a terrible waste. If I'd have known you could have stayed here and slept it off with me.'

Susie laughed. 'Simon, did you take lessons in how to sound sleazy?'

'*Take* lessons? God, no – no, I taught them. Anyway, I just rang up to ask if I could take you out to supper.'

'On Friday? You already asked and I already said yes. I thought when you sobered up you might change your mind.'

'Not at all. Actually, I was thinking about maybe going out tonight as well. How are you fixed?'

Nina, perched on the overstuffed green armchair, was all ears, and busy making what-the-hell-is-going-on faces.

'Are you serious?' said Susie.

'You asked me that yesterday and the answer is still yes. Why wouldn't I be? It's a lovely day out there – perfect for the beach – and Ellie has got the hump with me *and* Jack at the moment. I've said that I'd give the pair of them some space and then I thought we could kill two birds with one stone. Jack and Ellie, you and me. *So*, how do you fancy a drive down to the coast? I know this brilliant little restaurant that does local seafood – this time of the week we won't have any trouble getting a table – how about it? Come on, say yes. Beamer with the top down, a walk on the beach, supper –'

'I'm at work at the moment.'

'I know that, but I could come over later, pick you up about seven? Say yes, we had such a great time yesterday, you know we did – come on, Susie.'

How could she possibly resist? 'Do I have to wear something slinky, tight and rock star-ish?'

'If you like that kind of thing, but I was thinking more jeans and tee shirt.'

'And some sort of spandangly jacket?'

'It works for Aerosmith.'

Susie laughed. 'I'll see you around seven.'

'*Who was that*?' said Nina, unable to bear the suspense. 'You went all pink and perky and, you know –' She wiggled her fingers to suggest something flirtatious and excited.

Susie was amazed to hear herself giggle.

'Which, obviously, given the state of play last week is a good thing,' added Nina. 'So –'

'So Ellie's dad asked me out.'

'Ellie's dad? *As in Jack's girlfriend's dad?*'

'Uh-huh, Simon Hammond, and before you say anything, I've already told Alice, it's not incest.'

Nina pulled a face. 'I didn't say it was, I was just trying to work out whether I've met him or not, and if so what he looks like.'

Susie got up. 'Let's go Google him.'

'Great idea,' said Nina grinning, already on her feet.

About ten minutes later they were at the keyboard of the computer in what passed for an office in the art department, with Nina staring at the image on the screen. It was Simon Hammond in his prime, at some awards ceremony, wearing a beautifully cut DJ, open at the neck, bow tie loose, with his arm around a tiny blonde. He was so good-looking it was almost painful.

'Was she the one who stabbed him?' asked Nina, pointing to his companion.

Susie shrugged. 'Who knows? Could be one of thousands.'

'And he's taking you out to dinner?'

'He said that ordinary was nice.'

'Well there's a turn-up for the books. Can I come? I'm *very* ordinary.'

Susie laughed and then flicked to a more recent picture, taken at another awards ceremony. This time he was flanked by a couple of curvaceous brunettes, but there was no doubt about it, Simon had aged well, even if some of it was quite obviously surgical.

'I'm serious,' said Nina. 'I wouldn't eat much, wouldn't get in the way, you'd barely notice that I was there.'

Susie flicked back to the main screen. 'You're not going to tell me I'm too old, ridiculous, misguided or mad to go out with him, are you?'

'God no, why on earth would I want to do that?'

'Or that he's far too handsome for someone as horribly normal as me?'

Nina narrowed her eyes. 'No, I wasn't going to say that either – is that how you feel?'

'Well, a bit. I mean, Simon is still gorgeous and he's a bit wild, dangerous, and used to bonking the rich and famous. Not to mention the young and perky. Not exactly my usual type.'

'About ten years ago I went out with a male model,' Nina began.

'You didn't tell me that.'

'Well, it was something and nothing at the time – it didn't last very long and it was all a bit weird. He was lovely, Bobbie. He'd done all kinds of magazine work, promotional stuff, acted a bit, and was just so damned gorgeous. You wanted to lick him all over. He was ten years younger than me, sunbed tan, perfect teeth, and I thought at first when he asked me out that he was joking. In the end we went out to dinner, really nice little bistro in Cambridge, soft lights, sexy couples – and all the time I was wondering what people would think. Him young and oh so pretty and me fabulously talented but oh so wrinkly. Would they assume I was his mother; would they think I'd paid him? All kinds of stuff can go through your mind.

'Anyway, I was flattered. It took me about a month to realise that Bobbie was the one with the real problem. He took shallow to whole new depths. He'd got no conversation, unless you counted talking about himself and what he wanted to do when he got rich and famous. He was so dull and so very, very boring. Between jobs he spent all his time in the gym and was terrified about losing his figure, his hair, whether his roots were showing. He drove me completely and utterly mad.

'We'd be in a restaurant and he'd be trying to catch a glimpse of his profile reflected in the windows. In bed, he'd be looking at himself in the wardrobe mirror. We were going out one night, with friends, nothing special, a barbecue I think, and he brought six outfits over to try on to see which one I thought he looked best in. That was it really. I just thought, it doesn't matter how pretty someone is, if they can't talk to you then once the sex is out of the way there's bugger all left. So don't be fooled, babe. If the only thing that opens doors for you is your looks, post-thirty you're on a hiding to nothing.'

'So you're saying I'm ugly and old, but talented?'

Nina nodded. 'That's about the measure of it. Now do you want some more tea?'

'May as well,' said Susie, holding out her cup. 'Or would you like me to astound you with my astonishing conversational skills?'

'I'd rather you passed the chocolate HobNobs.'

'Simon is good-looking and talented and successful.'

'With a string of broken relationships.'

'Uh-huh, and stab wounds.'

'Well, maybe you'll be the one to turn him around.'

Susie handed her the biscuit tin. 'And maybe there really is a tooth fairy.'

'You never know.' Nina paused. 'Okay, so maybe you do know, but I reckon a bit of fun is just what the doctor ordered.'

'You're right. And we're not talking happy ever after here.'

'And it'll give you something to think about other than Robert – and at least Simon won't be boring. Talking of which, how did you get on ringing Petunia?'

'Who?'

'The girl from the nursery, the one who –'

Susie's expression made Nina stop mid-sentence. Susie realised with a start that she hadn't mentioned catching Robert and Saskia in the garden.

'What? What did I say?' said Nina. 'You know who I mean, the posh girl with the plants and the four-by-four, cold eyes who –'

'Who is currently dating Robert,' Susie said.

Nina's jaw dropped. 'No? *No?* Really? My god, you really *have* had a weekend, haven't you?'

'You could say that.'

'Do you want me to ring her for you?'

Susie nodded. 'Would you mind?'

Nina shook her head. 'Not at all – actually I'd enjoy it. She really hated me.'

Simon was late. Although he was worth waiting for. When he finally did show up he was driving a low-slung shiny black sports car with a cream leather interior. He had the top down and on the passenger seat was a huge bunch of luscious dark pink roses.

Alice stood upstairs on the landing watching as Susie went down to let him in.

'Do you think he's compensating for anything?' Alice said, pointing towards the sports car as he pulled into the drive.

'I'll tell you later,' Susie replied, picking up her jacket from the hallstand.

Alice pulled a face while Milo peered up at her longingly. He would have loved a walk on the beach but Susie couldn't see Simon welcoming a smelly mongrel in the back of his sports car.

She had agonised over what to wear and had finally plumped for a pair of smart jeans, knee-high boots and a long-sleeved fitted cream shirt, silver earrings and a fitted charcoal grey jacket, a scarf, and a big soft brown leather bag to match her boots. Standing in front of the mirror she decided it was a good look, casual, uncontrived but arty, like someone easy in their own skin who didn't have to try too hard – and not at all, as Alice had said before, like mutton dressed as lamb.

As Susie opened the front door, Simon looked her over like a hungry dog surveying a fillet steak.

'You look absolutely gorgeous,' he said, leaning in to hug and kiss her gently. 'And god, you smell wonderful too. Here –' He handed her the roses. 'These are for you.'

From somewhere in the house Susie heard Alice making vomiting noises. Maybe the morning sickness had started.

Chapter 10

They served fresh Cromer crab at the Wherry Boat Inn and newly baked bread with local organic butter, so delicious that it made you want to cry with pure delight. Susie decided, as she took another bite of bread soaked in the juices from a huge dish of moules marinière, that this had to be one of the most telling definitions of middle age, when you could be overcome with emotion by a nice bap.

The head waiter, a small man with an impressive moustache, with whom Simon was on first-name terms, had found them a roomy table by the window with a view out over the salt marshes and little twisting creeks to the Wash beyond.

As the evening closed in, great flocks of seabirds and waders rose into the air. Dense as confetti, they wheeled and turned on the stiff breeze, taking in the last of the sun as it set, casting them in silhouette, while turning the sky into a palette of golds and pinks and rich raucous reds which, if Susie had put on a canvas, people would have sworn blind she was making up.

Even though it was Monday, the dining room was

more than half-full and around them there was a constant low hum of conversation and laughter. Throughout dinner Simon topped up her wine and they talked about art and music and relationships and love and children and ex-wives and ex-husbands and making big mistakes and reliability and all in all had a really nice time.

Simon rationed himself to one glass of wine and a lot of fizzy water, although he seemed to be just as indiscreet about the rich and famous with or without alcohol. 'And then,' he said, using his hands as visual aids, 'I climbed back in through the window in my underpants and there he was sitting bolt upright in bed, stone-cold sober, dressed as Napoleon, complete with medals – I mean, what do you say? Anyway, I didn't get the chance to say anything because he said, "Ah my dear Simon, if you'd care to hop in my wife won't be long, she's just interviewing the Prime Minister –"'

And yes, Simon was flirtatious and complimentary, and looked like *somebody*, even in a tee shirt, suit jacket and jeans. Susie was aware of several people glancing in their direction as they ate, but it was fine – better than fine, it was lovely. And he laughed, he laughed a lot, at his own jokes, at her jokes and at himself. It was way better than champagne.

They got back to Susie's cottage around midnight.

'Thank you. I've had the most wonderful evening,' said Susie, gathering things together, picking up the bouquet of roses and getting ready to get out of the car as soon as they pulled into the driveway.

Simon, one hand on the steering wheel, the other on the back of her seat, eyes alight with mischief, laughed. 'What? Don't you trust me now that the engine's stopped?'

'It's not that, it's nearly midnight.'

'And what happens then? You turn back into a pumpkin?'

'Actually, something a lot more mundane than that – I've got to be up early for work tomorrow.'

His mobile phone rang.

'And anyway,' said Susie, 'it looks like somebody wants you.'

'It'll wait.'

'Yes, but I'm afraid I can't – I really need to go in.'

He glanced at the caller display and then, smiling, up at Susie. 'So, Friday, you still up for it or did tonight put you off?'

'Not at all. Friday would be lovely.' Susie looked across at him, not exactly sure what to do next. Did she kiss him goodnight, or leap out of the car like a maiden aunt on a Sunday School outing and hurry inside? And if she did kiss him, then what sort of kiss? On the lips, a peck on the cheek, or tongue down his throat? What exactly was the etiquette of dating your son's maybe-ex-girlfriend's father?

Watching her from the driver's seat, Simon wasn't helping at all. And there was something else on her mind too. Although he had been great company and they had had a good time, Susie knew that she didn't quite fancy him. There wasn't that nice little buzz there and she wasn't sure whether that was a good or bad thing, or maybe it was that her fancying radar was all screwed-up, but it was definitely another thing to consider. What she didn't want to do was give Simon the wrong impression, or at the other end of the scale, hurt him. Or was she being naïve? Simon struck her as having skin like a rhino.

Finally, Susie swooped forward, pecked him on the cheek and, before he had time to react, hopped out of the car.

'Whoa, come back!' he called, getting out after her. 'Is that it? What about inviting me in for coffee, which we both know is shorthand for feeling me up in the kitchen while the kettle's boiling, moments before you have your wicked way with me on the sofa.'

'In your dreams, maybe,' Susie said.

He winced. 'Bit harsh,' he said.

Susie smiled. 'I've really got to go in –' And then she paused. He was right; it was a bit mean. 'Would you like some coffee?' she asked, not meaning any of the things Simon had suggested, but wondering now if he thought that was what she meant. God, this dating lark was a nightmare, however old you were.

He grinned. 'I might do, or would you prefer that I played hard to get?'

'I'd prefer you were expecting instant coffee rather than a quick grope.'

'Sure you were,' he teased.

And for some unfathomable reason they still didn't move, instead lingering just inside the garden gate, a neutral no-man's land between car and coffee and saying goodnight.

'So what happens next?' Simon asked, leaning in close. Susie was amazed to find herself being drawn towards him, almost as if the pair of them were magnetised.

'Well, I thank you again for a great night out, and then you say you had a great time too,' she said in an undertone, as his lips brushed hers. The man was slick and very sexy. She felt her body instinctively reacting to his. 'And then if you want coffee with no strings you come inside. And then –'

'And then?' he murmured, and as he spoke Simon began to play with her hair, stroking the nape of her neck, making her skin tingle all over. She knew without a shadow of a doubt that he had made this move countless times before – no one was this slick without lots of practice – but even so it was most definitely working. She could almost feel the heat rising between them and gasped as he kissed her harder.

'And then?' he repeated, voice throaty and seductive, making every molecule in her body glow. Talk about Pavlov's dog. She almost laughed aloud at the way her body purred in anticipation.

And then, just as Simon was leaning in to kiss her again, the security light flashed on and something warm and hairy pushed its way up between the two of them, begging for her attention.

'Milo,' she murmured, scratching him behind the ears as he danced merrily from paw to paw in a wild welcome-home jig, all wet nose, wagging and enthusiastic whimpering and yipping with sheer delight at Susie's return. Saved by the mongrel.

'Mum, is that you out there?' Alice called from the

doorstep. She was standing in the jaundiced glare of the security light, blinking like a dormouse as she peered into the gloom, pulling the sleeves of her cardigan down over her hands to keep them warm. At the same time Simon's phone started to ring again.

Simon laughed and stepped back. 'Looks like we're both wanted.'

'So would you like to come in for a coffee?' asked Susie with a grin.

Simon shook his head regretfully. 'Another time. Thanks for a great evening. You still on for Friday?'

Susie nodded. 'Why wouldn't I be?'

He glanced towards the house. 'How long did you say Alice is staying?'

Susie grinned mischievously. 'Oh, I don't know – end of the week, maybe the week after. Maybe she's home for good. Who knows?'

'Who needs a conscience when you've got kids?' he said, lifting his hand to acknowledge Alice, who – now that she had got the two of them firmly locked in her sights – was keeping a weather eye on both of them, her arms folded tight across her chest in a fair approximation of a seaside landlady.

Simon brushed his lips across her cheek, this time his touch the very epitome of a chaste farewell.

'So, did you have a good time then?' asked Alice a few minutes later, handing Susie a mug of hot chocolate.

Susie slipped off her boots and, perching on the arm of the chair, nodded, feeling a sudden wave of guilt. 'Actually I had a lovely evening, but, Alice, I've been a rotten host really, haven't I? The thing is, and I know it's not much of an excuse, but at the moment it's not a great time for me either.'

Alice waved the words away. 'It's all right, I thought we needed to talk but actually I just needed a break, a bit of time out of my own environment to think about what to do next. And being with you for a couple of days –' she paused '– to be perfectly honest, Mum, our views are so far apart that we'd probably not have a lot of common ground even if we did talk more. I mean, I've always been focused on my career, uni, management training, but it's been great to come here and step out of the rat race for a little while.' She lifted a hand to encompass the cottage. 'Nice for me to get back to my roots, you know. All your arty stuff and chaos, all the clutter is nice, really *homely*.'

Susie swallowed down a flicker of outrage. This, she sensed, was meant to be a compliment. So much for Alice graciously accepting her apology. 'So have you talked to Adam today?' she asked.

Alice rolled her eyes and looked heavenwards. 'Oh god, yes. Mum, the man is a complete Neanderthal. He seems to think that this is all some sort of hormonal hiccup and the little woman will come to her senses if he just humours her. I put him straight on that one, I can tell you. Adam can be so patronising at times. Anyway, I laid out my views on the nursery, clearly and concisely. And then I emailed him a copy of my current action points so we had something concrete to discuss, and then told him that I'm putting the baby's name down whether he likes it or not and to get over himself.'

'Some discussion.'

'See,' said Alice, holding her hand up. 'That's exactly what I mean, Mum. No common ground.'

'And what did he say to that?'

Alice hesitated. 'To the emailed discussion document? I'm not altogether sure, I was just explaining and the phone went dead. I wondered if there might be a fault on your line. I did try ringing back but he was constantly engaged.'

'Alice, for god's sake. Adam hung up on you and then left the phone off the hook. I would imagine he's really hurt. Relationships are about give and take, about compromise and discussion, especially when it comes to big decisions about your baby's future. Adam loves you very much and he's probably worried sick about you – but –'

'But nothing, you see this is exactly what I mean about us having differing views, Mum. I absolutely understand give and take. I work in HR for god's sake. I understand negotiation, discussion and compromise but one thing this is not is a love issue. I know Adam loves me and is concerned about me and the baby, but what I'm talking about here is not love, it's education and science.'

'Science?'

'Listeria, foetal alcohol syndrome and toxoplasmosis. Adam just doesn't seem to have any grasp of all the things that can go wrong – there are just so many things. They've been doing all sorts of research into sunspot activity and just don't get me started on sonar and mobile phone masts.' And as she spoke Alice's voice started to break and her eyes filled up with tears, and for an instant Susie saw a fleeting glimpse of just exactly how scared Alice was of what was happening to her. Pregnancy and babies were not neat – worse still, she had not planned this pregnancy, and all this threatened her carefully ordered universe. Nature was messy and dirty and unnerving.

Alice was the girl for whom the expression control freak could have been invented. She hated chaos, and Susie could see that she was doing her level best to keep it at bay with her plans and schemes and spreadsheets and signing junior up for nursery now. Alice was scared of the lunacy that hormones and human bodies brought with them, and as soon as she saw it, Susie was overcome with compassion.

'It's all right, baby,' she murmured, settling down alongside Alice on the sofa and slipping an arm around her shoulders. 'It's going to be okay. Science or no science, I love you, and even though I'm a rotten host and a lousy mother I want you to know that I think it's wonderful that you're having a baby. You'll be a brilliant mum. And I'll try to be the best granny I can be. And it will be all right – and if it isn't, we can cope with that too.'

And with that Alice turned round very slowly and leant against Susie's shoulder and cried softly while Susie stroked her hair until she was exhausted.

When Alice was safely tucked up in bed, and the house was all locked up and the lights off, Susie sat for a while with Milo in the kitchen. It was way past her usual bedtime and she knew she really ought to be snuggled up under the duvet, but instead Susie looked out into the darkness mulling over the events of the last few days.

Simon wasn't what she needed at all, especially not straight after Robert. Just how much pain did one woman need in a lifetime? Realistically Simon was a diversion, and she had no doubt that she was probably one for him too. Hadn't he already pointed out that there were no strings? She was a place-marker, holding the door open for the next little pop nymphet who happened by. She mustn't let herself get involved – even from this distance Susie didn't need to be a genius to see that it would only end in tears.

The good thing was there wasn't a trace of self-pity in her thoughts – if anything quite the reverse. Susie had a real sense of what was good for her self-esteem and her confidence, and, with the best will in the world, Simon Hammond wasn't it.

So, Robert had Saskia – the idea made Susie wince but it was undeniably true – Matt was probably snuggled up with Alex, and Jack was trying hard to make it work with Ellie. Alice was busy being Alice with Adam. What Susie needed, she thought briskly, was to give herself some time to heal, get on with her life, her job and her family, and then find someone for herself. It would just take a little time. And it wouldn't take Simon Hammond, even if he did make all the right moves. Even if he made her feel squiggling and smiley and horribly horny when he turned on the charm. She was certain that he could do that kind of thing with his eyes shut.

Internal pep-talk over, Susie put her mug in the dish-washer – sometimes the sensible voice in her head sounded an awful lot like Claire Rayner – and had a quick tidy-up.

Milo looked up expectantly. It would soon be time for bed and they would make their way upstairs, Susie to the pretty room up under the eaves with its view of the garden and the common beyond, and Milo to his basket on the landing where, as the closest thing to a faithful retainer Susie had ever had, he would stand guard all night long.

Susie stretched and got to her feet, and as she did she spotted a piece of notepaper tucked under the kitchen phone. It read:

Nina rang. Saskia Hill (?) says that she needs to talk to you. <u>URGENTLY</u>. She said it was personal. Please could you ring her back <u>ASAP</u>.

For a few seconds, Susie stared at the note, wondering what malicious little night demon had decided she needed to see the message now, just before going up to bed, rather than finding it the following morning.

On the bottom of the message, in Alice's meticulous handwriting, were two phone numbers, one a mobile and the other presumably Saskia's home number. Susie stared at them. It was far too late to ring now, she thought, but the perfect time to lie awake in the dark, staring unfocused at the ceiling wondering exactly what it was that Saskia wanted.

Maybe she wanted to let Susie know that she was

already pregnant. Maybe she wanted to invite Susie to the close-friends-and-family-only, very private wedding service, or maybe she was just ringing to gloat.

Susie groaned. One of the problems with having a great imagination was that, left to its own devices, it could spend hours, days, weeks even, coming up with ever more perverse worst-case scenarios. And the whole Robert–Saskia scenario was full of rich pickings.

It was a long, long night.

When Susie finally rolled out of bed just before seven she felt terribly fragile and way beyond tired out into the foothills of exhaustion.

With dark-rimmed eyes and a thumping headache, hair still damp from the shower, Susie was relieved to give up on the idea of sleep and make her way downstairs. She filled the kettle. While waiting for it to boil she watched Milo pottering around the garden, intent on his morning sniffing, rummaging and weeing ritual. Staring out into the brilliant sunshine, it felt as if someone had wire-brushed her eyeballs and then backfilled the sockets with sand. Sleeplessness was not something she did often or well, although, seeing that she was finally on the move, Milo grumbled optimistically and went to sit by the gate in anticipation of his early-morning constitutional. There was no point resisting him.

When Susie – who studiously avoided the path that took her close to Robert's house – got back, she discovered there was an enormous bouquet of lilies propped up on the front doorstep. They would look fabulous with the night before's pink roses, Susie thought, as she bent down to pick them up. Tucked into the lush green foliage was a little cream envelope and inside a handwritten note, beautifully executed on heavy notepaper, that read:

Thanks for a lovely evening, Susie. You're great company and one hell of a sexy woman. I can't wait to see you again. Remember you owe me coffee. Love, Sx

Susie felt her colour rising – not altogether a bad thing as she was pale as tallow – and looked around quickly in case he was somewhere about. The last thing she wanted was for Simon to catch her looking like the Corpse Bride. Then, feeling silly because he quite obviously hadn't delivered them himself, she picked the flowers up and carried them inside.

It was tricky not to feel flattered, and after the grim night she'd had, the bouquet gave Susie exactly the lift she needed. Okay, so maybe Simon wasn't good for her, but at least he knew how to schmooze a woman.

When she pushed open the door, Alice was up and in the kitchen smearing great gouts of marmalade onto doorsteps of hot buttered toast, having apparently declared some sort of amnesty on her self-imposed no-wheat, no-dairy regime. When she heard Susie and Milo come in she swung round, spotted the flowers and instantly broke into a huge smile.

'Oh wow, they're lovely, where were they?' she asked, making a grab for the bouquet as Susie was about to set it down on the draining board. 'I so love lilies.

Although I always pull the stamens out – you can't get those stains out, you know. And did you know the pollen can kill cats –'

'They were on the doorstep.'

'I heard the doorbell but I thought you were up and would get it. God, they are superb, aren't they? Adam can be *such* a romantic sometimes,' continued Alice, all flushed, eyes sparkling.

Susie stared at her. 'Adam?' she repeated.

'Yes,' Alice said, starting to unpeel the big cream bow and acres of cellophane. 'It's our anniversary today. Didn't I tell you? Four years since our first date. He took me to the zoo. Long stems, he shouldn't have, wow, they must have cost him a fortune.' She giggled. 'We usually go away somewhere, we went to Rome last year, remember, but this year's different. You know, what with the baby – and this –' She glanced round. 'You know, time apart to think, my escape. Bless him. I didn't think he'd remember – all that stuff last night about being at the end of his tether.' She giggled throatily. 'I knew that deep down everything was all right. He's just stamping his foot, me caveman, you Jane – I mean it is all right, but it isn't, if you know what I mean. He just needs to be a bit more reasonable, that's all.' She held out her hand towards Susie. 'Let me see the note.'

'What note?' said Susie, hot and uncomfortable now, desperately crushing the sheet of paper and envelope into a tight ball. The thick paper was unwieldy and bit into her fingers. She'd have eaten it if only she could think of some way to palm it into her mouth.

Alice's tone firmed up. 'The note you were holding

in your hand when you came in, Mum. I saw it. I want to see what he said.'

'Oh that, that was nothing,' said Susie with forced jollity. 'Something else entirely. Is there any tea left in that pot?'

'Mum,' said Alice emphatically, her expression like granite. 'Give me the note. What are you saving me from? I bet he feels such an idiot hanging up on me last night knowing that this lot was on the way this morning.' She smiled and, leaning forward, inhaled the heady scent of the lilies. 'Just give me the note. Now.'

Susie stared at Alice. In a war of wills Susie really ought to win hands down. 'Alice,' she began, wondering if an explanation would be less painful than written evidence.

'Now,' repeated Alice, and held out her hand like a primary-school headmistress.

Susie handed her the crumpled paper. Very carefully, Alice put it down on the countertop, smoothed it out with the flat of her hand, and read the message, every last word. Twice. After a few seconds, she folded it up into neat quarters and slipped it into the envelope.

'Sorry about that,' she said in an embarrassed undertone, passing it back to Susie. 'What a twit. My mistake. Silly, really. I was hoping, you know –'

'Alice,' said Susie, throwing herself into the void.

'No, no, it's fine,' Alice said, far too quickly, holding her hands up like a shield. 'My mistake.'

'Alice, for goodness' sake. There's plenty of time for Adam's flowers to arrive yet. It's barely eight o'clock. I mean, the post hasn't been or anything.'

Alice looked up, blinking back tears. 'You're right,' she said, without conviction. 'It's silly really, it's just that Adam's always been complete crap with dates – I always remember, you know what men are like – but I thought that maybe this year, with the baby and everything, he might make the effort, and then these –' She waved towards the great extravagance of lilies which Susie was currently wishing would spontaneously combust. 'I thought this was some kind of sign. Showing he cared, that he was growing up, that he remembered. I suppose it was a bit naïve really.' Alice backhanded away a tear that had escaped and was busy trickling down her cheek. She sounded horribly sorry for herself.

Susie looked down at the lilies; it was an awful lot to ask a bunch of flowers to do. And so very hard too for Adam, who lived with a romantic pragmatist, to stand any chance of second-guessing the right thing to do on any single occasion.

Alice picked up the note from the table and turned it over in her long, thin fingers. 'Sounds like you had a nice time last night. I'm really pleased for you. Now if you'll excuse me I'm going to go upstairs and get dressed. I've got a huge pile of work to do.' She slunk off, shoulders slumped, head down, looking as if she was on her way to an execution.

Susie nodded, and then she picked up the lilies and dropped them into a bucket of water in the utility room. It felt too much like gloating to put them in the sitting room or, come to that, even in a vase.

* * *

On her way to work Susie tried phoning Adam and then left a message on Simon's answering machine to thank him for the flowers. She convinced herself that there just wasn't the time to ring Saskia before she pulled into her parking space by the art room – maybe she'd call at lunchtime. And maybe she would give up chocolate, and Radio Four, and the Pope would convert to Buddhism.

Susie turned off her phone just in case Saskia was desperate, and headed inside. Nina was waiting inside for a blow-by-blow account of her date with Simon. Instead she got the lilies, which Susie had stuffed in the boot before she left for work.

'Are you sure?' Nina said, looking down at the enormous bouquet, hastily rewrapped in cellophane.

'Absolutely. I can't leave the bloody things in the house, they feel like an accusation of neglect.'

'So what did you say to Adam?' asked Nina, busy unpeeling the bouquet.

'a) That it was their anniversary; b) that if he valued Alice he would get something organised PDQ; c) that I understood Alice could be a complete pain in the arse but that he had to realise how scared she was at the moment, and d) that if I was him I would have probably strangled her by now.'

'And he said?'

'Nothing, I got his voicemail.'

'And how about Simon?'

'Voicemail.' Susie looked across at her. 'I thanked him for a great evening and great flowers and tried very hard not to gush.'

196

'Uh-huh. And how did you get on with Poison Ivy – she was very keen to talk to you?'

'Saskia? I thought that I'd probably had enough aggravation and mobile-phone time for one day so I gave that one a miss.'

Nina's expression suggested that wasn't the answer she was looking for.

'Okay,' said Susie. 'My plan is to ring her later when I've got more time to talk about whatever it is that's on her mind.'

Nina looked at her and raised an eyebrow. 'You know, Susie, you really are the worst liar.'

Susie waved the words away as if she was flicking away a troublesome wasp. 'Stop nagging me. I will ring her, I'm just not sure that I want to hear whatever it is she's got to say. Now, what's on the agenda for today's meeting?'

'Guess,' said Nina.

At which point Austin showed up, and then Colin from ceramics. Nina whipped out a folder with the current list of VIPs and RSVPs for people, along with a couple of sample buffet menus and Saskia Hill's promise of a horticultural display to remember, and everyone got on with the job in hand.

When the meeting was over, Nina went off to the ceramics department to find a vase for the lilies and Susie got down to the business of the day. She didn't bother to check her phone for messages, just in case there were some.

The long, sunny days at the end of the summer term were always a bit of a muddle. With the end of the academic year in sight, every class was torn between wanting to bunk off to enjoy the good weather and focusing on getting their projects finished. And not just finished for the exhibition either, but finished for exams and coursework and accreditation, all of which had to be handed in to all sorts of examiners and examining bodies by the end of term. It was a logistical nightmare to make sure everything and everybody was in the right place at the right time with the right documentation.

Through the art rooms, alongside Susie's normal classes, there was a steady stream of comings and goings, some panic, some eleventh-hour single-mindedness, some resignation, and a lot of stoic hard work to get things done by the early summer deadline. Some pieces had to be finished, some photographed, some mounted and displayed, some wrapped carefully and posted off. The usual rhythm of the days was broken, and so it was almost half past two by the time Susie and Nina finally stopped for lunch.

Susie flicked on her mobile between mouthfuls of a sandwich and waited. There was nothing, not a message, a text or a missed call. She didn't know whether to be relieved or disappointed. Nina, meanwhile, had been out to rustle up some greenery and twigs and fussed the lilies up into a floral arrangement that wouldn't have been out of place in a state room on the QE2. Good news was that as soon as Nina started pimping it Susie lost any sense of deprivation or ownership.

It was nearly six by the time the last of the students ambled out. Susie was exhausted. In previous years she'd taught a couple of evening classes each week, and now that she had given them up, wondered where the hell she had ever found the energy.

Driving back towards the cottage, Susie realised that the day had been so full she had barely had time to think about Alice or Simon or Saskia, but as she turned left into the common she could feel them closing in around her like wraiths.

She really ought to ring Saskia, if only to ensure that the promised floral displays hadn't been cancelled in a fit of pique – at least if she knew then Susie could come up with some kind of contingency plan. Alice might need comforting or congratulating depending on what Adam had managed to come up with. And Simon? Well, it wasn't that hard to work out what Simon had in mind.

As she rounded the corner Susie could see that her driveway was full of cars. One she recognised as Simon's – the low sporty job he had picked her up in the previous evening. The smart little black Corsa was Alice's, the battered Discovery Matt's, and the other – a dark green Rav 4 – rang no bells at all. Susie pulled up behind the Jeep and headed for the front door, already feeling frazzled at being invaded by the world and his wife after a long, hard day, and annoyed at having to park in the road outside her own home.

Through the kitchen window she could see Matt and Jack sitting at the table drinking tea, Simon holding court, and Alice – well, there was no sign of Alice, but there was a huge vase of sunflowers and rich purple irises standing in a big glass vase in the hearth near the Aga. Milo wagged his tail when he saw her and gave a half-hearted bark before heading to greet her. Susie rubbed his muzzle as she opened the door.

'Some guard dog you turned out to be, you're meant to keep people out, not invite them in and let them help themselves to tea,' she said as he wound himself round her legs.

He wagged some more and yipped a bit and the others looked up. Simon was busy looking even more tanned and gorgeous since she'd last seen him; Matt and Jack both looked pleased to see her; and from somewhere close by she could hear Alice yelling, 'You just don't understand how much this means to me, do you, you bastard?'

Which meant that presumably the Rav was Adam's.

'Well,' said Susie, looking from face to face, 'to what do I owe the pleasure, gentlemen?' Before anyone had a chance to speak, a stream of expletives came from the sitting room, so Susie kept on walking past her unexpected house guests, closed the door into the sitting room and then the hall door so that Alice could reach critical mass in private.

'I was in the area and thought I'd just drop by,' said Simon brightly, as the swearing and sobbing became muted hysterical rumblings.

Susie turned. 'You happened to be in the area? Simon, you live miles from here.'

He aped pain or maybe contrition at having been caught out.

'And how about you two, what are you doing here?'

'I just came over to pick my gear up,' said Jack, indicating a large heap of something khaki and indefinable stacked up by the back door.

'And I offered to give him a lift,' said Matt.

'With the Italian dig postponed I've got bugger all to do all summer,' said Jack, 'so I'm going to be staying here for a while.'

'Here?' said Susie, looking round the cottage. 'You don't mean *here*, do you?'

'No, not here. But I do need to find somewhere to live.'

'I've already told him he can stay with me till he gets himself sorted out,' said Matt.

Susie laughed. 'I don't think either of us have got that many years left.'

At which point the noise from the sitting room revved back up a notch.

Jack got to his feet. 'Fancy a cup of tea, anyone?'

Susie nodded. 'How long's Adam been here?'

'Long enough to put some sunflowers in a vase and get his arse well and truly kicked by her ladyship,' said Jack, refilling the kettle. 'Poor bugger.'

Simon said, 'We were just saying what a great evening it was for a barbecue.'

'Actually, Simon, it was *you* saying it was a great night for a barbecue,' corrected Jack. 'We were more concerned with Adam's wellbeing and how long we leave it before we go in there and drag Alice off him.'

'I was thinking of barbecuing in terms of a diversionary tactic. So how about it?' said Simon to Susie, totally ignoring Jack's comments.

She stared at him in amazement. 'How about what?'

'How about we pop down to the local supermarket, fill up on steaks, burgers and beers and have ourselves a little family get-together, you know – me and you and the kids –'

'Have you been drinking?' she asked suspiciously.

'No, I'm just – just –' For once Simon seemed at a complete loss for words and looked at Susie. 'I like it here. We had a great time last night, didn't we? I missed you. I'm lonely – I needed somewhere to go, somewhere I wasn't going to get in trouble.'

Susie shook her head. 'I don't know what's going on, Simon, but if you want a barbecue knock yourself out. It's been a long day and I'm totally and utterly knackered. Oh, and I need to take these shoes off.'

'I thought you'd come with me, show me where the shops are,' he said.

'Well you thought wrong, you're on your own, chuck,' she said with a tired smile. 'Denham Market's three miles that-a-way – you can't miss it, follow the signs,' she said, pointing down the path.

'I'll show you if you like,' said Jack.

Simon, caught out, looked first at Susie and then at Jack and then nodded. 'Okay, I'll get my car keys.'

'Any chance I can drive?' asked Jack.

'What about my cup of tea?' protested Susie as the two of them headed back out the door.

'Don't worry,' said Matt, 'I'll do that while you grab a shower.'

He was such a good chap. Susie grinned. 'My hero.'

From the sitting room came the sounds of Alice shrieking, then a door slamming and feet thundering up the stairs. Susie sat down at the kitchen table. 'Actually I'm not sure I can cope with life upstairs just yet.'

Matt made them tea. 'So, how are things going with you?' he asked, sliding the mug across the counter as Susie sat, sandals off, alternately wriggling her toes and then pressing them onto the cool flagstone floor.

The conversation was punctuated by the sounds of more banging and more yelling coming from upstairs.

'Would you mind if we went outside and had this conversation?' Susie asked, picking up Milo's lead. 'We could walk across the common. I often take a mug of tea with me.'

At the door she slipped on walking shoes while Matt gallantly held her tea and Milo's lead and then they headed off across the rough grass together leaving Alice and Adam to their own devices.

'I was really sorry to hear about Italy,' she said, as they fell into step along the main footpath.

'Me too,' said Matt, 'but we should be back later in the year if they can sort out the paperwork. It's just one of those things, we're reliant on outside funding and all kinds of other people for this project – it's just the way it is, but it's bloody frustrating.'

'I can imagine,' she said.

There was a little pause and then Matt said, 'I wanted to ask you something. You're not serious about Simon, are you?' He said it suddenly, almost as if he was apprehensive about asking her.

It took Susie by complete surprise. She turned to look at him. 'Sorry?'

'Simon, you're not serious about him, are you? Jack had told me a lot about him, but meeting him – well –' Matt looked uncomfortable, obviously aware that he was prying into her personal affairs, but he seemed hell-bent on pressing on nonetheless. 'I do know that it's none of my business and I can obviously see the appeal – the whole wounded-bad-boy thing – but the man is a complete shyster. I mean he's charming but it's obvious he is a total rogue.'

Susie wasn't sure whether to be flattered that Matt cared about her or just plain outraged that he thought he had the right to interfere in her private life. 'I'm not totally blind, Matt, or stupid come to that,' she said. Maybe going upstairs after Alice had been a better option after all.

'So why on earth are you going out with Simon Hammond?'

Susie stared at him. If she didn't know better she would think he was jealous. 'I'm not going out with him – well, I am, but not in the way you mean, not on a proper date. He asked me out to dinner, no strings, no nothing, and I said yes, because I really fancied being schmoozed and fancied for a change.

'God, what is it with everyone? I'm a grown-up, I can make my own mind up about who I go out with. Alice gave me a lecture about Simon the other day as well. This is nobody's business but mine. All right? And, remarkably enough, I do know exactly what Simon is, and to be honest, at this moment in time, I don't care. This is what I need at the moment: no strings, no forevers, no false promises, just some good old-fashioned fun. And it's all right for you preaching from the high ground, Matt. Jack told me you had a date this weekend. Part of the reason he didn't want to stay at your place was because he didn't want to play gooseberry.'

Matt blushed furiously and looked as uncomfortable as she had seen him since they met. 'It wasn't a date, it was Alex,' he said, shifting his weight.

'Well, that's wonderful, I hope it went really well,' she snapped. 'Which brings me back to my point: What business is it of yours who I go out with?'

For a few seconds he hesitated, and then he said, 'Look, Susie, Jack's one of my best friends, he worries about you, and I care about him – and you – I don't want to see you get hurt and –'

'And Simon is the kind of man who is going to hurt me, that's what you're trying to say, is it?'

'Yes,' he said finally. 'And I presume that you can see that too. Although I can absolutely see why he's good company.'

'Well that's big of you,' Susie said icily.

'But –' he began again.

Susie held up a hand to silence him. 'Matt, you don't have to tell me what Simon's like. I already know. But a dinner date and a man barbecuing in your back garden is not a marriage. All right? Now, let's talk about something else, shall we? How did it go with Alex?'

He hesitated, caught off-guard. 'Alex?'

'Yes, you said it wasn't a date, it was Alex.'

'I did, didn't I? Well, it was okay . . .' He shifted uncomfortably. 'But not particularly easy – we're talking again. I suppose that's a start.'

'Are you hoping you'll get back together?'

He made an odd shrugging gesture which didn't tell

Susie very much at all. She was about to ask him whether that was a yes or a no, whether it was Alex's idea or his that they gave it another go, when a 4x4 pulled up alongside them. For a moment Susie thought it might be Adam escaping in the Rav, but realised an instant later that it was Saskia Hill, and she was leaning towards them, anxious to attract their attention.

'Hi Susie,' she said, flicking a stray blonde tress back over her shoulder. 'I thought it was you, I was wondering if maybe we could have a few minutes?'

Caught on the back foot, Susie stared at her for a few seconds, trying to work out what to say. 'What, now?' she said eventually, trying to regain her composure. 'It's not very –' But Saskia was ahead of her.

'I was hoping that you'd ring me back,' Saskia said. 'And then I wondered if maybe you hadn't got my message. Can we talk?'

Susie looked at Matt and then back at Saskia. 'Actually it's not very convenient at the moment. What is it you wanted to talk about?'

Saskia reddened and bit her lip nervously, the sophisticated veneer that she wore so well in the office dissolving. 'I really need to talk about Robert,' she said in a tiny voice. 'And I'd really like to talk about him now.'

Chapter 11

Susie stared at Saskia, uncertain exactly what to say next. Should she say yes? Or no? Or maybe tell her to bugger off? From her expression and her body language, Susie got no sense that Saskia had pulled up to gloat, or to play games, and she could only imagine the balls it had taken for her to first of all phone, and now to ask Susie face to face.

'Why do you want to talk to me?' she said.

Saskia reddened. 'Well, you know him, and I don't – and there's no one else really.'

Almost in spite of herself, Susie found herself nodding. 'Okay,' she said.

Saskia looked relieved.

Susie didn't move, feeling unsettled and, now that she had agreed, slightly uneasy. 'But not here,' she said, glancing over her shoulder; they were standing within a couple of hundred yards of Robert's front door. If he was upstairs he'd be able to see them from his bedroom window, which didn't make her feel any better. Although knowing Robert he'd probably think he'd got the pair of them fighting over him.

'We could go for a drink if you like, find a pub?' suggested Saskia.

That was the last thing Susie wanted. What she wanted was to go home, find that everyone had left, make a pot of tea, turn on the radio and unwind with a dose of evening sunshine, something nice out of the fridge, maybe a quick Delia moment and a lot of Radio Four.

'Why don't I take Milo back for you?' said Matt helpfully, holding out his hand to take the lead and Susie's mug. 'And then you two can have a chat and sort this out.'

Sort it out? Have a chat? Was the man mad? Susie turned to glare at him, pulling a face that she hoped would indicate that she had no idea what was going on – worse still, she had no idea what Saskia wanted or was expecting from her, and she was certain they hadn't got a hope in hell of sorting anything out over a nice cosy chat.

'I'll save you a burger,' said Matt.

Susie held the glare, while he shrugged philosophically and turned for home with Milo in tow.

Meanwhile, Saskia leant over and undid the passenger-side door of the 4x4. As Susie climbed in she thought about all those warnings she'd given and received over the years about not getting into a car with strangers. It crossed her mind as they pulled away that she didn't really know anything at all about Saskia Hill. The icy blonde could quite easily be stark staring mad, a bunny boiler, a complete raving maniac for all Susie knew.

'You've got no idea what a relief it is that you've agreed to talk to me,' said Saskia. She didn't sound or look like a loony, but then again maybe that was the trick. 'I don't really know who else to talk to about any of this. Robert told me that you were his best friend.' And then, more anxiously, she added, 'You won't tell him about this, will you?'

Susie stared at her, not sure what the right answer was, still trying to get past the best-friend line. Seconds ticked by. *Best friend*. It occurred to her that if Robert had said they were best friends maybe Saskia didn't know that she and Robert had been having a relationship for the past three years. Which put Susie in a really peculiar position.

'You won't say anything, will you?' Saskia repeated. Susie realised that Saskia had taken her silence for reticence about keeping their meeting a secret from Robert.

'No, no,' said Susie quickly. 'Of course I won't. It's all right, I won't say a word. What else did Robert say?'

Saskia looked increasingly uncomfortable. 'That you'd been seeing each other casually for a while, only a couple of months, both of you were at a bit of a loose end, and you got on really well – as friends, you know – but that you'd both decided that it wasn't going anywhere. You wanted different things – and so you split up, but you stayed friends, which I think is really nice.'

Really nice? Susie felt her colour rising. It felt as if someone was busy squashing all the air out of her lungs. *Stayed friends*, this from the man who Susie had thought was going to propose to her a few days ago. She made

209

a real effort to swallow down the wave of pain and the bright red plume of anger that threatened to engulf her.

She had to remind herself that it wasn't Saskia's fault that Robert was a complete bastard, and if Susie wanted to find out what was going on then screaming at Saskia really wasn't going to help at all. And maybe what was more disturbing was that Susie also realised that she did want to know – there was part of her that was desperately curious to find out what was going on between Saskia and Robert, and what Robert had been saying.

'It is nice, isn't it?' asked Saskia, seeking reassurance. 'I mean I think that shows the kind of people you both are.'

'Yes, I suppose it does,' Susie said as casually as she could manage. She thought it showed him up as a lying two-faced snake, but didn't plan to say so unless really pushed. 'And how long have you been seeing him for?' She made every effort to sound casual.

'Robert?'

Susie struggled to stay calm. Who else did Saskia think she meant?

'Oh, I've known him for a while now; I've always been a bit shy – ' She bit her lip again. 'Not easy having a job in sales but I'm getting there, anyway we met through work, but he only asked me out two or three months ago. But you know what it's like when you first meet someone –' Saskia laughed self-consciously, colour rising. 'All that mad stuff, always on the phone, texting, it's all been a bit crazy really. And now that the air is clearing –'

Two or three months ago?

Susie didn't give a tin shit about the air clearing, instead she watched Saskia's mouth moving up and down without really registering anything else that she was saying. Her brain had got itself all tangled up in the first sentence. *Two or three months ago?* Two or three months ago, when Susie had been thinking that everything was okay between her and Robert, when she thought that they had a future together. Two or three months ago, when they had been planning a weekend away before the summer rush; when they had gone out to dinner and sat hand in hand watching the sunset; and when they had walked Milo on the beach and Susie thought that Robert loved her. All that time he had been pursuing Saskia.

How could she have been so bloody stupid? How could she not have known? *How could she not have seen?* Susie looked away, feeling as if the bottom had just dropped out of her world. She stared out of the window, unseeing, while Saskia talked on and on.

How could he? All the time they had been talking and planning and making arrangements Robert had been sniffing round Saskia Hill. Had he been thinking about Saskia when they were talking over supper about going on holiday? Planning when he was going to see Saskia next as they were picking out carpets for his sitting room? If he was that smitten how could he not have been? Was it Saskia's face he'd seen when they were in bed together?

Susie felt sick. 'Can you stop the car?' she said quickly, holding her hand to her mouth. 'I need to get out.'

'What?' Saskia said, caught mid-sentence.

'I said will you please stop the car. I've got to get out.'

Hastily Saskia pulled into a lay-by. 'Are you all right, you look as if you've seen a ghost?' she asked anxiously.

Susie clambered out of the Jeep. Bent double, she struggled to catch her breath. Saskia, meanwhile, was out of the car and beside her, hand on Susie's shoulder, anxious, solicitous, all wide-eyed, windswept and gorgeous. Susie was torn between gratitude and wanting to punch her lights out.

'I'm so sorry,' said Saskia, handing her a tissue. 'Here. Can I do anything? I didn't realise that you weren't very well. Do you want me to take you home?'

Susie held up a hand to silence her. 'I'm absolutely fine, really. Just give me a minute. I'm not sure what came over me,' she lied, taking deep breaths.

They had pulled off the bypass into a long, tree-lined lay-by on the far edge of the common, maybe a mile or two's walk from the little hamlet of cottages built around the green where Susie and Robert lived. On the far side of the road, skirting around the golf course, was a right of way that went off into adjoining woodland.

'Do you mind if we walk for a bit?' said Susie, indicating the path. 'I need some fresh air.' It wasn't strictly true but she had no great desire to get back into the 4x4 with Saskia, or head home to Alice and the rest of the crew for that matter. A walk in the woods seemed like the best of several unpleasant possibilities.

'That would be great,' said Saskia brightly. 'I'll just lock up if you're sure you're all right?'

'I'm fine,' said Susie grimly.

'The thing is,' said Saskia, as she reappeared around the side of the Jeep, pulling on a little jacket. 'Most of the boys I've dated before Robert have been just for fun, you know, kind of jokey and a bit silly and I didn't – well, they didn't –' She fidgeted, tugging at her sleeves and hair, a study in discomfort.

'Robert is my first, like, proper relationship.' She giggled, which made her suddenly look and sound incredibly young. 'I started late, I've never really had a serious boyfriend before. I was really shy when I was a teenager, bit of a geek. Me and my brother played the cello and the viola. I was a bit bookish, I went to ballet, and all that stuff, but I never mixed very well, and then I went to the local college and then my dad got me a place on this really good business course.'

Saskia was rambling, finding it hard to get to the point – or maybe, Susie thought, not even sure what the point was. As Saskia carried on, Susie glanced across at her. The closed, icy aura that she projected at work was completely at odds with the rather breathy, child-like creature here. She could see how easy it would be to misinterpret her shyness as standoffishness.

'Sorry, I'm talking too much, aren't I?' Saskia said, colouring as she caught Susie looking at her. 'I don't know who to talk to about this. I haven't got that many friends really and most of them are dating guys the same age, and you seem – well, you seem nice, and you know Robert.'

'How old are you?' asked Susie.

'Twenty-three, nearly twenty-four,' Saskia said defensively. 'But in lots of ways I've always felt old for my age, I'm naturally drawn to older people.'

Susie smiled. For a split second she had a vision of Alice when she was little, sashaying unsteadily around Susie's bedroom in borrowed high heels, a toy phone tucked under her chin, trying out what it felt like to be grown up.

'I mean, I've always imagined I'd end up being with an older man. I can't stand boys my age, they're so immature and so juvenile – but Robert, well, he's great. He's so mature. You know what he's like. It's so nice to be with someone who knows how to behave in a restaurant, which wine to order, how to treat a woman.'

Oh yes, Robert knew how to treat a woman all right, thought Susie grimly, and for one so mature he could behave like a spoilt three-year-old at the drop of a hat, plus his evident delight when farting was something that had to be seen to be believed, but Susie decided it was better to keep mum. She didn't want to spoil the surprise.

It was such a tricky situation for Susie to find herself in. Part of her wanted to warn Saskia off, tell her to run away while she still could. She knew from experience that what Robert called sensible and cautious was actually dull and mean, and that he would eventually bore the life out of her, and then another part of her wondered what right she had to interfere. What right had she got to deny Robert his chance of happy ever after? Or Saskia's, come to that? Maybe Susie was wrong, maybe this was a match made in heaven, maybe Saskia would change him. How the hell did she know? Thinking about it was giving Susie a headache.

Saskia, meanwhile, appeared to be waiting for some kind of comment, a judgement on Robert's prospects. Susie nodded noncommittally and hoped that it was enough, and apparently it was because Saskia smiled and carried on.

'The thing is, I know that Robert really wants to settle down, and I know he said he'd take care of me, but I'm not sure that I'm really ready yet. I mean it's a big step to take, after all he is pretty old.'

Susie bit her lip. Pretty old and with a biological clock ticking away nineteen to the dozen. 'Have you thought about a family?' she asked, trying hard not to meet Saskia's eyes in case she gave herself and Robert away.

'You mean, like, babies and stuff?' said Saskia, slightly incredulously.

'Uh-huh.' Like the babies and stuff that Robert was so desperate to have that he'd dumped Susie.

'Well yes, I'd like kids eventually, but not yet.' Saskia lingered over and emphasised the word *eventually* as if it was a distant land far off beyond the horizon that she had been told about but could barely imagine. 'I was thinking like maybe when I'm, say, thirty, thirty-two. I mean there's no rush, is there? And there are loads of things I'd really like to do first: I'd like to travel, I've been looking at buying a house – and then there's the business. There are just so many opportunities in the whole gardening thing right now. It's so popular. And my dad is really keen for me to develop that side of things.'

Susie nodded. 'And how does Robert feel about that?'

'What? About the gardening?' Saskia looked bemused.

'No, no – about the travel, all the things you want to do.'

Saskia smiled. 'Oh that, well, he is really supportive. You know what he's like. In some ways he's a bit like my dad. He says that he understands that there are things I need to do and that he'll support me and help me. But . . .' The smile held but it looked an effort. 'I'm not so sure. In some ways I really want to do stuff like that on my own, you know, like an adventure?' She wrinkled her nose. 'But he's already said if we were together I could do all those things and lots of other stuff too, but I think he just thinks he means it. I get the feeling that he'd really like settling down to mean just that.' She laughed. 'Pipe and slippers and a dog and his garden. But that's kind of sweet too, really, isn't it? Maybe I'm reading it all wrong. He can be such a funny old thing, huffing and puffing about, it's quite cute really.'

Susie, pretending to concentrate on the winding track that ran between the trees, was torn. There was no way that she could come out of the present situation smelling of roses, whatever she said. Still deep in thought she scooted left around a stand of bracken to avoid a big pile of dog crap – it seemed like an omen.

While Susie was still weighing up her options, Saskia dropped the final bombshell. 'The thing is, and you've got to promise that you won't say anything – I wasn't going to say anything to anyone else because I haven't told my parents yet – Robert has asked me to marry him.'

Susie swung round in amazement. Saskia, bright-eyed and flushed with delight, sounded excited, euphoric.

The dog had been busy, and as she turned Susie stepped bang into a pile of poo the size of a bowler hat, and swore furiously.

Saskia's face crumpled. 'You're his friend. I thought you would be pleased for him. And for me.'

Susie stared at her. What was it with people who thought you should be pleased at babies, marriage and, and . . . Susie shook her head. 'I'm not swearing about you and Robert,' she said, and looked around for something to wipe her boot on.

'So have you said yes?' asked Susie a few minutes later after she had scraped most of the muck off the bottom of her boots.

Saskia shrugged. 'Not exactly, I told him I need some time to think. It's a big step,' she said, as if defending her decision. 'And I only want to do it once. I'm not sure I'm ready or, to be honest, if he is the one. I think if he was I'd know – but maybe it's something that grows. He was a bit hurt really. But I couldn't just say yes to humour him, could I?'

'Of course not,' said Susie, warming to Saskia in spite of herself. 'You did the right thing. When did he ask you?' Susie knew that she was prying but just couldn't help herself, although if Saskia said last Friday night there was a possibility she might just lose it totally.

Saskia's colour rose furiously. 'Just now. I mean he'd got a ring and everything. He did the whole down-on-one-knee thing. I thought he was clearing up a pile of magazines. I feel awful.'

Susie looked up from scraping her boot. 'Just now?'

Saskia nodded.

'*Just* now?' repeated Susie.

She nodded again. 'About ten minutes before I stopped to pick you up.'

'Robert asked you to marry him, *and then you left*?'

'I'd been trying to tell him that I'd got a delivery to sort out and that I couldn't stay very long but he kept – well, you know what Robert's like. He's got a plan and he likes to stick to it.' She laughed. 'He rang me this afternoon and kept saying that he had something important he wanted to ask me and that he wanted me to come over, so I made the effort to get away, and then when I got there he didn't want me to go.' Saskia's colour deepened and she began fiddling with the buttons on her cuff. 'He said that the ring was his mother's.'

'So he asked you to marry him and then you left?'

Saskia pulled a face. 'It sounds awful, doesn't it, but yes, more or less. I did tell him that this was our busy time – we've got two lorries due in from Holland this evening.'

'So is that where you should be now?'

'The lorries don't arrive for another couple of hours, I could have stayed for supper but I felt a bit pressured.

I need more time. Robert was really excited and then he was kind of upset.'

Susie smiled. 'I can understand that.'

'He is my first proper boyfriend,' repeated Saskia.

Susie could understand that too; everyone had to start somewhere, and who in their right mind married the first man that came along? Or the first man who asked you? Saskia needed more time in more ways than one. Susie could see her mulling the possibilities over in her mind and, oddly enough, felt nothing but sympathy for her. Whatever decision Saskia made now could alter the course of her whole life, whether she said yes or no it would have some kind of impact on whatever came next.

'What does your heart tell you?' Susie asked, horribly aware that it sounded like a bad cliché.

Saskia smiled. 'I like him.'

'And do you think that's enough?'

She sighed. 'I don't know. It's such a big question, isn't it?' She paused. 'Do you want to hear what I really think?' It was obviously a rhetorical question because Saskia continued, 'It's flattering but it's too soon. It's kind of freaked me out a bit. I don't think we know each other well enough to be talking about getting married, at least not yet – maybe in six months or a year or something, but I've only been going out him for a few months. It's crazy.'

Susie nodded. 'Then I think you should go with what you feel,' she said gently.

Saskia smiled, looking relieved.

Susie smiled too. Saskia's good sense had saved Susie

from having to drop Robert right in it, which was her next option.

'So what should I say to him?'

'What you just said to me.'

'That it's too soon? That I need more time?'

Susie nodded.

'I don't want to hurt him. I do care about him.'

Susie looked Saskia up and down. She was gorgeous and full of the ripe vitality that only blesses the young. She had her whole life ahead of her, and what Susie wanted to say more than anything else was 'For god's sake get away from Robert now, find someone to have fun with, someone who makes you laugh, someone who you can travel and have adventures with, someone who understands that young isn't forever. And it doesn't have to be the same someone.' But, even as she thought it, Susie knew that she couldn't say any of those things aloud.

Instead she said, 'Of course you do – but it would hurt him a lot more if you said yes and really meant you weren't sure, or said yes and went along with it just to humour him.'

'I knew I could talk to you,' Saskia said. 'I wanted to talk to someone who knows him.'

Susie nodded. Oh, she knew him all right.

And with that they fell into step for another couple of hundred yards, this time walking in an easy silence. Susie was the first to break it. 'Shall we go back?'

'Would you mind?' Saskia asked, sounding relieved.

'Not at all, you've got a delivery to sort out and I'm knackered.'

As they turned and headed back through the trees towards the Jeep, Saskia said, 'Would it be okay if I rang you again sometime? Maybe we could have lunch – we'll need to talk about the displays for the exhibition – my treat. The thing is, I can't talk to my mum.'

Her mum? Susie slowed; realistically it was the last thing she wanted. She had hoped this little heart-to-heart was a one-off.

Saskia dropped Susie off at the bottom of the lane that led back to her cottage. 'Thank you,' she said, as Susie clambered out of the Jeep. 'I really appreciate you giving me the time. Robert told me that you were special.'

Special? She managed a smile. The most powerful emotion in amongst the many was an almost overwhelming sense of relief that Robert wasn't hers to worry about any more. However complicated, however hurtful, however downright boring, it wasn't her problem. Susie turned for home with the feeling that somewhere down the line she had had a very lucky escape.

Walking back along the lane towards the cottage Susie could see what appeared to be smoke signals rising in great black billows from her back garden, and as she got to the gate she heard the sound of raised voices.

'Well I didn't know it was fucking Armani, did I? Who wears Armani to barbecue in, for Christ's sake?'

'Will you look what you're doing with that?'

'Now look what you've done – Jesus H. Christ, it'll never come out.'

'It's all under control now, just get back to whatever it is you were doing.'

'It's bloody grease –'

Alongside all of that Susie could hear Milo yipping and whining with excitement, which suggested things weren't under control at all. He enjoyed a little chaos did Milo. As Susie rounded the corner of the cottage he ran up to her, wagging and barking happily, while further down the garden, Rome was burning.

Across on the far side of the terrace Matt was busy beating out a bush fire with a broom. There was a raging inferno in the barbecue pit and Simon was trying to wipe what looked like marinade or barbecue sauce off the front of his jacket with a horribly charred tea towel. Jack, meanwhile, was busy hopping from foot to foot, making lots of noise and flapping his arms around, in a way that was uncannily reminiscent of his father in a crisis. There was no sign of Alice or Adam. The dog skittered to and fro getting more and more excited and appeared to have accumulated a little heap of raw sausages rolled in compost under the table on the terrace.

'So what time's supper?' asked Susie, closing the gate behind her.

They looked in her direction, all apparently expecting love and understanding.

'It was all his idea,' said Jack.

'He spilt sauce all over my jacket,' Simon whined in protest at around the same time as Matt's broom burst into flames.

A mother's lot, thought Susie grimly as she unrolled

the garden hose, wrestled the barbecue into submission, sprayed Matt's burned hand with hydrogel, spot-cleaned Simon's jacket and aped gratitude an hour or so later when they brought round a tray of unidentifiable burnt things on a bed of limp, over-dressed supermarket salad.

Alice came back to the cottage around ten, while Susie was busy clearing up in the kitchen. The dog was asleep on the kitchen floor, happy as Madge and fat as butter on the accumulated stealings and leavings of the four of them. He didn't stir as Alice opened the door. Pale as milk with red-rimmed eyes, Alice came in, dragging her handbag along the flagstones. She looked like a tired, very grumpy vampire.

Outside on the terrace Simon was feeding the fire with twigs, while sipping Perrier with slices of lime. Matt was drinking red wine and Jack, apparently the designated driver of the pair, was on orange juice. No one seemed keen to be the first to leave.

'Have you eaten? There's some food left,' Susie told Alice, indicating the heap of burnt offerings on a tray on the kitchen table.

'I wouldn't call that food,' sniffed Alice, perching herself on the edge of the table. 'But it's all right, Adam and I went to that little place in town, the brasserie on the High Street – anniversary treat, great food.'

'That's good. So Adam hadn't forgotten then?' Susie asked cautiously.

Alice said nothing.

'So how's it going, love?' she asked, sliding plates into the dishwasher. It wasn't a question Susie particularly wanted to hear the answer to, but she had a huge sense of fair play, and realistically it was Alice's turn to make her life difficult, even though Susie was exhausted and wanted nothing more than an early night and an empty house. She momentarily toyed with the idea of asking Alice where Adam was, but decided that if she needed to know Alice would most likely tell her.

Alice sighed and threw herself down into one of the armchairs by the Aga, prised off her shoes using her toes on the backs as leverage, dropping them to the floor, and then wriggled her toes. 'God, that feels so good; I think my feet are swelling. Do they look swollen to you?' She pointed her toes and turned them this way and that to get an informed opinion. 'Did your feet swell when you were pregnant with me and Jack?'

'Not that I can remember, but it is hot tonight – you should maybe sit with them up for a little while.'

Alice teased a stool closer with her feet and settled down, legs at full stretch, body the same, like a long, slim cat, as close to horizontal as she could manage. She knitted her long, thin fingers together and rested them across her non-existent belly, closed her eyes and yawned.

'I'm so tired, but I think we've sorted a few things out,' she said after a minute or two. 'The fundamental problem is that Adam and I see things very differently.'

'Well that is often the way, darling, people are different, we all have different opinions and views about what's right and what's –'

Alice sat up. 'I understand that. The issue is, can we find a compromise and can we live together, and we've come to the conclusion that instead of knocking our heads against a brick wall we're going to join the TA brigade for a while and see how that works out.'

Susie stared at her, utterly bewildered. 'TA, what do you mean the TA? Territorial Army? What's the army got to do with having a baby?'

Alice laughed. 'No, Mum. *TA* means Together Apart – we've talked about it and Adam's agreed to move out by the end of this week. And don't pull that face, it's all right. Lots of people do it. We're going to carry on in a committed relationship, still be a couple, see a lot of each other, still be there for each other and the baby, we're just not going to live together.'

'I thought you were going to get married?' Susie said lamely.

'We still can, one thing doesn't preclude the other. Lots of people have jobs that keep them apart.'

Susie knew without being told that all this had come out of Alice's head, not Adam's.

'We're committed to each other rather than being committed to an institution,' Alice said. 'Which, actually, is what will happen if I have to spend another night under the same roof as Adam.'

'So what does Adam think about this? And where's he going to live?'

Alice looked a bit sheepish. 'Well, short-term he's going to go and stay with his mum, but longer term he'll probably find a house-share or get a little place of his own.'

'But Alice, you've just taken out a huge mortgage –'

'I know, I know, but we'll work it out, Mum, you

don't need to worry. We love each other, we just can't live together.'

'At the moment.'

'Well, maybe not at all, but as I said, you don't have to worry about it. It'll be fine. I was thinking maybe I could get a lodger.'

At which point Jack came in for a refill. 'Who wants a lodger?'

Alice stared at him thoughtfully. 'I do. Know any good paying house guests?'

'Well, there's me. I'm more or less house trained, and homeless. You already know all my unpleasant personal habits and you wouldn't need to check out my references.'

Susie could see Alice was mulling the possibility over. 'What about your job at university? It's too far to commute and I need someone who can pay proper rent, not chip in fifteen quid towards a takeaway.'

'Not a problem. I just need somewhere to stay for the summer really, or until I can sort things out with Ellie. I could help you sort the flat out. We both know that Adam is about as much use as liquorice plimsolls when it comes to DIY. Meanwhile you advertise for someone for the autumn term, some nice prissy teacher, and by the time she moves in everything in your flat will be tiled, emulsioned and slick as a BBC2 makeover.'

Alice nodded thoughtfully. 'That's not a bad idea actually, although we still need to talk money.'

Jack sighed. 'Women, eh? All the same.'

Susie got to her feet. 'I'm staying well out of this.

I'm just going to go and say goodnight to the rest of the gang and then I'm off to bed. Alice, will you lock up?'

Jack looked affronted. 'You can't go to bed, Mum, you've got a house full of guests.'

'Who invited themselves,' Susie reminded him.

At which point Simon appeared. 'Hi sweetie,' he said, leaning in through the kitchen door as if he owned the place. 'Do you want me to pour you a glass of wine, and have we got any more ice anywhere?'

Susie shook her head. 'No thanks, and no *we* haven't, and just for the record I'm not your sweetie, or anyone else's come to that.'

'Pity.' He grinned. Susie made a sterling effort to beat her libido back into its box.

'Oh come on,' he purred when she didn't react. 'Relax. Come out and have a glass of wine. Take the weight off. It's still really beautiful out there and I'm missing you.'

'No thanks, some of us have to be up for work in the morning,' she said, aware that she sounded like a Victorian schoolmarm.

'I know, sweetie, it's been a long day. I was wondering,' he said, eyes bright and full of mischief, 'if I could maybe stay over – I mean it's getting late and it's a bit of a hike back to my place.'

'Simon, you're a professional rock tart – this is the middle of the afternoon for you.'

'Aw, come on, Susie, give a guy a break. I'd like to wake up with you in the morning, make a pot of coffee, sit out in the garden, share a croissant.' He spoke slowly, letting the words roll off his tongue.

Susie's expression didn't soften. 'Nice try, but there's no room at the inn. Alice is in the spare room. And the only thing I'll have time for in the morning is a quick cup of tea and I'm out of here.'

'I could always crash on the sofa,' he said, his tone implying that it most certainly wasn't where he planned to end up.

Jack pulled a face. 'Simon, please, do you mind not leching at my mother in front of me? I've got a weak stomach.'

Susie couldn't help smiling. 'And I was really hoping that you'd make a bit more of an effort. Whatever happened to good old-fashioned romance and sweet talk?'

Simon looked all hangdog and hard done by. 'I thought you'd have seen through all that and be bowled over by my honesty and complete lack of subterfuge. I didn't have you down as shallow or taken in by smooth-talking charmers.'

Susie laughed. 'Simon, *all* women can see through that, but we enjoy it – and besides, it takes more than a fish supper and a plate of burnt chipolatas to get me in the sack.'

Simon groaned. 'Really? Okay, well, in that case I was thinking – this weekend, how about we fly over to Paris? I know this great little hotel in the Latin Quarter. Gothic, four-poster beds, used to be a bordello. We could sail down the Seine, sip champagne – there is this fabulous little restaurant I discovered last time I was over there, their *agneau aux cinq épices* with rice has to be tasted to be believed – and they do *caviar d'aubergines.*' He pressed his fingers to his lips and mimed an explosive, appreciative kiss.

'Better,' said Susie, with a wry expression.

'I think I'm going to be sick,' said Alice.

'Me too,' snorted Jack.

'No, no, I mean really,' said Alice, and hurtled out of the kitchen clutching her hand to her mouth.

Simon held Susie's gaze. She felt her stomach do that weird backflip that accompanies desire. 'Well?' he purred. 'Stick the dog in kennels, let the kids take care of themselves – you won't regret it, I promise you. Now, about tonight . . .'

'Oh please,' said Jack. 'I'm going to go and see how Alice is.'

'Simon, you're about as subtle as a pile of house bricks. If you don't want to drive home, ring your driver, book into a hotel,' said Susie. 'You're not staying here, is that clear?'

'Benny is still on holiday, and besides, I've had a great evening, to be honest I don't want it to end.'

Susie, suppressing a smile, made an effort to hold on to her stern expression. 'Bugger off home.'

Chapter 12

Wednesday morning and Susie woke up alone. Alice was still in bed, the sun was shining and all was well with the world.

Susie left checking her mobile until she got out of the shower – there were text messages from Saskia and Simon, one thanking her for being such a nice person and one accusing her of being a terrible tease and a gorgeous, sexy woman. Simon missed her and couldn't wait to see her again apparently. Both were highly flattering.

As she did her hair, Susie looked in the mirror, liked what she saw and drove into college with the car windows wide open, singing along at full pelt to her favourite CD.

As she pulled into her parking space, her mobile rang but she ignored it; it was too much to expect that good news, like bad, came in threes. The double doors to the studio had been wedged open, the whole place was bathed in sunlight, and for the first time since Robert had dumped her Susie felt good. Really good – not to mention calm, wonderful, sexy – and, most of all, free.

Inside, Nina had already got the coffee on. There was music playing, and lots of students were already in and working despite it still being early, everyone buzzing about industriously.

'Shame they can't be this dedicated all year really,' commented Nina as Susie headed over towards the computer where Nina was sitting. Between glancing at the screen and typing, Nina was rifling through pages of the disembowelled exhibition files that were spread out on the desk in front of her like a deck of cards.

Susie picked up one of the sheets. 'Now what?'

'Now nothing, touch wood it's all coming together. I've just been emailing a few people who need chasing up. Oh, and your friend Saskia has really come up trumps. Last night she emailed us a whole load of pictures and sketches of what she's got in mind for the front foyer and asked if we'd considered theming the rest of the exhibition – at this stage that's probably not possible but worth thinking about next year. Meanwhile,' Nina opened up the file attached to Saskia's email, 'lots of big palms in the front, lots of foliage and big-impact plants, and then inside she was thinking vines and – well, here, come and take a look.'

Susie leant over to take a peek. 'Wow, those look brilliant, is it actually those plants or ones like them?'

Nina scanned the email. 'Nope, I think we're getting these, big planters and all.'

'Great. Has anyone discussed insurance?'

'I'm on the case. Although to be perfectly honest I'm way more interested in what Ms Hill wanted to talk to you about.'

'Yes, but that's because you are a nosy cow. Can you scroll down so I can see the rest?'

'If I must. For a woman with a broken heart you're very perky this morning,' Nina said as she clicked onto the next image that Saskia had sent.

'These are amazing,' said Susie.

'I know, apparently someone ordered a container-load of stuff to dress a film set – Hill's were the importers and once the shoot was all done and dusted they were the people asked to clear it all away.'

'Fab.'

'So?' said Nina.

'So it looks like we'll have a truly stunning foyer and forecourt display.'

'Wrong answer.'

Susie pulled a face and mimed incomprehension.

Nina sighed. 'Oh for god's sake, Susie. *Did you ring her?*'

'No.'

Nina grimaced. 'Oh come on. You're going to have to talk to her sooner or later.'

'I didn't say that I didn't talk to her, far from it. She stopped me on the side of the road last night.'

Nina looked horrified. 'Oh my god, do you think she's stalking you?'

Susie shook her head. 'Worse.'

'Worse?' repeated Nina.

'Uh-huh, she thinks I'm a really nice person and I have a text message to prove it.'

'Will you just tell me what she wanted?'

Susie settled herself down on the stool by the desk.

'Okay. The short version is that Robert asked her to marry him. She wanted my advice about what she should do.'

'Bugger me,' Nina said. 'That man doesn't hang around, does he?' And then Nina's mouth dropped open as an idea percolated through. 'Oh my god, don't tell me, she's not already pregnant, is she?'

'Nope, well at least not so far as I know, and from what I can gather having kids is pretty far down on her to-do list – after backpacking to Bali and buying a pony.'

'But he wants –'

'I know what he wants,' said Susie.

'So when's the big day then?'

'Well, as far as Saskia's concerned a way off yet.'

'But she's said yes?'

Susie shook her head.

'*She said no*,' said Nina incredulously. 'My god, that girl has gone up in my estimation. So is it all over? I mean, Jesus, that would just be so ironic.'

'Neither. She told him that she needs time to think.'

'I'm still impressed.'

'I don't think he was.'

Nina smiled wryly. 'The girl's got her head screwed on. Every time anyone asked me I said yes just in case it was a fluke and nobody ever did it again. Trust me, it's not a great idea as ideas go, although I've had some great engagement parties and I've still got more household gadgets than John Lewis. So what did Robert say? Presumably she told you what he said?'

'Well, she thought he was hurt. But picking through

the wreckage, it sounds to me like Robert's lied to her about what he wants. She wants to travel, build up the family business, maybe buy a house, and he's said he'll be right there beside her holding her hand and shouldering her rucksack.'

Nina pulled a face. 'Oh please. The man gives reptiles a bad name.'

'She thinks he is wonderful, supportive, kind. Nina, what the hell could I say to her? Sorry, but Robert is actually a lying tricky little sod who is desperate for a baby and is trying to lure you into motherhood on a pretext of fatherly understanding and boundless patience?'

Nina considered for a few seconds. 'Well, that would have done for a start; I would have probably added that he was a boring, miserable, grumpy old fart. Presumably she's already noticed the bald spot and those ears.'

Susie laughed in spite of herself. 'I can't do it, Neen. She has to find out for herself – and the worst thing about it is, despite how much I would like her to be a complete cow, she isn't. She is a really nice girl, young for her age and quite shy –'

'Really? I got the impression she was stuck up and miserable?'

'It's a bugger, isn't it – apparently she really is shy.'

'Damn, and just when I was really getting into loathing her. Although that's all the more reason to tell her,' growled Nina. 'How would you feel if it was Alice he was going out with?'

'We can't make our kids' mistakes for them.'

'You sound more like Claire Rayner every day,'

groaned Nina, shuffling off her stool as the first class of the day trickled in. 'Anyway,' she tapped the computer screen, 'good plants.'

Susie nodded. 'Uh-huh.' It was such a shame she was dating Robert.

Nina paused. 'Proposing is a bit heavy at this stage though. Bit of a whirlwind romance – I mean, how long have they been going out together?'

'Don't ask.'

Nina's expression registered understanding. 'Oh, okay. Something of an overlap?'

Susie nodded. 'And then some.'

'I told you the man was a bastard,' said Nina, putting a hand on her shoulder. 'You know you're well out of it, don't you?'

'You took the words right out of my mouth,' said Susie. 'Now, best we get on.'

At lunchtime one of the students came over to where Susie was working and said, 'Scuse me? Susie, there's someone looking for you. Some bloke – says it's urgent. I told him to wait in the office.'

Susie, between bites of a tuna and sweetcorn baguette, looked up from behind the camera that she and Nina had set up in one corner of the ceramics studio. That was just what she needed. Some bloke – just when she was up to her eyes in work. He was bound to want something. So far the morning had been crazy. For the last hour and a half she'd been working with second-year art and design, taking pictures of their finished pieces, some of which were enormous not to mention fragile. A few weren't quite finished and everyone was slightly edgy and overexcited about the idea that, finally, the whole thing was coming together.

So far there had been a lot of to-ing and fro-ing and careful manoeuvring – and then there was a problem with the lighting, and the ply sheets they'd built an impromptu photographic studio with weren't proving to be that stable, despite the frame that the guys from metalwork had put together for them.

One of the students had a stomach bug and kept disappearing; another couldn't find her work and another had just managed to spill tea all over her tissue-paper collage, which had taken many painstaking, nitpicking, self-denigrating weeks to get to a state where she wasn't fretting about it and everyone had agreed was finally finished. Half a cup of builder's tea at an acute angle and it now looked like a heavy night in a nightclub lavatory. But was it art?

After an initial panic they'd found her a hair dryer and a couple of sun lamps from the health and beauty department, while the student had sobbed uncontrol-lably, which made the sculpture damper. Susie had suggested she fixed it with spray varnish a couple of weeks earlier, but apparently the girl had forgotten or not bothered or something. It was fate, apparently. Losing her masterpiece at the eleventh hour went along with her whole Goth angst Emo princess take on life. A couple of the other students tried to persuade her it looked better after the tea incident, while her best friend had pulled out her sketchbook with the preparatory drawings and was busy trying to tease the mangled pulp back into shape. So Susie didn't need any more stress, certainly not stray blokes.

She stepped back behind the camera, feeling like a beachside photographer as the next student rolled up with three finished canvases and a selection of other work neatly packed in a banana box. It felt a bit like taking photos of their children. Very carefully the boy unpacked his treasures.

Susie stared down through the viewfinder. The current subject caught in the frame was a series of sepia, gold and black blocks made up of newsprint, photos and giant shiny black text forming a stunning image of Marilyn Monroe and the word Icon. It was a great piece of work and one that deserved her full attention. She didn't have time for visitors. She altered the focus a fraction.

'So what do you want me to tell this bloke?' asked the boy, who fancied himself as the next Damien Hirst.

Susie wanted to tell whoever it was to bugger off, she hadn't got time to see them – but then again it could be anyone. 'Can you just tell them that I'll be there in about five minutes? Thanks. I'll just finish this series off and then I'll be there. These look really good – a few more –' she said, looking up at the owner of the Marilyn collection, who looked on soulfully, or maybe it was just relief that his babies had nearly finished their moment under the spotlight. The shutter clicked, she finished with the long shots and then shifted the tripod and went for a series of sharp close-ups before standing back to make sure she'd covered all the angles.

Nina took a look down the viewfinder. 'Nice composition, Ms Bailey.'

'How's the collage coming along?' she said, moving one of the panels a little.

'Drying out nicely . . . I reckon as long as it doesn't catch fire it'll be good to go in about an hour.'

'Be just our luck.'

'Uh-huh. I've got a couple of people on suicide watch in case it spontaneously combusts.'

'Have a camera on standby just in case. Catch its final moments.'

Susie moved the tripod back, taking another couple of shots, and then she stood back, finished. 'They look really good,' she said to the work's creator and then to Nina, 'Would you mind helping Daryl here to dismantle this set and start on the next one? I've got someone waiting for me in the office apparently.'

'Do you want me to go over and sort it out?'

Susie considered the idea for a couple of seconds. 'Whoever it is asked for me, said it was urgent.'

Nina grinned. 'Probably some rep trying to sell us Swarfega.'

'Again?' joked Susie. She ruffled her hair with her fingers and fiddled in her pocket for a mint, as an amused Nina looked on.

'What?' demanded Susie.

'Who do you think it is in the office?'

'I've got no idea,' she said, which was true. It could be anybody, but she realised at least part of her was hoping that it was Simon. She ran her tongue over her teeth checking for stray bits of sweetcorn.

Nina stuck her hand in the pocket of the brown shop coat that she wore when she was at work and pulled out a tube of lipstick. 'You want to borrow this, or do you think you'll do as you are?'

'Don't mock. I could get us a great discount on a case of brush cleaner.'

Susie hurried off through the rabbit warren of inter-connecting studios, storerooms and workshops back to the art room, checking out how she looked in the windows as she scurried across the quad.

She smiled to herself. Simon was truly incorrigible: no boundaries, no sense of decorum, just what she needed. Even if it was going nowhere it was exciting in a way that being with Robert never was. Time to grow old disgracefully. Susie swung in through the double doors, slowed down to a more relaxed pace, palmed another mint and did one more quick ruffle of her hair.

'Susie?'

'Robert?' Stunned, Susie felt her mouth drop open in genuine surprise – and disappointment. Robert was standing by her desk, dressed for the office, although she noticed that he had had his hair cut and that just had to be a new tie, which surely must be down to Saskia or some pushy salesman. Susie couldn't imagine him choosing a red, white and black chequered silk number without having had *some* outside influence.

'What on earth are you doing here?' she said before she could stop herself.

He looked hurt and then slightly put out. 'Sorry, were you expecting someone else? I was rather hoping that maybe we could go out for lunch or something. I did text you.'

She looked at him incredulously. 'What?'

It had to have been the text she'd chosen to ignore. Susie made a mental note that sometimes, even if it was bad news, it was probably better to be forewarned.

'Lunch. I was thinking we could maybe go out and grab a sandwich or something. Although obviously if it's inconvenient . . .' His voice trailed off. He tried smiling instead.

Susie stared at him. Three years he had had to drop in and whisk her away at lunchtime, and in all that time *nothing*, not so much as a whisper, and now it was too late, whatever the reason.

She shook her head. 'I'm sorry, but this is a really bad time, I'm up to my eyes in work – incredibly busy. Thanks anyway.'

He looked hurt. She was almost sucked in until it occurred to her that she owed Robert nothing. Zilch, zippo, nada. The thought was so liberating that she smiled, which gave Robert the green light to have another go.

'I was hoping we could talk,' he said. 'I did pop by last night. I was going to call in but you seemed to have a houseful. Didn't want to gatecrash.'

'Yes, it was a bit hectic. Look, I've got to get on, Robert. I'm really busy with the end-of-year show.'

'So I see,' he said, obviously not wanting to leave. To the uninitiated the studio looked like the anteroom of a particularly obscure realm of hell. In one corner a girl, whose work involved real faces pushed through holes in a giant canvas, was busy painting her best friend's face bright blue and sticking on giant false eyelashes. Her second volunteer, a vision in fuchsia, was drying in front of a fan heater. 'Maybe another time.'

'Robert, look, I'm sorry but I'm in the middle of something very important,' Susie said.

'Oh I see,' he grumbled. 'And so I'm not important any more.'

It was such a blatant attempt to make her feel guilty that Susie laughed. 'Robert, don't do this. You finished with me, remember? Now if you'll excuse me, I'm working.' She turned to go.

'It won't take long.' Truth was, he did sound desperate. 'I need to talk to you.'

In exasperation, Susie swung round. 'No, you don't, Robert. You don't need to talk to me at all, that isn't my role any more. You've got someone else, go talk to her.'

He flinched as if Susie had hit him. 'I can't,' he said.

Susie shook her head. 'Robert, this is not my problem, now please leave. I've got way too much to do to get caught up in your problems.' And with that she made for the door, trembling.

'But I thought you were my friend,' he called after her. 'Please, Susie –' She didn't dare turn around.

'I'll ring you,' Robert said desperately. 'Or maybe drop by later?'

Susie couldn't bring herself to reply.

'That was quick,' said Nina as Susie pushed open the door to the ceramics room. 'I was just coming over to have a little look –' And then she saw Susie's face and her expression and tone changed. 'Who was it? You okay?'

Susie nodded.

'So it wasn't Simon, the rock prince?'

'No, no, it was Robert.'

'Robert? What the hell did he want?'

'My thoughts exactly,' said Susie, peering down the viewfinder of the camera. 'Good news is whatever he wanted he didn't get it. Now –' She looked over towards the far end of the studio where a Goth was waiting expectantly, twisting his latest piercing in a frenzy of first-night nerves. 'Come on, let's make a start, shall we? I was thinking we may need to adjust the lights just a little bit more. The canvas looks great, though. We can do some of these in monochrome. Do you want to come and take a look?'

Susie indicated the camera and the Goth headed her way, tall, pale and skinny as a steeple in his platform New Rocks. She hoped he didn't notice just how much her hands were shaking.

There was no one at her house when Susie got home, except for Milo, who was busy guarding the house from the comfort of his basket on the landing. For the first time in god knows how long Susie eased her car into the garage and closed the doors behind her so that should Robert drive by, he couldn't see that she was home, and then she relocked the front door in case Simon, Jack or Matt just happened to try to walk in with or without the makings of a barbecue. Just to be certain she slipped out and locked the side gate.

There was a note from Alice on the kitchen table which read:

Needed to go home to sort a few things out and go for antenatal check-up – am feeling much better, will ring you later. Love A xxx

Susie turned the paper over. She had no idea when it was written. Eight that morning? Nine? Fifteen minutes before she got home from work? Did this mean Alice would be back later or that she had gone home for good? And why hadn't she said anything before going to bed last night? It occurred to Susie that she really ought to ring Adam to see how he was, but actually at the moment she didn't want to talk to anyone, especially not anyone who might need anything.

Instead, Susie woke Milo up and let him outside for a wee, plugged the kettle in and sat down in the kitchen with her feet up, revelling in the cool, the quiet and the total calm. After half an hour or so she changed out of her work clothes into shorts and a tee shirt and walked Milo down to the river, going the long way round to avoid Robert's cottage and the roadway in case Saskia was lying in wait. Once clear of the cottages and any possible interception, she spent the rest of the time planning a Delia moment, involving a grilled chicken breast and a watercress, orange and cashew-nut salad lightly tossed in a tamari dressing, served up with new potatoes and maybe a glass of wine, eaten out on the terrace in the last of the evening sunshine, all on her own with a soundtrack of her choice. Bliss.

As Susie walked back towards the house she had an odd sense of something coming to an end. Over the last few days, besides being busy and rushed off her feet with guests, work and god knows what else, she had also been too raw and far too hurt to think about what losing Robert actually meant in practical terms.

Even though they hadn't lived together, Robert had been a big part of her day-to-day life. They had been together almost every weekend for the last three years, met up during the week for films or impromptu suppers, DIY sessions or gardening projects, or sometimes just to have someone else to share the sofa with at the end of a long day. In fact, how he had managed to slot in his fledgling relationship with Saskia was almost beyond her. Maybe they'd met up for lunch? Or on Sunday evenings, when he pleaded ironing and paperwork? Susie's pace slowed to a crawl.

The truth of it was that for all his faults she had loved Robert, and part of her still did, although there was a world of difference between loving and being in love. She hadn't quite let go of Robert yet, but she would. It was something that would fade slowly rather than vanish overnight, and heal into a shiny new scar to go with all the others that, if you live a life, you collect along the way.

What she needed to do now, Susie decided, was plan for the gap Robert left. She needed something to fill the void. And if she had any sense at all it wouldn't be Simon.

She bit her lip and wished Robert and their happy-ever-after farewell.

Wandering back towards the cottage, Susie made up her mind to get a grip. Maybe she should go online and sign up with a dating agency. Look through the local papers at the personals and the what's-on section. Book a holiday. God, there were so many films, places, shows and exhibitions that Robert had refused to go and see since they had been together. She'd got three years of culture and DVDs to catch up on for a start. She felt excited at the idea of a clean slate.

When Susie got in the phone was ringing. She hesitated for an instant before answering, taking a look at the newly installed caller display. Seeing Simon's number made her smile. She picked up the handset. 'Well hello there, now what do you want?' she said brightly.

'Hello,' said a female voice. It caught Susie by complete surprise and took her another few seconds to realise that the voice was Ellie's. She didn't sound wildly pleased either.

'Sorry, I thought it was your dad,' Susie said, keeping her tone light.

'Well that answers my first question,' said Ellie.

'Which was?'

'Whether my dad was over there with you.'

Susie smiled. Maybe he was on his way. 'What time did he leave?'

'He didn't come home last night.'

'What? Oh my god – have you called the police?'

'Why on earth would I do that?' retorted Ellie.

'Because he's missing.'

'He's not missing, he's gone AWOL. Trust me, he does it all the time,' snapped Ellie.

As she continued speaking, Susie glanced out of the window. What if he'd turned up and she'd been on the common with Milo; what if she'd missed him? Worse still, why did she care? Was fancying Simon creeping up on her like flu or blue mould? Or was it that she needed someone to fill the gap left by Robert? The thought made her uneasy.

Ellie sniffed. 'I've been trying to track him down. He's supposed to be meeting someone this afternoon.'

'A client?'

'God only knows. There's a snotty message on the machine and about fifty missed calls all from the same number. To be honest, I have no idea how he manages to get anything done. His whole life is a mess of missed messages and broken promises; he's never here, he's so vague, we never know where he is or where he's been or what he's up to – the man is a complete nightmare.'

'Maybe he's just not used to having you around, and he is a grown-up,' protested Susie, somewhat stunned to find herself defending him. What was it with the Alice and Ellie generation that they felt they had to parent their parents?

'Well you wouldn't think so the way he behaves. He was supposed to be meeting someone yesterday – he promised faithfully – and where was he? At yours, apparently. Barbecuing. He sent me a text and then switched his bloody phone off.'

'Perhaps he can reschedule it, I mean these things happen?'

'Oh yes, they happen all right, mostly to my dad.'

'He told me that he was out this way.'

Ellie's tone was icy. 'He was out your way yesterday because he was supposed to be going to Stansted Airport.'

'Stansted Airport?' parroted Susie.

'He was supposed to be there to pick my mum up at six o'clock. When she told him she was coming over and planned to get the train, Dad said, "No, you don't want to do that, honey, don't you worry, I'll drive over and pick you up." And you know what? After all these years she still believed him. Mad cow. I don't know who is the craziest really, him or her. Anyway, she's stuck at the airport, furious, and ends up having to get here by train, which is a nightmare – it takes ages – and then she misses her connection and then when she gets here she finds out that his nibs is out with another woman. I won't tell you what she said.'

Susie didn't know what to say, but settled for, 'So where is your mum now?'

'Here with me. Her and Nika have gone down to Tescos because there's nothing in the house to eat. The man is a total liability, whatever you do, Susie, please don't get hooked up with him. My dad is about as reliable as a cheap watch. He makes me so angry – Mum *said* me coming to stay here with him was a bad idea. I should have listened. Anyway, if he isn't with you we've got no idea where he is or what time he'll be back.'

Finally, Ellie ran out of breath. Despite herself, Susie could see why Simon wanted to be out of the house;

she somehow doubted the atmosphere between Ellie, her mum and Simon was going to be convivial happy families.

'I'm sure he'll turn up,' she said lamely. 'You never know, something could have happened to him?'

'Oh please,' snorted Ellie. 'My father happens to other people, and besides, we'd have heard by now if he'd had an accident. Bad news travels fast. No, the only thing that's likely to have happened is either he's blind drunk and can't drive home, or he's pulled some cheap little bimbo and *won't* drive home. He'll just hole up in a hotel room somewhere till he thinks everything has blown over. He'll turn up when he's slept it off or kicked her out of bed or both. Meanwhile he'll let someone else pick up the pieces. Mum is livid and so upset.'

'I'm really sorry, Ellie.' And then, before she could stop herself, Susie added, 'You will let me know he's all right, won't you?'

'Oh he'll be all right,' Ellie said. 'It's the rest of us who always end up suffering.'

As Susie hung up she felt queasy. It hadn't occurred to her at all that Simon might be out with someone else. Maybe Ellie was just being catty, after all she was angry and had every reason to be. Susie picked up her mobile and flicked through the text to the latest flirty one from Simon and then pressed the call button. Unsurprisingly, Simon's phone went to voicemail. There wasn't anything she wanted to say to him, or at least nothing she wanted recording.

Technically there was nothing between them other

than one supper, a barbecue and . . . and it suddenly occurred to Susie that the reason Simon hadn't wanted to go home the night before had got nothing to do with wanting to end up in her bed, so much as not wanting to end up in his own.

Susie stood for a few seconds, phone in hand, thinking about the implications. How much worse would she feel now if she had taken him up on his ham-fisted proposition? She reddened. How could she have been so naïve – and how was it that now, when she was supposed to be older and wiser, she was so much less perceptive? Ellie was right, Simon was a self-serving bastard.

At which point the phone rang. Susie peered at the number – it was Simon. She felt as if somehow she had managed to conjure him up, and stared at the number and the name, and decided to let it ring. After five rings the machine clicked in. And then it rang again and she ignored it and started on supper, slicing through the chicken breasts like a true professional, and then it rang again. At which point Susie, annoyed now, snatched up the receiver.

'What do you want?' she snapped. Except of course, sod's law being what it is, it wasn't Simon third time around but Alice, who didn't take kindly to being snapped at.

'Oh, sorry I disturbed you. I was just ringing to let you know how the antenatal check went,' she said, sounding wounded and probably rightly so.

Susie grovelled for a full ten minutes, then eventually asked, 'So will you be back this evening, only I'm just about to cook supper. Would you like me to cook you some?'

'No,' said Alice. 'Adam said he'd pop by later. He was going to come to the check-up with me, but I said there wasn't much point in the two of us sitting around for half the afternoon. I asked the girl on reception why it always takes so long for them to see everybody – I mean it said two fifteen on the appointment, and if it says two fifteen then I'm sorry but I expect to be seen at two fifteen – and she got quite sniffy with me. I did say it was all right for those people who'd got nothing better to do all day.

'Anyway, I popped into the office on the way back and they are making a total pig's ear of things there, so I'm going in tomorrow. I had planned to come back to the cottage, but to be honest there is so much that needs doing here – and then Jack will be moving in.' Alice paused. So far she'd made it sound as if she had been doing Susie a favour by staying, but then her tone softened and she added, 'Thank you for letting me come home, Mum. You've got no idea how much it meant to be with someone who I didn't have to explain myself to. I needed to get away.'

Susie sighed. 'It's all right, sweetie, and you know if you need me I'll always be here. Don't think you're ever on your own.' She wished there was a better way to say the things she meant. 'I love you,' she said simply.

'Thanks, Mum,' said Alice, and then, reverting to type, continued, 'Anyway, I've got to go. I'm just fixing supper.'

'Something horribly healthy and wheat-free?' teased Susie.

Alice giggled. 'Actually I'm sending out for pizza,' she said. 'I've had this real craving all day for a king-size Hawaiian with double pineapple, added anchovies and a great big pile of sliced black olives. I'm thinking of ringing back and ordering extra anchovies – god, even talking about it is making my mouth water.'

Susie smiled. 'Enjoy.' She hung up and went back to Delia-ing. The food was sublime – *a summer feast, ideal as a supper dish or a light lunch* – made all the more enjoyable by the fact she unplugged the phone.

Chapter 13

In the studio Jack's portrait was coming along well. Susie wiped her hands on a rag and stood back to admire the progress she'd made over the past couple of days. The tentative lines of the charcoal sketch had gone now, to be replaced by broad energetic brush strokes that she thought really caught the coltish vibrancy of her son. She was pleased with the quality of light and shade and the angle of his chin and the texture of his skin as he looked down towards the bench, although from experience she knew that in ten minutes' time she could easily think the whole thing was complete rubbish.

While she'd been working Susie had kept the phone in the studio switched off and the doors and the back gate locked. It was something that she hadn't done since she'd started dating Robert. It struck her as she stood in the warm, clear light from the big studio windows that she had been altogether too available over the last three years.

Over the weekend Susie planned to take the dog to the beach – he was currently asleep under the bench dreaming of rabbits and sausages yet to be caught – and maybe treat herself to a massage at the beauty parlour in town, get her hair cut, rent a couple of really good DVDs, maybe buy a bottle of Baileys and some expensive ice cream and luxuriate in her uncluttered, stress-free singledom. And if things got too lonely she'd ring Nina and invite her over to lunch, or maybe suggest a drive out to a stately home or a garden. She had had a catalogue of open gardens sitting by the TV since February. It would be great to go and nose about with someone who was actually interested. She'd decided the secret to recovery was to keep busy and to spoil herself a little bit. It was nice to have the house back to herself too, with no Jack, no Alice, and no Robert moaning about what was on the telly and then hogging the remote all evening.

Susie stretched. The muscles in her neck and shoulders ached but she really felt as if she had achieved a lot. She had been into town early, before it got too busy, and moseyed round the market, bought flowers and fruit and felt wildly continental filling her wicker basket up with all sorts of goodies like a woman on a postcard in Provence.

Sometimes there was a little stall that sold olives and feta and good ciabatta, and today she decided that instead of Delia she might try for a young Sophia Loren, or maybe that girl who had been in the film about chocolate – Juliette Binoche – and wished that instead of jeans and a shirt she had been wearing a floral-print dress and sandals, possibly riding a bike with a basket on the handlebars.

But now Susie just felt like an artist who had had a long day. She planned to go inside, run a bath, pour in some of the expensive bubbly stuff someone had bought her for Christmas, soak for as long as the fancy took her, rub in loads of moisturiser and then put on her pyjamas and spend the evening eating bread, cheese and olives, washed down with a couple of glasses of wine while watching gardening programmes on TV. What more could a girl possibly want? Except for chocolate. She toyed with the idea of driving up to the garage for a chunky Kit-Kat and a packet of Maltesers before going inside.

It wasn't that Susie had totally cut herself off from the outside world. She was still picking up her email. There were ten days until the opening night of the end-of-year exhibition, and there were things to be completed and chased up, which she had dutifully done. Nina had sent her an email to say that the last of the stands and display units had been finished by the guys in the carpentry shop, attached was a copy of the nibbles menu that the head of department had signed off on, and they had had confirmation that two of the three local newspapers were going to be there to record the event for posterity. A local arts magazine had promised to send along one of its staff to take lots of photos. So too a man from some gardening magazine, who Saskia had invited. Nina also mentioned in passing that Saskia had asked if she could bring someone along to the private viewing.

Susie bit down on the end of her paintbrush. You didn't have to be a genius to work out who that might be.

She turned to start clearing away, and as she did something caught Susie's eye. Something white glided elegantly past the studio window, spiralling on a slow arc down towards the pond. A dove, she thought – years of cat-free living and a resident dog and wildlife lover meant the garden was a haven for birds. And then, a moment or two later there was another one, except this didn't look like a dove so much as a stealth bomber, and then before she could really take it in there was another one, this one a little like Concorde, which banked left, nose-dived sharply and plunged into the shrubs. Susie stared, trying to make sense of what she was seeing.

Someone was throwing paper aeroplanes into her garden. She turned off the radio and went outside just as another one looped the loop and then swooped down gracefully to land right in the middle of the fish pond.

Susie hurried round to the back gate and unlocked it. Standing in the lane outside her cottage was Simon. Holding a paper aeroplane. Case closed.

'Hi,' he said, lifting a hand in welcome. 'How's it going?'

There were several misfires caught in the roses on the trellis, a couple of others in the gutter and several by his feet.

'I'd just about got the trajectory right,' he said, indicating a line drawn into the sandy soil on the verge. 'Over-arm from here. Nice smooth movement. Couple of them have gone next door but it's all right – I didn't write anything too rude on them. I did think about climbing over the gate but I thought someone might see me and call the police. You really ought to have a go, gives you a real sense of achievement when one goes over – there –' As he spoke he launched another paper plane over the roof of her studio with great gusto. This one sailed up on some unseen breeze and banked gracefully left before vanishing below the roof line. 'Isn't that wonderful?'

'What the hell are you doing here, Simon?'

'Your phone's not working,' he said, very matter-of-factly.

'I know, I switched it off,' she said. 'I wanted a bit of peace and quiet.'

'Fair enough,' Simon said. 'Are you packed?'

Susie stared at him. 'Packed?'

Simon nodded. 'Yes, you know, packed – frilly little numbers and thongs and things. Evening dresses and stuff to look drop-dead gorgeous in.' When she didn't respond he looked crestfallen. 'Packed, passport, Paris? You must remember.' He pulled his own passport out from the inside pocket of his jacket and waved it at her. 'Friday night, you said you'd come out with me. And then you refused to let me stay over and you said you needed to be wooed or something, and I said –'

'You said, "This weekend how about we fly over to Paris – I know this great little hotel in the Latin Quarter. Gothic, four-poster beds, used to be a bordello. We could sail down the Seine, sip champagne . . ."'

He grinned. 'There. See, you *do* remember. Now come on, we've got a flight in – err – ooo, just long enough for you to throw something slinky in a bag.'

'Simon, are you completely nuts?'

'No.' He looked mortally offended. 'Not at all. Well, not totally, maybe a little eccentric – misunderstood maybe.'

'When you said it I thought you were joking and then I didn't hear from you. And I spoke to Ellie.'

He pulled a face. 'You know, letting her come to stay at my place was the worst day's work I've done in a long time. Nag, nag, nag, pick, pick, pick. It's a complete bloody nightmare. Your Jack is well out of it if you ask me – she's just like her mother.'

'Who you left at the airport,' countered Susie.

'Ah.' Simon faltered and mis-launched the next plane. It spiralled out of control and crashed into the climbers by the front door. 'For someone who's not interested in me you know an awful lot about my private life.'

Susie, sensing the trap, stayed silent, so Simon continued. 'She emotionally blackmailed me into saying that I'd meet her, and anyway I don't know what she's moaning about, I paid for her bloody cab. If Benny hadn't been off bloody waterskiing I would have sent him. You know he sent me a postcard? *Wish you were here.* Cheeky bastard.'

'Ellie said her mum had to come by train.'

'See – everything's got to be a bloody drama with those two. I said grab a cab and I'll pick up the tab once you get to my place. End of. Train, my arse; she wouldn't know where to find one. Christ, she thinks taxis are public transport.'

'Ellie said that you didn't go home on Wednesday.'

'Do you blame me? I'm not completely crazy. The

pair of them wanted my balls in a bucket. They'd have ripped me to shreds. Okay, okay, yes, I said I'd pick her up; no, I wasn't there; yes, she had to find a cab; and yes, I stayed out all night.' He grinned. 'You had your chance, sweetie. You had first refusal.' He threw another paper plane; this one sailed effortlessly over her rooftop and on into the wide blue evening sky. 'So – Paris,' he said.

'I'm not sleeping with you.'

He aped hurt. 'Did I ask you to? Did I mention it? What kind of a man do you take me for?'

Susie didn't bother to answer, instead she just stared at him.

'Separate rooms, no strings, cross my heart,' he said.

'What about Milo?'

'I'm not into men.'

'He's not a man, he's my dog.'

Simon held up a hand. 'Don't even go there.'

'I *meant* I can't take him to Paris with me.'

Simon nodded. 'So you're coming then?'

Which was why just under an hour later Susie was on Nina's doorstep with a bag of Bakers Complete, Milo's lead, two bowls, a packet of leather chews and a bag full of assorted dog paraphernalia.

'This dog has just farted in my car,' Simon yelled from the kerb.

Nina peered past Susie to take in the view. Simon, with a spray-on tan that made his eyes even bluer, was dressed in a ginger long-line linen jacket, black jeans, white collarless shirt and boots. He looked almost edible.

'Wipe the drool off your chin, Neen,' Susie said, handing her the dog food. 'I've brought a packet of dog poo bags and his blanket is in that bag. Are you sure you don't mind doing this?'

Nina purred salaciously. 'I'd rather be doing what you're doing.'

Susie laughed. 'You're my best friend. You're meant to be giving me a lecture on how stupid I'm being, how I'm bound to get hurt, and how he is obviously a total and utter bastard.'

Simon had got out of the car now and was busy fooling around with Milo, who was obliging by fooling right back. 'He is really cute.'

'Milo?' asked Susie, raising her eyebrows.

Nina looked heavenwards. 'For god's sake, woman, take the broom out of your butt, the man is really easy on the eye. Enjoy.'

'And he knows it, Neen. Will you please talk me out of this. The man's a lecherous womaniser, who is going to seduce me and break my heart.'

Nina put her hands on her hips. 'You want me to take the bullet for you, is that what you're saying?'

Meanwhile, Simon made his way down the path, grinning. Milo was carrying his lead in his mouth, wagging his tail with pure joy and coming a very close second in the who-would-you-like-to-take-home-with-you stakes.

'No, that isn't what I want, what I want is for you to tell me this is a bad idea,' said Susie.

'Well, it is, but it's good sport if you can get it,' Nina said with a grin, as Simon turned up the charm.

'You must be Nina,' he said, leaning in close and kissing her on both cheeks. 'Shame I didn't know you were free,' he said to her. 'We could have stuck the mutt in kennels and you could have come too. You know what they say, two's company, three's so much more fun.'

'As long as you're supple,' Nina said, refusing to be fazed.

He laughed and then said, all serious and concerned, 'Now you're okay about having Milo, aren't you?'

'Whoa there, cowboy, don't come over all paternal – that's *my* dog you're talking about,' said Susie.

'I'll be just fine – me and the mutt are old friends,' said Nina, looking first to Susie and then Simon. 'Now you kids run along and have a good time, me and Old Yeller here will keep 'n' eye on the ranch till you get back,' she continued, lapsing into a deep southern drawl, and then added in a normal voice, 'Oh, and I want something luxurious and unlikely from Paris.'

'Something strapless and silky?' suggested Simon.

'Surprise me,' Nina purred right back.

'Oh please,' said Susie. 'Will you just stop it and get in the car.'

They flew out of a little airfield near Stansted. Susie made every effort not to be impressed or overwhelmed as they drove out to the private jet in a silver-grey 4x4 chauffeured by a man who looked as if he would be more at home in a Bond film.

Inside the plane, which sat ten people comfortably,

were large leather seats, lots of leg room, plush carpet and expensive-looking fixtures and fittings, a pilot called Carl, a co-pilot called Henry and a steward called Antoine, who announced as they taxied down the runway that they would be arriving at Paris, Le Bourget airport in around an hour and meanwhile he suggested they relax and enjoy the flight, adding that the pilot would point out anything of interest if they wanted and if not the whole crew would be as quiet as Carmelites.

All this was in sharp contrast to Susie's usual experience, flying El-Cheapo Air, where, having queued for hours before finally fighting her way to a seat, Susie normally spent the entire flight surrounded by screaming kids, furious middle-aged men, an old lady with an indefinable smell, all the while knowing that her luggage was being flown club class to Gdansk.

'Impressed?' asked Simon as they began to climb up into the skies above East Anglia.

'It's hard not to be. This yours?' she said, looking round the sleek interior, trying not to look too awestruck.

'I wish. Actually it belongs to a good friend of mine.' Simon unfastened his seat belt. 'Fancy a glass of champagne? There should be some in the fridge.'

'I'm already on the case,' said Antoine from somewhere behind them. 'God, some people, no patience, no manners, no class,' he said warmly – obviously he knew Simon well.

Susie sat back in her oh so comfortable seat and

breathed a sigh of contentment. Who could resist? Flying across the Channel drinking pink champagne and eating canapés just had to be the way to live.

'So tell me about Robert and your work – oh, and the exhibition – how's it all going?' said Simon, steepling his fingers and watching her closely.

Susie looked at him. 'Are you serious?'

'Never more so. Whatever Ellie told you, I can do empathy.'

'I'd rather talk about what you do, and why you've asked me to come to Paris for the weekend when you could be coming over here with a pneumatic twenty-something.'

'I prefer my twenty-somethings two at a time; no staying power, the younger generation,' he said with a grin. When Susie didn't respond he continued, 'Well, you wouldn't let me stay the other night despite the burgers, so I thought I'd better make a bit more of an effort.'

Susie lifted an eyebrow.

Simon made a dismissive hand gesture. 'What's to tell? I mean, young and perky is great but once you've shagged them what do you talk about? Don't get me wrong – it's huge fun at the time, but they need a lot of attention, when they've got a problem the whole fucking world's got a problem – and to be honest I'm fed up of all that. And then there's the texting. It's terribly disconcerting when you're chilling out, enjoying a little post-coital bliss, and they're there, rooting around in their massive handbag, tap-tapping away with those nasty acrylic nails with leopardskin patterns on them.' He did a spiteful mime. 'I mean, what are they writing about, for fuck's sake? Are they giving me marks out of ten to their mates? Ordering a take-away? Finding out the cricket scores? It's completely beyond me.'

He topped up their glasses and then helped himself to another blini before pushing the tray in her direction. 'God, have one of those,' he said, mouth full, pointing to a little parcel of something wrapped in filo pastry and fastened together with a shred of seaweed. 'Prawn and something creamy, fab, they're my favourites. They always make sure they have an extra tray of those on board just for me – and those are really nice too.' He poked at something green and white in a little pastry case.

And then, as Simon picked up one of the little parcels, he leant towards her, and kissed her. Susie gasped with surprise and then Simon kissed her some more, in a way that went very slowly on a sliding scale from something chaste – like the kind of kiss you'd give your aunty at Christmas – to something you'd probably have to pay for under other circumstances. Susie felt her whole body responding instinctively. God, she'd forgotten just how good a decent snog could be. Robert had never been keen on public displays of affection – and wasn't wildly demonstrative in private either. Against all the odds she could feel herself melting.

When they finally eased apart, Susie felt dizzy and Simon was smiling, eyes bright with amusement and desire.

'Ummm,' he purred. 'Aren't you glad that you said

you'd come? We're going to have *such* a good time this weekend.'

There was a sense of unreality about the whole situation. She stared at him as he settled back in his seat and made an effort to throttle her libido. 'Simon, I've got to be really upfront about this. I'm not interested –'

He sighed theatrically. 'Really? For a woman who isn't interested you kiss very convincingly.'

Susie reddened. 'I feel as if I'm here under false pretences. You're not my type at all.'

Simon pulled a face. '*Now* she tells me. So what? Are you planning to use me and cast me aside, heartlessly? Like a worn-out shoe?'

Susie couldn't help but laugh. 'That's just the thing,' she said. 'I don't really know what I'm doing here. And I *certainly* shouldn't be kissing you.'

He waved the words away. 'Susie, baby. You think too much. And, trust me, I wasn't the only one doing the kissing just now – here, have some more champagne. I said before you agreed to come: no strings, no catches, separate rooms – honest.' He paused, 'But then again, if you're overcome by lust or I can persuade you . . .' His eyes were full of mischief. 'My advice would be just enjoy it.'

'Being persuaded?'

'Well, yes, that too, but actually I meant the whole thing. I needed to get away from all the constant whining from Ellie and her mother. Think of coming to Paris with me as a mercy dash, a charitable act – you're doing me a favour. Trust me, I'd far rather have

264

you for company than go on my own. I'd get myself into all sorts of trouble. No, you'll be good for me – a calming influence.'

Susie wasn't sure whether that was a compliment or not. And then the pilot pointed out the south coast and, unlike in a normal aeroplane, she could move from side to side, seat to seat, to get the best view of the white cliffs of Dover as the plane headed out over the Channel.

And then they had more champagne and canapés and Simon told her outrageously indiscreet stories about the guy who owned the plane and a member of the royal family, a couple for whom the term close personal friends might have been invented, and then just as they were getting to the bit with the police-woman and two tubs of Häagen-Dazs, they landed.

'"A few miles north of Paris, Le Bourget was the home of the Paris Air Show and also housed the French Museum of Air and Space. Once the only airport serving Paris, it was now used exclusively by business jets. It was also famous for being the landing site for Charles Lindbergh's famous solo transatlantic flight."'

'Yes, all right, Carl,' said Simon, as they taxied down the runway to the disembodied voice over the intercom. 'If we'd wanted the full tour I'd have hired a fucking sherpa.'

Antoine laughed as he tidied away and helped them with unfastening their seat belts. Half a bottle of cham-pagne and Susie's fingers were like chipolatas.

There was a car waiting for them on the apron, which, once they'd cleared customs, drove them straight into the centre of Paris. The sun was setting as they made their way across the city, the evening light casting everything in soft golds and reds. And the hotel, far from being a modest little place tucked away on a back street, as Susie had imagined, was just off the Champs-Élysées. As they pulled up in front of the portico a uniformed footman opened the car door for Susie while another opened the boot and started to unload their luggage.

Susie stared in astonishment at Simon, who shrugged. 'What can I tell you? The Travelodge was full,' he said, retrieving his jacket.

Once inside, the huge foyer was unbelievably ornate and exquisitely over the top, decorated with miles of marble, acres of gold leaf, and god knows how many square yards of elegant furniture arranged around low tables. The walls were hung with tapestries and there were the most beautiful floral displays on every side table and in every niche and alcove.

'God, if I'd known I would have brought completely different clothes,' hissed Susie.

'You women are all the same. Don't panic, we can go shopping tomorrow,' he said. 'Meanwhile, you could always go naked.'

Susie glared at him and then turned slowly to take it all in. The ceilings were ornately worked with cornices and gilded panels and all manner of complex plaster-work in peacock blue and red, each ceiling panel finished off with a huge art deco chandelier. Susie tried very hard not to stare and even harder to act cool. It was a losing battle.

'It is amazing,' she murmured as they headed for the reception desk.

'They refurbished it a few years ago – it's what happens when the French run out of magnolia and woodchip,' Simon said sotto voce as the girl on reception smiled warmly at him.

'Mr Hammond,' she said, with just enough of an accent to make her sound unbelievably sexy. 'How nice to see you again, are you well this evening?'

'I'm just fine, Monique.' He grinned. 'And how about you? You look beautiful, as always.' The girl reddened slightly and turned her attention to the forms behind the desk.

Meanwhile Simon picked up a pen to fill in the registration form she handed him. Formalities complete, the girl waved over a porter who took them up in the lift. As the door closed, Susie decided that the lift was more luxurious than most hotels she had ever stayed in.

They eventually stepped out into a broad corridor, once again set with ornate side tables, more flowers, more pictures and another mile of carpet. Simon turned sharp left and Susie scurried after him, not wanting to be left behind. The porter unlocked a set of double doors and then, having stepped aside to let them in, walked ahead to open the doors into the main room of their suite. They had their own entrance lobby – with a corn-coloured marble floor and side table on which was a huge bowl of hydrangeas.

As the porter opened the second set of double doors, Susie gave up any pretence of playing it cool and stood with her mouth open. Beyond the doors was an enormous sitting room with French windows and a terrace giving way to a stunning view out over the city skyline. To the right was a bedroom, doors currently open to reveal an enormous king-sized bed, all dressed in the most opulent turquoise, green and cream silks. There were more flowers everywhere. The porter handed the keys to Simon.

'Enjoy your stay, Mr Hammond,' he said, as Simon discreetly tipped him.

'Well, what d'ya reckon to this then?' said Simon, throwing himself onto a cream silk sofa that probably cost more than the whole of Susie's household contents put together. 'Your bedroom's over there. Mine's there.' He indicated a second set of double doors further down the long, elegant room. 'There's a kitchen but I'm assuming you don't want to cook, so shall we order up a TV dinner or do you want to pop out for a kebab?'

Susie looked at him and laughed. 'Simon, this is crazy. Can you afford to stay here or am I going to have to hock the family silver to settle up?'

'You've got family silver?' he said. 'God, in that case I'll order up a couple of filets mignons and a bottle of Cristal.' He picked up a leather-bound file from one of the side tables and then looked up at her and grinned.

'Relax. It belongs to the same guy whose plane I borrowed. It's okay. Now how about we eat? I'm famished. You want to eat here or shall we go take a walk and find somewhere else?'

Susie stared at him as he handed her the menu. 'You'll owe him one after this.'

Simon laughed. 'Actually he owes *me*, big time. Now what do you fancy?'

Susie shook her head. 'I have no idea, you choose. I'm going to go look round my bedroom, unpack, explore.'

'Fair enough, if you're not back in an hour I'll send out a native tracker.'

Susie's bedroom was decorated in cool blues and greens and creams, with floor-to-ceiling drapes framing a view out over the Paris skyline.

It was almost too much to take in. There were antiques on every available surface, making it more like a sumptuous townhouse or an over-stuffed film set than any hotel room Susie had ever stayed in. The walls were hung with original oil paintings and heavy gilt mirrors, and the room was dominated by the enormous bed, which had a silk canopy over it, the folds and drapes picked out in the room's themed colours. On the bed itself there were more shams, cushions, bolsters and throws than in a Sunday colour supplement. On the dressing table, which was subtly lit with soft lamps, stood a great bowl of pink roses, while overhead in the middle of the moulded plaster ceiling hung a chandelier. Cosy and understated it wasn't.

The en suite bathroom was cream, green and blue marble with a central bath and matching bidet, shower, hand basin and enough fluffy white towels to fill the average airing cupboard. Alongside the bath was a little recess filled with toiletries, the same on the vanity unit by the circular sink. Susie unscrewed the top of something that promised to be a bath essence and sighed with pure delight as she breathed in the heady perfume of ginger and lilies with an undertone of something sharper.

'Well?'

Susie looked up. Simon was leaning against the bathroom door, watching her.

'I was just thinking I might spend the whole weekend in the bath,' said Susie, putting the bottle back on the side table.

'Fair enough, it's big enough for two – they've got a spa here too, fitness room, pool. Although if you fancied getting out of the bath I thought maybe tomorrow we could do the Louvre and the Tuileries, or if you want we could shop – or a little of both. Or we could hit the tourist trail and do Versailles, or maybe drive out to Fontainebleau, take a look round Barbizon, sail down the Seine. Whatever you fancy – the world is your bi-valve.'

'Simon, why are you doing all this?'

'I was bored, and besides it was worth it to see the look on your face when you clambered on board the jet –'

'So are you trying to impress me into bed?'

Simon shrugged. 'The thought did cross my mind, but to be honest I've done all that kind of stuff before and I'm not that fussed really. You're easy company.'

'Well, thanks,' said Susie. 'That makes me feel a whole lot better.'

'I said easy company, not easy. See, a man can't win, can he? What I meant was, let's have fun, me and you. Life is complicated and painful enough. If we end up in the sack, great; if we don't then just having good company will be fine.'

'You mean that, don't you?'

For a moment he paused. 'Maybe, maybe not, maybe it's a double bluff. Anyway, I've ordered some grub – they have got the most amazing chef here.'

'And your friend won't mind?' said Susie.

'Who said he was a friend?'

Susie's face must have registered her anxiety because Simon said hastily, 'No, he won't mind. Now stop whittling and have a bath or something. Supper will be here in half an hour or so – meanwhile, d'you fancy a mug of tea?'

She looked at him and laughed. 'Tea? Really?'

'Oh god, yes, they keep a stock of Yorkshire tea bags in the kitchen for when we come over. Now, how do you like it? White? Sugar? Do you want it in the bath – use plenty of bubbles, and I promise not to look.'

Chapter 14

'Oh my god, that sounds fantastic. And then what happened?' asked Nina, all ears, as they sat almost knee to knee in her tiny conservatory.

'Well, the food showed up and, trust me, it was out of this world – and then, halfway through, Simon's mobile rang and it was someone – I've got no idea who – and he went off into the bedroom to take the call, and when he came back he said, "Okay. Change of plans. I've got to go back to London." And I said, "That's a shame, when? Tomorrow?" And then he said, "No, now, but there's no need for you to come back with me. It's complicated, you'll be in the way, so take your time, enjoy – and don't worry, I'll get the guys here to sort you a flight out for Sunday. Go shopping, see the Louvre – knock yourself out. Put it on the tab. I'll give you a ring in the week."'

'Just like that?' Nina was incredulous.

'Uh-huh. He didn't apologise or anything – I mean, I know that it sounds a bit churlish given that I'd been flown to Paris in a private jet, and given a suite and carte blanche to eat my way through the hotel menu, but I felt really let down –'

'So you *do* fancy him then?'

Susie laughed. 'Daft thing is no, not really. He's good company and very funny, totally unpredictable, but no, I can honestly say with my hand on my heart that I don't fancy him.' Although even as she said it, Susie was thinking about how he made her feel when he kissed her. Was that chemistry or just chemicals? Maybe she should give it more time.

'So you went to the Louvre?'

'No, I planned to but the queues were horrific, and besides it was too nice to be inside, so I walked through the Jardin des Tuileries. Then I took a bus to a flea market that the girl in reception recommended, wandered round looking at amazing things, drank lots of coffee, looked in lots of shops, ate good bread and pretended that I spent every weekend exploring Paris from a suite in a posh hotel – oh, and I bought you these –' Susie rummaged through her bag and handed Nina a small package beautifully wrapped in rose-pink tissue, all tied together with a pale silk ribbon. 'The lady did it for me on the stall. You should have seen the things she had on there. Oh, and there are these –' she took a little bottle of bath oil and another of shampoo out of her bag '– which I took from Simon's bathroom in the suite. I mean, he wasn't going to use them.' Meanwhile, Nina was setting about the parcel. Inside, wrapped in layers of crinkled tissue paper, were two hand-painted bone hair-combs and a marcasite mantilla comb.

'Oh, they are just gorgeous,' said Nina, leaping to her feet to peer in the mirror, desperate to try them out. Nina had a real passion for hair furniture; as soon as Susie had seen them on the stall she just knew her friend would love them. But Nina's delight and Milo's enthusiastic welcome home didn't quite take the bitter taste out of Susie's mouth.

The truth was she had probably had a far nicer time in Paris without Simon than she would have had with him around. Certainly, she'd felt relaxed and less stressed, not having to second guess what was coming next, but even so she still felt cheated.

Paris was such a lovely city in the early summer. The gardens were gorgeous and no one carried off clothes with the style and panache of French women. With an artist's eye, she had found herself a café table in the shade and enjoyed observing the passers-by – it would have been fun to have done that with Simon. She also guessed he was familiar with Paris in a way she wasn't and probably knew places she would never find in a million years.

On Sunday morning Susie took a boat trip down the Seine – apparently already booked and paid for – and looked longingly at the couples snuggled up together as the breeze tugged mischievously at their hair and clothes and made them snuggle all the closer, and for a little while she felt horribly alone.

On Sunday afternoon Susie had the hotel arrange a chauffeur to take her to the airport, and she had flown into Heathrow, business class thanks to Simon.

'And then what happened?' asked Nina, tinkering with a comb.

'I was going to take the train home, and went to the

cash machine and the bloody thing ate my card. Talk about back to earth with a bang.'

'You should have rung me.'

'I was going to, but when I switched my phone on there was a message from Matt asking how I was, and I don't know what possessed me really but I rang him and – I suppose I was upset – he just said, "Sit tight, buy yourself a coffee, I'm already on my way." Which was the nicest thing.'

Standing in the airport all alone without her fare home, Susie had had some sense of what Ellie's mother must have felt like. Seeing Matt's face in the crowd had given her such a sense of relief.

'Your ride, m'lady?' he'd said, tugging an imaginary forelock as he took her bag.

Susie smiled and then hugged him. 'God, Matt, you've got no idea how pleased I am to see you, thank you for coming.'

'Rough time?'

'Yes and no – let's just say the weekend was a game of two halves.'

'Uh-huh – and?'

'And you don't want to know.'

He laughed. 'Come on, that's not fair. Surely I get to hear all the ins and outs of how come you've ended up stranded at Heathrow.'

Susie had reddened. 'Simon invited me to Paris for the weekend.'

Matt raised his eyebrows. 'Simon?'

Susie nodded.

'So what happened?'

'How long have you got?'

Matt had looked at his watch. 'We can always take the long way home.'

Matt Peters riding to the rescue was something Susie certainly hadn't expected. As they'd talked, he'd whisked her through the concourse, carrying her luggage, getting them coffee, all bright and cheerful. On the drive home she'd told him all about Paris and where she'd been and the suite and what a shit Simon was. Nothing like a gay man and a shed-load of gossip to pass the time. Back at the cottage he'd dropped her off, waving away offers of payment or petrol money. 'You sure you don't want to come in?'

'No, you're fine. I've got some stuff to do. Did I tell you we'd got work this summer?'

'No.'

'The Shetland Isles. You want to come?' he asked casually.

Susie laughed. 'The way things are going at the moment I might take you up on that.'

He climbed back into his car. 'Offer's definitely open, we can always do with a good artist and photographer on site.'

'So has he rung you since?' Nina was saying, as she teased her hair up in the antique combs.

'Who, Matt?'

'No, not Matt, *Simon*.'

'No, no, he hasn't, but he did say he was working – I'll ring him when I get in,' Susie said as casually as she could manage. She tried not to sound miffed. 'But Matt rang on his way home to make sure that I was all right.'

Nina sighed. 'See, it's right what they say – all the good men are either married, taken or bent as a box of frogs.'

It was dark when Susie got back to the cottage with Milo. It felt like weeks since Friday evening. There were no lights on. No mystery callers, no exes, no unexpected children showing up, nothing, and for a moment as Susie pulled into the drive she could feel the tears welling up. Wedged halfway up the wall in one of the creepers was a mangled paper plane.

Chapter 15

Once she got inside, Susie fed Milo, put her washing in the machine, switched on the lamps, and made every effort to pull herself together. This was crazy. Madness. She didn't fancy Simon, so what was she so upset about for god's sake? She was far more touched by Matt rescuing her from the airport than Simon's abortive attempt at a weekend away. Jesus, the man had done her a favour leaving her in Paris on her own. She had had a far better time without him than she could ever have had with him. Probably. So why did she feel so deflated?

Maybe he'd call to apologise, to say he missed her, to say that he'd been really looking forward to spending the weekend with her – after all, it wasn't every man who chased you with paper aeroplanes and real live jets. Maybe it had been a life or death emergency. Maybe . . .

She picked up the phone. There were no messages on her answering machine. She rang Simon but his mobile went straight to voicemail. Although she felt annoyed, the more rational part of Susie's brain reminded her that he was probably still working. She felt she ought to tell him that she was home safe and sound, thank him, and say that he'd missed out on a great weekend. She made an effort to sound cheerful and bright – after all, the world was full of sullen, difficult women, who, actually, she thought when she hung up, often seemed to get treated a lot better than the nice ones. Maybe she shouldn't be so easy to please.

Alice wasn't answering either. Jack's mobile was switched off and Susie's father's answering-machine message sounded as if he had recorded it under water while wearing a snorkel – which, knowing him, was always possible – although she doubted if he would be able to pick out her message between crackles, pops and pings. There was no way she was going to ring Robert, so she rang Matt.

'Hi, how's it going?' he said, sounding genuinely pleased to hear from her.

'I just wanted to thank you again for bringing me home. I've never been rescued before. It was so nice of you. I'm not disturbing you, am I?'

'No, not at all. I'll just turn the music down.' Susie heard something soft and classical fade down to the edge of audible. At least it wasn't Barbra Streisand.

'Did you want to talk to Jack? Only I'm afraid he's not here. He's borrowed my car to take some stuff over to Alice's place. Do you want me to get him to ring you?'

'No, it's fine,' Susie said.

'Are you okay?'

'I'm fine,' she lied. 'Just a bit tired, that's all. It's been

279

a long day.' Susie was hoping he wouldn't ask why she'd rung because self-pity wasn't a very commendable reason.

'Well you don't sound fine, what's the matter?' he asked.

Susie sniffed back a tear. 'Nothing, really. Sorry, I shouldn't have rung you. I'm just feeling sorry for myself and there's no one to talk to.' Damn.

'I'm flattered,' he said in that low gentle voice he had. 'Come on, talk to me. We all need a shoulder sometime.'

'Really?'

'Oh yes.'

'Promise you won't give me a lecture?'

'Nope, but I will listen.'

And he did. And then Matt suggested he came over and took her out to dinner sometime soon, and they talked about Paris again and the exhibition at college for a while and how she was getting on with the planning, and she invited him to the private viewing and he accepted. And when she finally hung up Susie felt better. A lot better.

Simon didn't ring on Monday or Tuesday. Susie thought about ringing him again, but didn't want to look desperate. By Wednesday she was starting to get angry; on Thursday, working from home was worse, even though Susie tried very hard not to think about him. Not that it was difficult as she was up to her armpits in work and organising things for the exhibition, but between times, in lulls and quiet moments, there was something about the whole thing that hurt and set every alarm bell in her head ringing. Twice on Thursday evening she dialled Simon's number but hung up before it started to ring.

On Friday she had promised to go and help Nina set up the exhibition. Just as she was about to leave Alice rang to say that the whole Together Apart thing was working out better than she could have possibly hoped for, and Adam was beginning to see things more rationally – Alice-speak for *her way* – and Jack was moving in over the weekend and everything in that garden at least was rosy.

By Friday lunchtime Susie had given herself a good talking to and decided that Simon and his weekend away were just a flash in the pan.

'The thing is,' said Nina that afternoon, as if they had been talking about it, which they hadn't, as they were manhandling a plinth in front of a backdrop of unbleached hessian. 'If Simon treats you like this at the beginning of a relationship it's not going to get any better, is it? I mean, they usually do make *some* kind of an effort, at least at the beginning. Online dating – it's the way forward. Get your groceries delivered and get them to send round half a dozen blokes on approval.'

Susie fired up the staple gun and re-fixed the fabric where it had pulled away from the framework as they'd re-sited the plinth. 'Will you get out of my head – I've already told you I don't fancy him; who said anything about this being a relationship?'

'No one, but you know. Taking you away for the weekend to Paris sounds like someone who means well.'

'Someone who means well, who hasn't rung back since. What does that say about the man? Was it so awful that he needed to bail out before we got to the coffee and liqueurs? Or is it just that he is a complete waste of time and is messing me around?' Susie grimaced and fired in another staple, imagining it was Simon's head. 'Besides, to be honest, I think Simon Hammond is the kind of man who spends a lot of time taking strange women to exotic places. No, I'm going to chalk it down to experience. Good god, it wasn't even a one-night stand. Can you give me a hand with this? It just needs to be stretched,' she said with some effort.

'It seems an awful lot of trouble to go to just to mess you about. He could have done that without leaving his armchair,' said Nina, getting hold of the trailing edge of the hessian and helping to pull the lining fabric taut while Susie fixed the next section.

'I know, but I'm still not sure what the hell is going on with him. I do know that I can live without any more aggravation in my life.'

'There, that's better?' asked Nina, tucking a raw edge inside.

'Great – now for stage two.'

They both looked over towards the beautiful, wildly contorted piece of driftwood that made up the exhibit. It had been exquisitely sanded and drilled and waxed until it glowed with a life of its own. It was one of half a dozen similar pieces created by one of their most promising third-year students. This was the largest one, and it was currently hanging like a bizarre aquatic baby in broad canvas strops from a hoist more often used for manhandling engines in the metal shop.

Nina nodded. 'Well, it's now or never,' she said, beckoning the hoist closer. The two women slipped on muslin gloves – the highly polished surface of the wood would show every mark, every fingerprint – and eased the hoist closer.

One of the male technicians helped manoeuvre the sculpture and then, very gradually, they lowered it into position. It wasn't something that could be rushed. The large wave-shaped plinth had a steel tube set into the top that would slide, with luck and a little guidance, to fit snugly into a hole drilled in the base of the driftwood.

'Nina, Susie,' called one of the students just as they were inching it down into position. Susie glanced round. Why was it that people never wanted you when you were sitting around twiddling your thumbs?

'There's a bloody great lorry out the front and some woman says that she wants you.'

Meanwhile, the sculpture worked its way very slowly down towards the tube – *easy, easy* – as the technician turned the handle on the winch. Susie caught herself holding her breath as between them they swung the heavy piece of wood over the steel pole and edged it home into the hole. As soon as it was in place it carried on downwards, sliding silently over the metal column down towards the soft rubber washer on which it would eventually sit.

'Go and tell her that we'll be there in a couple of minutes,' said Nina over her shoulder as they guided the wood gently down until it seated itself onto the heavy asymmetric block base. For a few seconds when it was home, everyone paused, letting the sculpture settle, and then they stood back to admire their handiwork.

The great curling twist of wood looked amazing, a subtle blend of something sea-born and the tree it came from, part animal, part reptile, part arboreal and all art.

'Lighting will need a tweak,' said Nina after a moment or two, with a more critical eye, standing a little way back to gauge the effect. 'Maybe we need to angle those down towards the back?' She pointed to spotlights screwed onto the light rack above them.

Susie nodded. 'Uh-huh, and we need to make sure that the guy who made it is happy with the way it's set up.'

Nina laughed. 'He bloody well better be, I'm not moving the damned thing now.'

Susie stretched. 'Best we go and see what the lady with the lorry wants then.'

Around them the whole of the college foyer was a hive of activity. In some ways the large uninspiring space made a far better gallery than it did a lobby. With the displays and plinths and good lighting it felt alive. Set out in the entrance on a large table was a key to the various exhibits, made by a second-year model maker as part of her final assignment, which was currently being used as a reference for everyone helping with the set-up.

Tuesday was their opening night, the prestigious

private view, and everything had to be ready, hung and lit by then. If other years were anything to go by they would all end up working for most of the weekend to ensure everything was in place and perfect, but it was always fun. There was a low hum of determined activity – a year's worth of concerted effort and they were almost there. 'Like the Blitz' was one of Nina's favourite comments as they'd find themselves sorting out some eleventh-hour panic that always seemed to resolve itself by the time the mayor or the principal made their way in through the main doors, smiling for the camera.

'It's full of plants,' said the student who had brought the message, falling into step alongside them. 'The lorry. The woman wanted to know where the forklift was.'

'That'll be your Ms Hill then,' said Nina to Susie. 'I've arranged to borrow one from the lads in the built environment, they've already said they'd be more than happy to unload anything that isn't a pallet-load of breeze blocks. I'll go and tell them the lorry's here. It'll give me a chance to check on the progress in the studio while I'm down there.'

'She's not *my* Ms Hill,' Susie grumbled as she went out through the main doors.

Outside, on the college forecourt there was a flatbed lorry, with high wire-mesh sides, full of what looked like a gift-wrapped jungle, slowly reversing its way up towards the front doors, warning signal beeping loudly. On board there were palms and tree ferns and cannas, cordylines and banana plants and god knew what else, all wrapped in a fine mesh to help protect the foliage

285

while it was in transit. There also appeared to be some kind of stainless-steel curves and curls in amongst it, which Susie guessed from the plans were probably water features.

Saskia, standing on the kerbside, was watching the lorry's progress, her face totally impassive. It looked as if she was back to ice-maiden mode, although she did manage a brief smile and to lift a hand in acknowledgement when she saw Susie heading her way.

In contrast to Susie's khaki cargo pants and tee shirt, Saskia was wearing another perfectly tailored black trouser suit and had her hair up in a faultless French pleat that gave her the look of a young Grace Kelly, although Susie couldn't remember a time when Grace Kelly had ever been caught carrying a walkie-talkie, clipboard and hard hat.

'The plants look wonderful,' Susie said as she reached her. 'Do you need a hand to unload or anything? Nina's just gone off to get the forklift, but we can whip up some bodies if you need a few extra pairs of hands.'

Saskia shook her head. 'Thank you, but I've brought a couple of guys from the yard with me to help landscape the entrance and then dress the main exhibition area. It's not like we're planting up or anything, it's more a case of arranging. We do a lot of this sort of thing so they know the score. They know the plan and know what they're doing.' She paused and then smiled again, this time more slyly, the façade slipping.

'Oh, but there is something else I wanted to show you.' As she spoke Saskia extended her left hand, fingers down towards Susie, and waggled them ever so slightly.

It took a couple of seconds for Susie to work out the significance, and then she saw it. There on Saskia's ring finger was an engagement ring. Susie stared at it, feeling her heart sink.

'I was going to call you, but I wanted to tell you face to face.' She blushed and then giggled nervously. 'I said yes,' she said, somewhat unnecessarily. 'I just wanted to say thanks again for listening to me the other night. It was really kind of you.' Her attention moved back to the ring. 'It's platinum, apparently. Solitaire – Robert says it's been in the family for donkey's years. He showed me this gorgeous picture of his mum on her wedding day wearing it.'

Saskia turned her hand and spread her fingers to admire it, oblivious to Susie's discomfort. 'Although Robert did say if I didn't like it he would buy me another one.' She laughed. 'He is such a sweetie, he was afraid I might think he was being mean. And fashions change, although I think this is lovely, don't you?'

Susie couldn't bring herself to answer, so instead she said, 'So, you made your mind up then, congratulations.' Her tone was as warm as she could manage.

Saskia pulled an odd face that Susie couldn't really interpret. Was she pleased, relieved, or had she accepted just to humour Robert? From Saskia's expression it was impossible to work out.

'Yes, but it's not like being married or anything, though, is it?' said Saskia quickly. 'I mean, in the end I had to say yes. We're going to Prague to celebrate – he was so worried and upset, poor old thing. He kept ringing me up at work and causing a fuss. He's such a sweetie, he really needs someone to take care of him.'

Susie stared at her. Saskia managed to make Robert sound like a crusty old uncle in need of day care.

'He's so stuffy and set in his ways, bless him. I've already told him that what he needs is a complete makeover. Starting with those clothes and that hair.' She threw her hands up in a show of despair. 'I mean, what's next, a combover?'

Susie, ignoring the sartorial criticism, said, 'Well, if it's what you both want then I'm really pleased for you. So have you set a date yet?'

Saskia shook her head. 'God, no – not yet. I was hoping that saying yes would make him back off a bit, although he's made it very clear he'd like it to be sooner rather than later. He's already suggested that I move in with him. I mean, pushy or what? I'm already staying there most of the time as it is. I've told him I'll think about it.'

That would be just great, Susie thought darkly – bumping into Saskia every morning as she reversed the 4x4 out of Robert's drive.

And then, all of a sudden, Saskia's face lit up with childlike enthusiasm. 'He's said I can have a puppy, though, I've always wanted a dog but my mum and dad wouldn't let me – a little fluffy dog – oh, and a kitten. I was thinking of a Yorkie or maybe a Shih Tzu – we've been looking on the Net. And I've seen these cute little crosses – between a Yorkie and a poodle, they call them Yorkiepoos, isn't that just so sweet? Robert says if we can find one he'll get me one.'

'Really?' said Susie in surprise. If memory served,

Robert thought the only good dog was a big dog – a gun dog, a Labrador or a springer. Anything smaller – with the possible exception of a Jack Russell – was a canine joke, and as they'd walked Milo he'd often point out the fey morons with their fluffy rats on ropes. It would be interesting to see how he looked with a Yorkiepoo tucked under his arm. Obviously the saying 'there's no fool like an old fool' still had plenty of mileage. The fixed, cheery smile on Susie's face was beginning to make the muscles in her face ache.

'That'll be nice,' she said.

At which point a tall, good-looking man arrived, carrying an expensive camera. He kissed Saskia on both cheeks and whispered something in her ear that made her blush crimson before, rapidly regaining her composure, she turned and said, 'Susie, this is Calum Fox, he'll be doing the photos for the gardening magazine I told you about.'

Susie extended a hand. Calum's handshake was firm and dry, and there were no two ways about it, he was gorgeous: big blue eyes, gone slightly crinkly around the corners, a few grey hairs in amongst his thick dark hair, and this great big warm smile that was impossible to resist. All that good-natured charm, he probably had to beat women off with a stick.

'And we'll get a couple in the local press as well, maybe something national if we're lucky,' he said. 'Pleased to meet you, Susie. Do you mind if I take a few shots of the rest of the exhibition while I'm here?'

'No, not at all,' said Susie, 'although we're just setting up at the moment.'

He nodded. 'Uh-huh, you know I think that some-times that's where the best shots often are. It gives you something more three-dimensional, more vital and accessible than the finished article, don't you think?'

Susie nodded, while her brain was busy taking notes. Five ten, maybe six foot, nice broad shoulders, great hands. Calum Fox looked as if he had just come back from a trip to the Med. He was suntanned, sinewy, maybe late thirties, certainly not much older, and fit as a butcher's whippet.

Behind him, two guys in polo shirts with paunches appeared who had been in the lorry, and the driver began the process of powering the stabilisers out from the lorry body so that they could use the crane arm on the back to unload the heavier trees.

'Ciao, got to go,' Calum said, still smiling and turning his attention to the lorry and its contents.

'Nice guy,' said Susie.

Saskia looked uncomfortable. 'He's just a family friend, I've known him years,' she said, picking at some imaginary lint on her jacket. 'I need to be getting on too. See you later.'

'Bye,' said Susie as Saskia hurried away.

Susie watched for a few minutes as the trees and shrubs in soft bags began to be set down on the tarmac around the steps up to the entrance. The planters they had brought with them were wonderful, great galvanised tanks in odd shapes and exquisite terracotta pots as big as armchairs. There was a long metal arch that unfurled to frame the entrance porch – it was hard not to be impressed. As the men worked, Calum moved to and fro, supple as an eel, capturing it all for posterity, following Saskia around like a bodyguard.

By late afternoon a second lorry had arrived and Saskia and her troops had created a broad walkway lined with date palms from the front entrance down into the forecourt – a tropical terrace along the front wall and an arboretum in the main foyer.

Saskia, carrying her clipboard, strode over to where Nina and Susie were still busy working.

'All done,' she said brightly. 'I just need someone to sign this to say you've taken delivery and you're happy with the results.'

Susie smiled and straightened up, surprised to see that Calum was still around, hanging back, his camera now all packed away.

'It looks absolutely wonderful,' she said. 'People have been commenting since you started setting up. Do we need to do anything?'

Saskia shook her head. 'No, I've organised staff to come in and do the maintenance while everything is on site, and a couple of the horticultural students are going to give them a hand, shadow them really.' She glanced at her watch. 'Anyway, got to go.'

'That's right,' said Calum. 'All work and no play makes Sassie a dull girl.' His tone was light and teasing. 'You know what she's like,' he added, tapping her lightly on the bum.

Saskia's face flushed scarlet. Susie could almost see her squirm.

'Calum is taking me out for a drink,' she said as she handed Susie the clipboard. As she retrieved it, Calum stepped forward, smiling, and caught hold of Saskia's elbow in a way that struck Susie as over-familiar. Having waved a hand in farewell the pair of them vanished through the double doors, now framed by banana trees. There was a distinct spring in Saskia's step.

Susie was left with mixed feelings as the two of them disappeared into the evening sunshine. In an odd way she was kind of relieved that Calum was so obviously interested in Saskia. If she was into older men, better one like Calum, who laughed and was obviously good fun and looked a million dollars, rather than Robert, who got heat rash, whined constantly and didn't like foreign food, but then again she cared enough about Robert – bastard or not – not to want to see him hurt, and whichever way you looked, from where Susie was standing he was headed for a fall.

It was nearly seven when she got home. Everything for the exhibition, at least all the important things, were more or less finished, including her. She was completely knackered. Milo looked at her accusingly from his basket as she eased off her shoes.

'I'll take you for a walk in a minute,' she said, opening the door so he could potter out in the garden. 'I'll have a cup of tea, check my messages and then we'll go out. Promise, cross my heart.'

'Talking to ourselves, are we?' said a familiar voice.

Susie swung round in amazement. 'Simon? What the hell are you doing here? I've only just got back.'

He was framed in the back door, looking as well-groomed and louche as ever.

'I know. I've been here for ages. I thought you worked from home on Fridays?'

'Where were you?' she said accusingly.

'In the back garden. Your neighbour came round to let the dog out at lunchtime and took pity on me sitting outside in the car.'

'You've been here since lunchtime?'

'On and off. I nipped out about three for a sandwich but I told the old girl next door that I'd be back. She let me in.'

'Why didn't you ring?'

He looked all hurt and hard done by. 'You didn't ring me.'

'Oh for goodness' sake, Simon, I rang you on Sunday when I got back from Paris. I left a message.'

'You sounded angry.'

She looked at him, toying with the idea of saying something conciliatory, and in the end said, 'That's because I was, and I was hurt too – you buggered off and left me.'

'Something important came up.'

'You see, there's the problem, Simon,' said Susie. 'Although I'm all grown up and I know that shit happens, there is a part of me that would still like to believe that at that moment – whenever that moment is – there's nothing more important in the world than me.'

'It was an emergency.'

'So you said. Just don't try to make me feel guilty,' she said, not taking her eyes off him. 'If I want any more guilt in my life I'll ring my children.'

Simon moved closer and ran a finger under her chin,

tipping her face up towards his. 'I promise you that it won't happen again,' he purred.

Susie looked at him, trying hard not to laugh, and wished for all the world that it might be true – but that was one of the things about being the other side of forty: you could smell bullshit a mile off, even if you did nothing about it.

'Too bloody right it won't,' she said.

But before she could point out that Simon was the most terrible liar, he leant a fraction closer and she guessed he was going to try and kiss it all better – not such a bad idea – but in the instant before he did there was a kind of strangled stagey cough, at which point Milo finally rallied himself into some semblance of a guard dog and barked a couple of times – not that anyone was convinced.

'Sorry, am I interrupting?' said Matt from the step. 'I knocked but nobody answered so I thought I'd come round the back. The door was open.'

Susie looked up. Matt was carrying a large bunch of flowers, a bottle of wine and what looked like a bag of groceries, a French stick peeping from the top. He was wearing a cream shirt and jeans, had a pale pink sweater draped over his broad shoulders and looked artfully windswept. 'I promised you dinner – I'm just sorry I couldn't make it earlier in the week. I thought I'd come round and see if you fancied some bread and cheese, grapes –'

'And a glass of wine,' said Simon, relieving him of the bottle. 'How very civilised. What a thoughtful chap you are. Not a great wine, but not bad, not bad at all.

Come on in. Pull up a chair. Susie's shattered. We were just about to think about supper, weren't we, babe? How's life – sorry to hear about the dig, mind you Italy is bloody hot at this time of the year.'

'Simon –' Susie began.

'Don't worry,' he said, holding Matt's wine out like a raffle prize. 'I'm already on the case, I just need to track down the corkscrew. I'm sure it'll be fine when it's had a bit of time to breathe.'

Susie wanted to say something that would stop Simon in his tracks but nothing came to mind. The man was insufferable. He began searching the cupboards for glasses.

Matt said, 'I did ring –'

'Nice sweater by the way,' said Simon.

'Thanks, Alex bought it for me,' said Matt.

Susie turned, wishing that Simon would disappear. 'I'm sorry, I haven't checked my messages yet. I only just got in from college. We're still setting up the work for the end-of-year exhibition.'

'God, that's all she talks about, work, work, work. How *is* that coming along by the way?' said Simon, easing the cork out of the bottle with a satisfying tock sound. 'And what time is kick-off?'

Susie stared at him. 'You're coming?'

He nodded, filling the glasses. 'You invited me, remember, last Friday in Paris?'

'Right,' said Susie slowly, not daring to catch Matt's eye.

'And you know, I wouldn't miss it for the world. Now what else have you got in that bag of tricks, then, Matt?'

Simon had the skin of a rhino. Half an hour later they were eating out on the terrace, and Matt was telling them about a dig he'd been involved in in Ireland, having been cajoled into telling them a story by Simon. Simon could make small talk for England and had the gift of making people feel as if he was totally entranced by what they were saying – something Susie suspected was a great asset in the world of show business.

Susie had had more wine than was probably wise and had no idea how she was going to end the evening politely. Around ten the phone rang. No one moved. A few minutes later it rang again and then again.

'Do you think you should answer that?' asked Matt.

Susie hesitated. Damn thing tended to bring more problems than it solved in her experience, but the incessant ringing was getting to be a bit of a drag. She got to her feet a little unsteadily and made her way inside. She walked slowly, working on the assumption that as soon as she got there it would stop ringing anyway. Except, of course, this time it didn't.

'Thank god you're there,' said Robert without any preamble. 'I really need to talk to you.'

Susie shook her head. 'I'm afraid you've got the wrong number, Robert. I'm your last girlfriend, remember? I've got Saskia's number here if you've lost it.'

'Oh that's right, you don't take anything seriously, do you? I need to talk to you.'

'So you keep saying, Robert. There's just one problem – I don't need to talk to you. Now, is there any reason why we should carry on this conversation, because if not I have guests.'

There was a moody silence and then Robert said in a voice barely above a whisper, 'I think I've made the most dreadful mistake.'

Chapter 16

Robert's words made Susie's stomach do a peculiar back-flip. She wanted to reply with something flippant, off the cuff, throw-away, but nothing came.

'Oh Robert,' she said, wondering where this conversation was leading. She bit her tongue, trying very hard not to ask what that mistake was, knowing full well that if she did she would get sucked right in and that she might as well tell Matt and Simon to go home now, because however much trouble those two could come up with between them, she suspected that Robert's was more likely to cause her the most pain.

'Can I come over?'

'I've already said I've got company.'

'Sorry?' He sounded surprised.

'Which bit don't you understand? I've got people here.'

'Oh really.' He grunted. Obviously it hadn't occurred to him that she might have any kind of life now he'd left her. Presumably he thought she was home reading *People's Friend* and listening to *The Archers* while darning socks.

'What time are they going?' He sounded annoyed now, which Susie thought was a bloody cheek.

'I've got no idea,' she said, while from the garden she could hear raised voices and peals of laughter coming from Simon.

'Who is that? Who's there?' he demanded.

It was too much. 'Robert, just bugger off, will you?'

'Susie, don't hang up. Please – I'm sorry – I didn't mean to – well, you know, I just need someone to talk to who understands me.'

'I'm afraid you've come to the wrong place if you're looking for sympathy. Goodnight.'

'Please,' he burst out. 'It's Saskia.'

Susie winced. That was the very last thing she needed to hear. 'Robert, stop right there, this is not fair. You really hurt me – it still hurts. But it's done now. The last thing I want is to be privy to whatever is going on between you and your new girlfriend. Oh, whoops, sorry, your *fiancée*. By the way, may I be amongst the first to congratulate you?'

Actually, Susie *did* want to know what was going on – curiosity was a horrible affliction – but experience told her that whatever it was, once she knew, life would get far too complicated and she'd end up feeling far worse than she felt now.

Robert groaned miserably. 'I thought I could count on you,' he said.

'Robert, I'm your ex-girlfriend not some character out of a war movie. You can't count on me – I'm not going to watch your back or take a bullet for you, or any of those other weird man things you're going to try and emotionally blackmail me with.' Susie looked accusingly at the glass in her other hand. Merlot as a truth serum, whoever would have thought it?

'Can I come round tomorrow then?'

Some people just couldn't take a hint. 'I've got to go,' said Susie.

'What time would be good for you?'

When hell freezes over and cellulite is sexy, thought Susie as she hung up. From outside she could hear the low roll of Simon's voice punctuated by laughter.

'Tall story,' Matt was saying as Susie went back out into the garden.

'With Simon are there any other kind?' said Susie. 'I don't like to be a party pooper, guys, but I'm knackered.'

'Me too – been a long day,' said Matt diplomatically.

'You were tired last time I came over,' Simon said. 'Have you thought you maybe need some vitamins or a bit of a break – you know, a tonic?'

'What I need is eight hours in bed,' said Susie.

Simon's eyes danced with mischief. 'I couldn't agree more.'

Matt got to his feet. 'I think it's time I was going. Thanks for a lovely evening – maybe we can do that dinner sometime?'

Susie realised with a start that of the two of them he was the one that she didn't want to leave. Real friendship over the chance of casual sex; she knew which she'd take every time.

Matt started to collect his things together. 'I'll walk you out to the car,' she said, wrapping her cardigan around her shoulders.

'Thanks,' he said. It was hardly a trek, but she wanted to tell him how grateful she was that he'd driven over, thank him once again for picking her up from the airport, and say how touched she'd been by him bringing supper – and that whatever he thought she wasn't going anywhere emotionally or otherwise with Simon.

'Thank you,' she said as they got to his car and he hugged her. 'We've barely had the chance to talk,' she said. 'I really wanted to see you.'

'Me too.' He smiled. 'But don't worry, we will. Unless of course your friend Simon is here all the time now?'

'God, no,' said Susie hastily. 'I haven't seen him since we went to Paris, he just turned up.'

'Right,' Matt said.

'How's Alex?' she asked, trying to cut through the funny little flutter of discomfort that arced between them. She knew Matt disapproved of Simon, and desperately wanted to be sure he knew she was equally wary.

'Alex?' He sounded surprised.

'Yes – the sweater – you know – I thought you two were seeing each other again?'

'We were. To be honest things are complicated there,' he said, slipping into his car.

Susie nodded, and then Matt turned the key in the ignition. 'It was nice to talk to you the other night,' he said.

'For me too.'

'Let's do it again sometime soon, catch up – maybe sort out a Simon-free supper.'

Susie laughed.

'Something funny?' said Simon, coming up behind her. 'Shame I missed the joke. I was just wondering where you'd got to, sweetie. Getting chilly out here, isn't it?' As he spoke Simon stepped alongside her and slipped a proprietorial arm around her waist. Susie glared at him.

'Drive carefully,' said Simon, leaning in towards Matt. 'Nice to see you again. And thanks for supper. Great cheese.'

Matt put a hand up and waved his goodbyes, easing out into the lane. Susie watched him go, Simon next to her. 'Well, thank god he's gone,' said Simon. 'I didn't think he was *ever* going to leave.'

Susie stared at him. 'What?'

'Well, honestly, just turning up unannounced like that, I mean talk about two's company.'

'Simon, what are you on about?'

'I thought you and I could maybe carry on from where we left off on –'

'From where you abandoned me in the hotel on my own while you went swanning off back to England in your mate's jet? Or the bit where you didn't return my call or ring me all week?'

He focused on her lips and traced their outline with a fingertip. 'Abandon is such an emotive word,' he murmured. 'Did anyone ever tell you you've got the most perfect mouth,' he said, slipping his other hand up the back of her shirt.

'Simon, do you mind?' she said, stepping away from him as her treacherous heart skipped a beat. 'I was serious when I said I needed to go to bed.'

'And so was I.'

She looked at the driveway and something suddenly struck her. 'Simon, where is your car?'

'Benny brought me over. Apparently waterskiing wasn't really his bag. He's thinking of doing a scuba course in September. Do you think I'm paying him too much?'

'But you said you went into town at lunchtime.'

'And so I did. I grabbed a cab. Nice bloke, apparently he retired here from London. Three kids, bought a house behind the high school.'

'Did he give you his card?'

'He did as it happens.'

'Well in that case,' said Susie, 'might I suggest you ring him and see how he's fixed to take you home.'

Simon grinned, brushing a stray tendril of hair off her face. 'Did anyone ever tell you you're beautiful when you're angry?'

'Stop it – I'm serious, you can't stay here.'

He pressed his lips to her neck, fluttering little kisses down her throat and shoulders, making her shiver. 'I would behave myself,' he murmured. 'Honest.'

'No,' she said, pulling away. 'No, you wouldn't.' Although Susie was realising more and more that Simon's well-honed lust didn't perturb her as much as her own reactions. There were bits of her that ached to be touched. She could feel her libido revving up like a racing car.

'Oh go on, you're so cruel,' continued Simon. 'We could have a great time, you and me – I mean, what is a little wonderful, meaningless sex between two or more consenting adults?'

'Home.' She squared up to him, pointing to the open road with her other hand on her hip. 'Now,' she snapped, before her libido changed up a gear.

'God,' he said, grin widening. 'I love it when you do that. You'd look fantastic in a leather corset and thigh boots. With a bullwhip. Have you ever done that kind of thing?'

'Simon, if you don't ring for a cab soon you'll be doing it while walking home.'

He looked heavenwards. 'I was hoping you might weaken. What does it take? Most women would have had their knickers off on the plane. Antoine usually has to hide in the galley and amuse himself flicking through back copies of *The Caterer's Quarterly*.'

Susie kept her expression fixed.

'One time we had to fly this girl band over to Copenhagen for a gig – three of them – wriggly and giggly as a sack full of turbot. The problem with trying to do anything worthwhile with three girls at once is that there's just not enough of you to go round. By the time we got there I was wrecked. I slept for three days.'

'And what? This is supposed to endear you to me, is it? To persuade me to let you stay?' She turned to go back inside. 'Night-night, Simon, enjoy your walk home.'

'The thing is, Susie, I can be myself with you, and you've got no idea what a relief that is after all these years. I'm pushing fifty, I just want to be with someone I can relax with – my life is so bloody complicated at the moment and I really enjoy spending time with you. I don't need to make any effort when you're around.'

'Charmed.'

'You know what I mean. Susie, let me stay. Please.'

'Simon, go home.'

'What if I beg some more?'

Susie went through the door, closed it and locked it behind her. The last thing she saw as she looked out of the bedroom window was Simon making his way up the lane towards the bypass, jacket slung casually over one shoulder. Within minutes Susie was in bed and fast asleep.

Chapter 17

It was around eight thirty the following morning when Susie woke from a bizarre dream involving a girl band turning up on her doorstep to reclaim Simon, who for some reason was dressed in scuba gear and whining miserably at the idea of being handed over to the baying bottle blondes. Except that when she surfaced and opened her eyes, Susie realised that it wasn't Simon who was whining at all, but Milo stalking up and down outside the bedroom door, snuffling and huffing and eager to be let out.

Susie stretched and yawned, pulled on a pair of pink polka-dot pyjamas and headed downstairs, with the dog ahead of her, wagging, happy to have been heard. Still yawning, hair like a haystack, Susie unlocked the back door and looked outside.

It was the most perfect early summer morning with just a hint of mist lingering over the flagstones and shrubs, adding a softness to the new day. Milo pottered around and then barked. Not much of a bark, but enough for Susie to look up and follow the sound, although when she did, she didn't quite believe what she was seeing.

'Oh thank god, I thought you were never going to

get up,' said Simon miserably. Susie looked and then looked again just to make sure that she wasn't imagining it. Simon was huddled over the table under the parasol, wrapped in some sort of dirty grey winding sheet. He looked like shit.

Susie was stunned. 'What the hell are you doing here?' she said.

'I couldn't get a signal on my mobile,' he whined. 'And then when I got back here the whole place was in darkness. I rang the bell.'

'It doesn't work.'

'Well, I know that now.'

'So where did you sleep?'

'I wouldn't go as far as to call it sleep.'

She looked him over. He looked too dry to have been outside all night. The sheet he was wrapped in was smeared and splattered with paint, blue and red and . . . Comprehension dawned. She'd been so anxious to leave Simon out on the roadside the night before that she hadn't locked the back garden gate, or, come to that, her studio doors.

'You know you're very lucky, I normally lock the whole place up.'

'There's luck and then there's fucking purgatory. Have you ever tried sleeping on that bloody bench in there? I really don't recommend it. I'm knackered, I ache all over and my back is killing me.'

She shook her head and laughed. 'You'd better come in and have a cup of tea.'

Very slowly, he straightened up and got to his feet. 'I thought you'd never ask.'

'And then you can ring what's-his-face and get him to drive over and pick you up.'

Simon grimaced. 'By god, you're a hard woman, Susie.'

'And you are something else entirely. Why the hell didn't you knock on the bloody door?'

'I did but you obviously didn't hear me, and besides you're scary when you're angry. You wouldn't have let me in, would you?'

Susie lifted her eyebrows, thinking about it. 'Probably not.'

'Anyway, I'm here now. I was hoping you might suggest we went back to bed, snuggle up. I'll get up later and cook you brunch, we could eat it in bed – spend the whole day up there. Snoozing and snuggling.'

And then he got up slowly and she could see that Simon really was in pain, and there was no doubt about it, he did look tired and cold and all in, and she relented. 'Why don't you go upstairs and have a bath while I make some tea?'

He grinned at her as he made the effort to straighten his spine and unfurl his shoulders. 'See, I knew there was a heart beating somewhere in that cold, hard chest of yours. Nice chest, though.'

Susie folded her arms across it. 'Do you never stop?'

'Did I tell you I've always had a thing about girls in pyjamas?'

'Don't push your luck, sunbeam,' she said, turning and going back inside, followed more slowly by Simon. In the kitchen Susie filled the kettle while

Simon made a great show of stretching and groaning some more.

'There are clean towels in the airing cupboard, shampoo, soap. Help yourself to anything you need.'

He grinned. 'I was hoping you might come up and scrub my back.'

'You've got more chance of seeing God,' said Susie, flicking the kettle on to boil.

Simon was in the bath for an hour and a half. For a lot of the time he sang at the top of his voice, while the whole house was filled with the heady perfume of her very expensive, a teaspoonful at a time, Christmas bath oil. Finally, around ten, he strolled back downstairs – damp hair slicked back behind his ears, wearing her pink fluffy dressing gown, looking all scrubbed up, bright, cheery and ache-free.

'God, that is just so much better,' he said, rotating his shoulders like a rugby player about to take the field. 'I really needed that. Do you mind if I use your phone to ring Benny?'

'Not at all, once you've put your clothes on. Tea?'

'That would be great. You look a little tense, you know you ought to go and have a soak. That bath is really comfy. What is that bath oil?'

'Mine. You've been up there an hour and a half.'

He looked amazed. 'Really?'

'I have to get washed and dressed and – and –'

'And?'

'And I promised Nina I'd go into college today to help her finish off.'

'Okay, not a problem, we can do that.'

'We?'

'Sure, I don't mind coming to give you a hand for a few hours. How long will it take you to get ready?'

Susie threw a tea towel at him. 'I would have been there by now if it hadn't been for you nancying about, using all the hot water.'

'Ring her and say you'll be there in what? Another hour, hour and a half. Come on, honey, I'll make the tea, you go and get ready. Have we got any bacon? I really fancy a bacon butty.'

Which was the precise moment Robert walked in. He didn't knock. Susie decided it really was high time she reviewed the whole open-door policy.

Robert paused mid-stride in a peculiar cartoon double take and stared at Simon, who was busy fiddling about in the fridge, resplendent in Susie's favourite dressing gown. Then he looked at Susie in her pyjamas before recovering his composure, pulling himself to his full height and saying, 'Ah, good morning – when you said you had visitors, I hadn't thought –'

'Well, obviously,' said Simon from the fridge. 'Would you like a bacon butty?'

Susie made an effort to wave Robert's unease away. 'Don't worry. It's fine, come in, Robert, it's not how it looks – I don't know if you remember, this is –'

'Simon,' said Simon, with a great show of bonhomie. 'How are you?' He grabbed hold of Robert's hand and pumped it up and down like it might jumpstart something.

Robert stared at Simon as if trying to place him, and then at Susie. 'Where's the other chap?' he said.

Susie felt herself colouring furiously. Simon turned with mock indignation. 'The other chap? Well, well, well, is there something you're not telling me, darling?'

'Simon, will you stop hamming it up and go and get dressed. Robert, this is probably not the best time.'

'Well, when is a good time?' he said crossly. 'I need to talk to you, it seems to me that you're always busy these days.'

'Don't mind me,' said Simon, holding up his hands. 'I'm just going to go upstairs and get me kit back on. Don't forget we're going out, Suse, so don't be too long before you hop in the bath. You can always give me a shout if you want me to scrub your back, babe.'

Robert looked at Susie in complete horror. 'I never thought, I mean I didn't think –' he began.

'That's true,' said Susie, cutting him off. 'Now what was it you wanted to talk about? I'm running late.'

'Well, you can hardly blame *me* for that,' he said indignantly.

'Robert –'

From upstairs came the cheery sounds of Simon whistling something by Van Morrison. Susie just hoped he wasn't planning to break into song.

'I think it might be easier if I came back later. What time will you be free?'

'I don't know.'

'Maybe if I rang you? The thing is, we're going out to dinner tonight with Saskia's parents.'

'We? That's nice.'

'The thing is I can't always get away. She's at work at the moment.' Robert pulled a face. 'They're totally

311

mad,' he hissed, glancing over his shoulder in case someone – presumably one of Saskia's parents – overheard. 'Her mother is a complete fruitcake, nice but not quite there, if you know what I mean – and her brother is – well, he keeps picking at his clothes and looks right through me. Apparently he's really clever, got a first in Physics or something. Whatever it is, it most certainly isn't in table manners.'

'Robert, you can be such a snob.'

'I'm serious. First time we met, her father said they were relieved that someone's taken her on.'

Susie looked at him. 'What?'

'Well, as good as, that's what her father said. That's what I wanted to talk about.'

'Saskia's family? That sounds so cruel. You're marrying her, not her family.'

'But that's just it, it isn't just her family. She's spending a lot of time at my place at the moment, which is nice in one way, but I'm really not used to having someone in my space. When I came home last week she'd got the painters in.'

Susie stared at him, well-aware of the euphemism, unsure that Robert was. 'Really?' she said, not sure exactly where the conversation was going.

'Oh yes – in the sitting room and the hallway. Dust sheets and ladders all over the place. Tropical peach. She's ordered curtains as well, floor to ceiling. Fully lined, in navy linen with wooden poles. They're going to cost a fucking fortune. She said I need a complete makeover. The house, me . . .'

'And do you?' Susie asked.

She would have loved to have been a fly on the wall when Robert came home. This was the man whose bed linen, well-washed and faded as it was, could have commanded its own slot on the *Antiques Roadshow*. One of his favourite suits had belonged to his father.

'She is a lovely girl,' said Robert, pointedly ignoring the question. 'But I'm beginning to realise that she's quite a handful. I mean, don't get me wrong, I'm sure I can do something with her. And she is lovely, really lovely, but she just expects so much attention. She's started to ring me up at work for a little chat, that's how she puts it, but she always wants to know where I am and what time I'll be home and what I'm doing. I feel like I'm being watched, I'm just not used to it. She threw my shoes out –'

Susie looked at him. He probably owned several pairs of shoes that were older than Saskia.

'She is lovely,' he repeated.

'So you keep saying, Robert,' said Susie, although she couldn't help wondering who he was trying to convince. 'The thing is, whoever you're with there is always a period of adjustment, sorting things out. It'll just take some time. I'm sure it will be just –' But Robert was on a roll. He wasn't listening at all.

'In the evening, for instance, I've got things I need to do in my study – notes, work, various bits and bobs – but she wants me to sit with her and watch TV or just sit and talk. About the day, about what she's done. What I've done – what we're going to do tomorrow. I mean, for god's sake! You know I'm not good with small talk.

313

She needs entertaining all the time. Sometimes it feels like having a child about the place.'

Susie wasn't sure what the right answer was. Surely a child was just what he wanted? 'I suppose you could always buy her some crayons and a magic painting book?'

Robert stared at her, and then to her amazement he laughed, and instantly the tension between them evaporated. 'I've already told her I'll buy her a puppy.'

Susie smiled. 'You should be relieved she only wants a puppy, a lot of children won't settle for anything less than a pony.'

Robert smiled sadly. 'So I've heard. Would you mind if I called back later? It would be really nice to catch up. Have a chat. Once what's-his-name has buggered off.'

Susie nodded. 'Yes, of course.' And this time she meant it. 'See you later.'

Robert hesitated as he reached the door. 'About your house guest.' He hesitated. 'Are you sleeping with him?' And then he reddened and backed down. 'Sorry – none of my business really, but I just wondered, you know –' He looked upstairs.

Susie let him squirm for a moment or two and then said, 'Just a friend. And it's still none of your business.'

'And the other one, you know, the other day?'

'Go home.'

'Right,' Robert said, lingering for a moment or two. 'Only, the thing is, I don't want to see you rush into anything or get yourself in a muddle or get hurt.'

'I know, Robert, and I appreciate that.' And for a

moment their eyes met and she knew without a shadow of a doubt that he missed her.

And then, lifting a hand in farewell, he headed home.

Susie watched him go and carried on staring into the open doorway for a while after he left. It felt like an age since they'd been a couple, and the longing and the loss, the pain and the grief she felt didn't seem to apply to him so much as an abstract sense of being part of something bigger than herself.

And Saskia was right; in some ways Robert *was* a poor old thing, with his bald patch and those odd little facial tics that she had never really noticed until now. The way he sucked his teeth before speaking, and grimaced like Popeye as he craned and then scratched his neck, currently red from an early-morning encounter with a razor.

Just a few weeks away from him, and the magical blind eye that loving someone gives you had cleared sufficiently to allow her to see Robert quite plainly – and her new view of him was altogether crueller and far, far more judgemental. Robert really was staid and grumpy and set in his ways with a bald patch and peculiar ears. It was quite sad really.

Susie went upstairs, switched on the bath taps and poured what remained of her bath oil into the turbulent swirling waters. Closing her eyes, she slipped down into the fragrant nest of bubbles.

'Are you awake in there?' Simon hammered on the door. 'Christ, you haven't drowned, have you?'

Susie jumped about a foot in the air. 'Bugger off, Simon, I'm soaking.'

'I thought you said we were late.'

'I said *I* was late, and I can't have been in here more than ten minutes.'

'What on earth are you doing?'

'Well I'm not singing Irish folk songs and soaping my balls.'

'Well, that's a relief. I just came up to say that your bacon butty's done and Alice just rang. She said it was important and she wants you to ring her back. She sounded really upset. Upset or angry, or maybe both – I have a problem working out which is which with women sometimes. Oh and I've taken the battery out of your smoke alarm. Kept going off.'

Susie sighed and slipped beneath the water. She could still hear Simon's voice through the froth but couldn't quite pick out the words. 'I'll be down in five,' Susie called as she resurfaced.

'Oh and I've put the tea towel in the bin. I couldn't see any point in keeping it really.'

Susie clambered out and wrapped herself in the only dry towel left in the airing cupboard. It was the one she usually dried Milo with after they'd been to the beach.

By some amazing coincidence, by the time Susie drove into the college entrance Simon's driver was there waiting for him. Nina was on the front steps enjoying a roll-up under one of the palm trees as Simon clambered out of his car, made his apologies, said his goodbyes and hurried over to the waiting Mercedes. So much for him giving them a hand.

'Ummm. Nice car,' said Nina, waving Simon off. 'Nice bum. Stayed the night, did he?'

'Yes, but not in the way you're imagining.'

'Pity, you see I think you're wrong when you said there isn't a relationship there. He's obviously keen.'

'Only on his own terms. I could never rely on him, and besides he is way too pretty. I'd be worried all the time that he was off after some perky little nymphet – and he is about as reliable as a two-bob watch.'

'Shows your age.'

'What does?'

'Two bob – who knows what that means any more?' Nina took a last long pull on her fag before nipping the end out. 'And how's the rest of life?'

Susie groaned as she realised she'd forgotten to ring Alice back. 'Too busy, too complicated – now what else have we got to do here?'

'The ceramics section down the far side. I'm three parts there but if you can just give me a hand with the last few pieces – there's those giant hand-coiled garden pots to shift yet.'

'Fantastic,' said Susie grimly.

And so the remains of the morning went, and a lot of the afternoon along with it, on the final nips and tucks and touches that finished the exhibition work. Last thing in the afternoon they walked around with the final draft of the catalogue to ensure that labels, position, numbers and items all tallied up, making any amendments and last-minute changes as they went round.

The exhibition did look stunning, even without the addition of Saskia's extraordinary plants.

'It gets better every year,' Susie said as they made

317

their way down the aisle of jewellery and body art, set out on tall, square crystal-clear glass cabinets. Beyond that was a wave of hats and headpieces hung in colour sequence on a crisp white board, and beyond that the first of the sculpture, each artist with a dedicated space, carefully lit and arranged to show their work off to its best advantage. Each of the different areas was divided from the next either by planting or, in some cases, by a great curving tower of stainless steel, which made up the down run for the water features. Each display carried discreet details of Hill's Nurseries and a phone number. The whole thing looked fabulous.

'Well,' said Nina, running her eye down over the list on her clipboard. 'I think that is about it. I'll get the catalogue emailed off to the guys in the printing department. We just need the bigwigs to come in and claim all the glory and it'll be all done and dusted for another year. When are you seeing Simon again? Have you –' she grinned salaciously '– you know, yet?'

Susie laughed. 'Don't hold back, Nina, say what you mean. And actually, no. And I've got no intention of having any *you know* with him. The man is a dog –'

'Nice-looking dog.'

'Neen, I'm really tempted but for all the wrong reasons. I don't just want sex with him. It would be like eating way too much chocolate when actually what I want is a good meal. I would end up feeling horrible about myself – and at the moment that's the last thing I want.'

'You know what they say, don't you? When you get old and look back on your life it's not the things you did that you regret, it's all the things that you didn't do that come back to haunt you.'

'So you're saying I should go to bed with Simon in case I regret it later? What kind of moral compass did you turn out to be?'

'Oh come on, neither of us is Mother Teresa, and to be honest, if you fancy him I can't see what the harm is. It would help you get over Robert – help you move on.'

Susie shook her head. 'I need to feel better about myself, not worse – and Simon is a little shit. Say we did go to bed together and then he didn't ring me the next day or didn't turn up for a week? To be honest, with him it could be for any number of reasons – that he'd lost his phone, that something else had come up, or that he was busy, but I would feel it was a reflection on me – and at the moment I couldn't cope with that.'

Nina sniffed and pulled out the half-smoked rollie from her pocket. 'My god, how sensible. You know your trouble is you think too much.'

'That's just what Simon said.'

'But what if this is *it*? What if Simon Hammond, against all the odds, is your happy ever after? I mean, why not? These things happen. They reckon there is someone for everyone. What if he is *your* someone?'

Susie laughed. 'I'd probably shoot myself. Now is there anything else we need to do or can I go home?'

'I would say go home,' said Nina. 'That's certainly my plan.'

* * *

The phone was ringing as Susie unlocked the door. It was getting to be something of a ritual. As she picked up the receiver Susie glanced out into the garden just to make sure that Simon hadn't found a way back in during her absence. She'd made a big point of locking everything down tight before leaving for college.

'Hel—' Susie began as she picked up the receiver.

'Where have you been?' snapped Alice. 'I've been ringing you all day – did you know that your mobile is off as well?'

'Well hello, Alice, hello, Mum, how are you? I'm fine, thank you, how about you?' said Susie through gritted teeth. 'I've been at work all day – oh have you, gosh, you must be tired.'

There was deafening silence from the other end of the line, so Susie pressed on. 'Alice, it's not that I don't want to talk to you, or that I won't talk to you, but I do have a life. If you leave a message I will always ring you back, maybe not instantly but I will ring you, you know that. I was going to call you as soon as I got a chance and could sit and talk as opposed to just doing the social niceties and then rushing off. And I've just this minute walked in through the door.'

'There was a man in your house this morning. It sounded like Simon Hammond.'

There was no way Susie planned to get drawn into that one.

'He called me, Alice.'

Susie didn't say anything.

'Are you still there?' said Alice after a few seconds.

'Yes,' said Susie. 'Now what was it you wanted to talk about?'

'It's Adam.'

Susie pulled up a chair and settled down for the long haul.

'Jack's here and that's working out very well. He's re-tiling the bathroom at the moment and the man downstairs wants him to redo their patio.'

'Good, I'm glad that's working out.'

There was another silence and then Alice said, 'Work is going really well. They're thinking about making me a grade three soon – with the possibility of a four once I'm back off maternity leave. Which will mean more work, obviously, and more responsibility – and more money.'

'That's good.' Susie had no idea what a grade three meant but it sounded like a good thing.

'And the baby is okay.'

'Wonderful.' She knew that Alice would get to the point when she was good and ready, no point in questioning her, rushing her or trying to push the river. She waited.

'Adam's got a job in Manchester,' Alice said all of a sudden. 'The thing is, Mum, he didn't talk to me about it or anything. Not at all – not a word.' Susie could hear the tears in Alice's voice as the words tumbled out. 'I mean, how could he do that without discussing it with me first? He says the money is loads better, and the hours.'

'That sounds great,' Susie began. 'What with the baby and –'

But Alice didn't want her to speak, just to listen, so she carried on talking over Susie.

'He says that as we were living apart he might as well take it. It's a big chance, he says. A real opportunity.' And now she was crying hard. 'He says he's going to look for a house share or a flat up there – *in Manchester*, for god's sake.'

'Well, surely this is what you wanted. And the house share or the flat makes sense, it'll be a lot cheaper than living in a hotel.'

'Mum, how can you say that?'

'Because it's true. It *is* cheaper. You're the one who wanted to live together apart, Alice. I can't see what the problem is – whether you live apart with him just up the road or up north, surely the principle is the same?'

'It's not the same at all. I want him close by, I want him at his mum's,' Alice wailed. 'He can't just go off and leave me like this.'

Susie shook her head in amazement. 'But you are the one who didn't want to live with him.'

Even though she was arguing Adam's point, Susie knew exactly what the problem was. Alice wanted the together-apart arrangement to be on her terms, not Adam's, and the idea that he might make an independent decision without consulting her obviously hadn't occurred to Alice.

'Surely you can see that from his point of view living with his mum is hardly a great option after having his own home.'

'He said he liked having his ironing done,' Alice snivelled.

'Yes, and I'm sure he does, but I bet he doesn't like her knowing all his comings and goings, and it can't

322

be easy for her either to have him move back in. Surely you must have realised that going back to live with his mum was only a temporary measure?'

'Why?' said Alice. 'His mum's is close to where he works. Why would he want to move out?'

'Because he is used to having his own home, his own family – surely you could see that when you did this? This was what you wanted.'

'Of course it wasn't, and anyway, Adam agreed.'

'I can't see that he had much choice, love.'

'There's no point talking to you. You're taking his side, Mum.'

'I'm not, Alice. I promise, all I'm doing is looking at it from both sides. You wanted to be apart, he's moved out, you can hardly dictate where he lives.' And then the line went quiet for a little while and Alice said in a tiny voice, 'But what if he meets someone else in Manchester, Mum? What about me and the baby?'

'Alice, Adam loves you, but you're not making it easy for him. You need to talk to Adam about this –'

'But he applied for this job without even telling me. He didn't even mention it until he'd got it.'

'Well, if you're only seeing him at weekends does it matter whether he comes to see you from just down the road or three hours away? You were the one who made him leave, love.'

There was a sob, and then another. 'How could he do this to me and our baby? How could he?'

'Oh, Alice, for god's sake ring him. He thinks you don't love him any more, he thinks you don't want him.'

'How do you know, Mum, has he rung you? Is that what he said?' Alice asked anxiously.

'No, no, he hasn't rung me,' said Susie, 'but if I was him that is how I'd feel.' She wondered how on earth it was that Alice couldn't see that for herself. Adam was such a good man and loved Alice so much – much more than she deserved in many ways.

'I don't want him to go to Manchester, Mum.'

'Then ring him up and tell him that yourself. But you can't expect him to live at home with his mum and live life on your terms. It's not fair.'

'Do you think I'm being unreasonable?'

Susie took a deep breath. Sometimes the only thing left was the truth. 'Yes. Yes, I think you are being unreasonable, and I think Adam was right about the hormones. It unbalances all of us.'

Susie braced herself for a broadside from Alice but instead she whispered, 'I couldn't bear to lose him. I love him, Mum.'

'I know, now ring him. I'm sure it will be okay.'

'What if it's too late? What if he's already made his mind up? What if he's already met someone else – what if he's moving up there because of her? What if . . .?'

'Alice, stop getting yourself into a state and just ring him and see what he has to say.'

Obviously Alice had inherited the family imagination. When she put the phone down Susie was exhausted. Was there a moment when you finally stopped being a mother, when it all got easier and the problems resolved themselves? She had a horrible suspicion that what actually happened as children got older was that they sorted out the easy stuff for themselves and only ended up asking your advice and help for the *really* tricky things in life.

So when the phone rang again Susie was tempted to ignore it but decided on balance that it was probably better to get it over and done with.

'Is it all right if I come round now?' said Robert. 'Only I was driving past and I saw your car in the driveway. Saskia won't be back until six. Did I tell you she's brought all her things over now – all her clothes and stuff? I've never seen anyone with so much stuff. She was saying that maybe we could turn the back bedroom into some sort of walk-in wardrobe for her clothes and shoes.'

Whatever happened to hello? Susie thought.

'Sounds like a nice idea,' she said. 'I mean, you don't really use the back bedroom for anything other than storage anyway, do you? It's full of –' Susie hesitated.

She was going to say 'crap', then settled on 'junk', but before she could say either, Robert said, 'Things. *My things.* I've got all sorts of things in there. Books and magazines, sports equipment, fishing tackle, all sorts of bits and bobs I've collected. Things I've had for years. I appreciate that they might not mean anything to anyone else but they're special to me. I've still got all the copies of the *Eagle* from when I was at school. Some of that stuff in there is probably worth a mint.'

And some of it, thought Susie, was just plain junk.

'Saskia said we ought to do a car boot. I mean, for god's sake. *A car boot?* I wouldn't dream of parting with my things, some of the fishing tackle in there belonged to my grandfather.'

And possibly Noah before him, thought Susie. How was it that people couldn't see things from anyone else's point of view? It obviously hadn't occurred to Robert that asking Saskia to move in with him meant just that.

'You can hardly expect her to camp out, Robert. By asking her to move in with you, you're asking her to make a home with you. She needs room for her things. She needs to feel that it's her home too.'

If only she could sort her own life out as well as she could manage everyone else's, everything would be great, thought Susie, ruefully.

'Well, I understand that. Of course I do,' said Robert, in a tone that suggested he did anything but. 'But she wants to change things. And she's got so much stuff.'

Susie couldn't think of an answer, maybe her sympathy gland was packing up. Not that it deterred Robert.

'Put the kettle on,' he said. 'I'll be over in a couple of minutes. Have you got any Rich Tea? Saskia says I'm not to have them, apparently I'm getting love handles.'

Robert was at Susie's for about an hour. He had two cups of tea, half a packet of biscuits, and started talking from the moment he got in the door, all the time he was there, and all the way down the path to where Susie said goodbye to him at the gate. Although he didn't plan to go directly back to his house, just in case Saskia was there, because even though she knew that Susie and Robert were just good friends, and that it was all over between them, and that Susie was a lovely person, Saskia found it hard to get her head around the idea that Robert still saw her and talked to her. And sometimes Saskia got upset about it – well, not so much upset as fretful and anxious.

And so, Robert headed back by a very convoluted route which would bring him out on the far side of the common, a long way away from Susie's cottage, on a path that couldn't be construed as leading directly from one to the other. A fact that seemed very important to Robert. It would probably take him half an hour to go round the long way, on the off-chance that Saskia might be at home – which made Susie wonder just how upset and fretful young Ms Hill could get.

Susie told him several times how happy she was for him, for them, and every time she did, Robert's expression settled into a mask of gratitude while behind it his eyes flared white-hot with panic, like a prisoner trapped behind bars.

All in all it was a very odd place to find herself. There was a part of Susie that was gloating over what looked like a horrible mismatch, and a part of her was terribly sad for Robert that he hadn't found the thing he wanted.

Susie had asked him about the baby thing, and Robert had looked really sheepish, not quite meeting her eye as he dipped another Rich Tea into his mug. 'I haven't pushed it – you know – the thing is Saskia's young. We've got time.' He tried to sound matter of fact, throwaway, as if it ought to be obvious. 'She's got things she needs to do and I think that is great.'

Susie stared at him. What she wanted to say was, 'But surely that was the whole point of this, Robert; you felt that you hadn't got time, which is why you wanted to be with someone younger.' But she had stayed silent, because although that *was* what she meant, it sounded too much like, '*Well that's crazy, because if you aren't pushing the whole baby business then you could still be with me. You pig.*'

And Susie knew that the bottom line was that at least with Saskia, Robert could have children at some point. So she hadn't said any of those things, instead Susie had nodded and waited for Robert to say whatever else it was he planned to say. And there was more, quite a lot more.

Robert had picked at his shirt. 'To be honest, and *let's be honest* about this, it's early days yet. There are a lot of adjustments for both of us, and Saskia has got plans. Lots of plans, apparently. This is her first proper relationship and I understand that, I do – I really do, so I haven't – well, you know . . .' His voice tailed off. 'I mean, it wouldn't be fair on her. She's lovely but she's quite young for her age and it's maybe a little too much pressure at this precise moment. So I haven't – well, you know – and I'd be grateful, if you ever speak to her, which I'm sure you will, that you don't either – please.'

Susie didn't ask him exactly what it was that Robert hadn't done because she knew. He'd lied. He hadn't told Saskia that he was with her because he wanted a womb and that his biological clock was screaming, 'Last chance, last chance,' so very loudly that he had lost any sense of what was good and what was an emotional disaster.

In which case, Susie thought, tidying away the remains of his visit, Robert deserved everything he got.

Just before he got up to leave, Robert had said, 'You know, I really miss you.' And Susie had to bite her lip and root around in the biscuit tin, but it wasn't quite enough to stop him. 'I think about you every day,' he said. 'It's just that we want different things from life, you and I. Our lives are different shapes – you've got your family.'

Susie didn't dare look at him in case all the healing she had worked so hard at got torn down. 'Robert, why didn't you talk about this – I never knew you wanted a baby,' she managed.

He nodded. 'Neither did I and then suddenly it seemed like the years had all gone and it was now or never.' He paused. 'I wanted to say that I'm sorry. I truly love you, Susie. And I didn't mean to hurt you.'

Susie papered a smile on over her hurt. 'Too late,' she murmured.

'I know, you already said,' he whispered, catching hold of her hand. 'But I need to do this.'

Susie nodded, because she didn't trust herself to speak.

Once he'd left, Susie watched Robert's progress down the back lane behind her house. It was always muddy down that way and brambly, which is why she didn't go round there with Milo. Robert had made light of it; he didn't want to upset Saskia just before they went to have supper with her parents. Susie watched him thoughtfully. She could just see his head above the hedge line, bobbing up and down as he found his stride, the sunlight glinting on his bald spot.

There were lots of things that went through Susie's mind as she watched Robert's progress. What on earth was he doing? Was he too bloody-minded to admit that maybe he was wrong? He wanted a younger woman, yes, but did it have to be *this* particular younger woman? Had he come round to try and win her back; did he expect her to rescue him? Susie stood at the window for a long time trying to work it out.

Chapter 18

Once she was certain Robert had gone, Susie rang Alice back. Alice had rung Adam, but apparently he was out, and his mum wasn't sure what time he was coming back. Which hadn't helped Alice's state of mind one little bit. Adam's mobile was switched off, so Alice had left a message on his voicemail and asked him to ring her when he came in. She had tried to sound apologetic, and as if she wanted to talk and not tell him what to do. And then she had cried and told him that she was really, really sorry and that she wanted him to come home. Although it was Jack who told Susie all about the phone call because he was the one who answered when Susie rang. He also said that once Alice had finished wailing on the phone, he'd put her to bed with a milky drink, two antacid tablets, and promised to wake her up if Adam rang. So far – nothing.

But yes, Jack was fine and busy, and no, he hadn't seen much of Ellie because her mother was over on holiday from Spain. And apparently Simon was seeing some woman and was being very secretive about the whole thing, which was driving Ellie and her mother crazy. Simon was never there, always showing up late, if at all, avoiding phone calls and all that sort of thing. Ellie said she'd forgotten what he was like. And then Jack went all cagey and said, 'He took you out a couple of times too, didn't he?'

Susie smiled. 'That's right.'

She waited for Jack to say something rude but instead he said, 'Well, if you ask me you're well out of it, Mum. He's driving Ellie mad, he is totally irresponsible. He promised to take her out shopping in Cambridge this week and basically just didn't show up. The problem with Simon is that when he does do what he promises it's brilliant, so you turn up the next time expecting to have a great day, and he doesn't show up at all, so he's always got the whip hand – it's a real power trip for him.'

'How's it working out with you and Alice?'

'Living here? Not bad. You know what she's like, all bark, lots of bite, but it's okay and her heart is in the right place. At least that's what they told her at the scan. The guy downstairs has offered me a bit of work, cash – which will be nice. And I spoke to Matt earlier, we've got a couple of months' work in the Shetland Isles over the summer. Not quite Italy, obviously, but you take what you can get. Oh, and by the way, he sends his love.'

The sound of his name made Susie smile. 'He told me about the dig. Matt okay?'

'Uh-huh, apparently he said you invited him to the private viewing next week. He was asking me what I thought he ought to wear.'

'Matt asked *you* what to wear?' Susie laughed. 'That has got to be a first, the boy who has got archaeological slobbery down to a fine art?'

'*Man*, Mum, *man*,' corrected Jack in a teasing voice. 'He just wanted to know how formal it was going to be, whether it was DJ or smart casual or what.'

'And you told him?'

'That the last one I went to I went in a Metallica tee shirt, combats and Nike sandals.'

'I remember.'

'So he said, "Smart casual then?" and I said "Yes". You didn't want him in a penguin suit, did you?'

'Well, no, I didn't.' When Susie had invited Matt it hadn't occurred to her that he might actually come or that he would take it seriously enough to ask what he had to wear. She smiled; he was such a nice guy.

'You know, you can come too if you like,' said Susie. 'You'd enjoy it. We've got a really good show this year.'

'I'll probably give it a miss. I've got to stay in and wash my hair.'

'I haven't told you what night it is yet.'

Jack laughed. 'Tell me and I'll reschedule my hair-washing programme so as to avoid it.'

'Philistine.'

'Guilty as charged, Mother. Anyway, I'm going to go, just in case Adam rings. Alice has stopped using her mobile in case it does something bizarre to the baby. I would have thought having her as a mother would have been enough.'

'Give her my love.'

'What about me?'

'I love you too.'

Next she rang Simon, smiling as she dialled the number at the idea of being described as *some woman*, although, true to form, it rang once and then went straight to voicemail. Susie was about to leave a message when she decided that actually she couldn't be bothered. Let him ring her. Or turn up, or fly paper planes over her roof or something. It was better to be chased.

Thoughts of Robert and Saskia started bubbling to the surface unbidden. Of Robert in particular.

Then the phone rang. The caller ID said Simon.

'Hi, how are you?' she said. Obviously not leaving a message was the way forward.

'Who is this?' demanded a woman. 'You rang this number a few minutes ago.'

Susie was taken aback. Maybe she'd got the number wrong the first time around, although that didn't explain caller ID on the return call. 'Yes, I did, sorry. I was trying to contact Simon Hammond,' she began.

'Were you? Were you indeed? Well, Simon don't want to speak to you, is that clear? He don't want to speak to you ever again – okay?' snarled the woman.

In the background Susie heard Simon's voice. 'Give me that here – come on – I've told you before, it could be business – here –'

And then she could hear the woman shrieking, 'Why is she ringing here – why can't she leave us alone, Simon? You tell me. Can you wonder I don't trust you, huh? Can you? You bastard.'

And then there were muffled, scuffling, cracking sounds, during which Susie could hear Simon saying,

'Come on, sweetie, please – come on, just give me the phone here – now. Please – it could be important.'

'It's a woman, it's one of your –'

'Hello,' said Simon, in an ultra-calm voice.

'Bad time?' asked Susie.

'Do you mind if I ring you back?'

'Sure,' she said, and hung up, feeling shaken.

Was the other woman drunk or crazy? As she sat down Susie realised that she was trembling. She assumed that Simon would ring back straight away, or at least pretty quickly, but of course he didn't and by ten she was tired of waiting and ready for bed.

There was a text when she woke up on Sunday morning. It read:

Sorry about that. See you at the private view, will explain everything then. Hugs 'n' kisses, Sx PS: Do you fancy going on somewhere afterwards?

Susie wasn't sure she did after the woman's outburst. Nor was she certain how to take the text exactly. Was it an answer? Or appeasing her? The most obvious thing was that she wouldn't be seeing him until Tuesday at the earliest, so when she finally got up, Susie drove down to the beach, taking Milo and her camera. As she pulled on walking boots and a lightweight windproof jacket, she planned lunch – shared cod and chips on the quay at Wells-next-the-Sea with Milo, by which time they would both be famished.

Meanwhile, a good brisk walk, looking at life through a lens, lots of fresh air, sunshine and canine company was the perfect cure for any kind of blues. As she strode across the fine, almost white sand, on her way down towards Holkham, Susie almost managed to forget about Simon, although it was far harder to block out images of Robert and Saskia coming home from their dinner party.

The great expanse of cerulean-blue sky above an almost coral-white beach was fabulous as always. On the landward side a great stand of pine trees that ran for mile after mile made it look more like Scandinavia than Norfolk, but today even they couldn't quite take Susie's mind off things.

In her imagination Robert and Saskia had been transformed into something out of a fifties black and white film, Robert in a DJ bearing a more than passing resemblance to Gregory Peck for the purposes of the fantasy. Saskia had come over all Audrey Hepburn, and was wearing a black evening dress with a hooped skirt and dinky little fifties slingbacks. She looked stunning – Robert too, come to that.

They were both so much wittier and warmer and in love in her fantasy and looked like the perfect older man, younger woman couple.

Grimly, Susie picked up a stick to throw for Milo. Not that he was much interested, on the rare occasions he made the effort to go-fetch she suspected he was only doing it to humour her, and more often than not he would watch the stick flying through the air and then scutter across the beach as if to say, 'So you didn't want that then?'

Today he trotted halfway and then sat down, wagging

cheerily, waiting for her to catch up. Meanwhile, in Susie's head, Saskia and Robert were busy making scintillating conversation with the in-laws, played by Susan Sarandon and Orson Welles, while in the background Simon was having a steaming row with a Penelope Cruz look-alike. Sometimes it was hell having an active imagination.

Susie tugged her jacket tight around her and stared out to sea, watching little boats tuck and turn and fight against the brisk wind. Eventually she knew, given time, that Robert and Saskia would fade. God only knew what would happen with Simon, but every indication was they were unlikely to live happily ever after.

'Excuse me – scuse me? Missss, Missss –'

Susie looked round to see a small boy running towards her carrying something that was ringing. It took her a few moments to work out that it was a phone, and by the way the boy was waving and yelling was most probably hers.

'You dropped this,' he said, panting hard, bent double to try to regain his breath. 'When you was throwing sticks for your dog, he's a nice dog.' Meanwhile, Milo trotted over to see what the fuss was about, and, seeing someone young and impressionable, came over all cute and grateful, wagging and whimpering and skipping around his new admirer.

'Thank you,' Susie said. 'That's really kind.' But the boy was already playing with the dog, who was now only too happy to retrieve anything. Sticks, stones, tatty old bits of seaweed.

Hussy, thought Susie, looking down at the missed-call

menu. It wasn't a number she recognised. For a split second she had an image of Simon crouched in a doorway with a stolen phone pressed to his ear, tapping in her number, while a blonde psycho with a knife stalked to and fro, sniffing the air trying to track him down.

Should she ring back? Maybe it was a wrong number; maybe it was someone ringing to offer her a mystery free gift. Whoever it was answered after the second ring.

'You called me?' said Susie cautiously. Given the earlier run-in she'd had with Simon's number, she decided to tread cautiously.

'It's me,' said a male voice, distorted and then torn away by the wind.

'I'm sorry,' said Susie, 'I didn't catch that. Me who?'

'Me, it's Matt,' said Matt. 'How are you?'

'Oh, hello, sorry, I can barely hear you. I'm fine. I didn't recognise the number.'

'Oh, sorry, it's my work phone.'

'I can hardly hear you. It's really blustery here,' Susie yelled, finger in her ear, mobile pressed tight to the other.

'Blustery?'

'Yes, I'm on the beach, with Milo.'

'Right, well that kind of answers my next question.'

'Which was?'

'If I could pop in for lunch?'

Susie laughed. 'Where are you?'

'On the A10 about five minutes from your place. I had to go to King's Lynn this morning.'

'Well we could meet up here if you like. Best fish and chips in the world. I'm buying. I owe you one.'

There was a moment's silence. 'Tempting. Unfortunately I've got someone coming over later.'

'Right,' said Susie, feeling oddly disappointed. 'Well, okay, maybe another time then – we're not doing very well with our lunch plans, are we? I'm on my way down to Holkham.'

'Great place. Sorry I missed you, sorry I'm not there. We'll catch up soon.'

'Sure,' said Susie. 'You can buy the fish and chips next time. And you're coming on Tuesday?'

'The private view?'

'Yes.'

'I'll be there.'

It was an odd conversation that didn't quite flow, but knowing that Matt would be there on Tuesday made her smile, although she couldn't work out whether it was because Matt was off-limits. As they said their goodbyes, Milo was still playing at being an obedient dog for the small boy, sitting and staying and rolling over until the boy's parents called him away and Susie headed off down the beach, at which point Milo reverted to type and dropped into a slow, casual amble alongside her.

Talking to Matt and knowing he had been thinking about her cheered her up no end and drove away the ghosts of Gregory and Audrey. Once the exhibition was done and dusted it would only be another couple of weeks until the end of the summer term. For the last three years she'd gone somewhere with Robert for the first week, before the schools broke up, and then spent the rest of the summer painting and sketching or going off with her camera, in between the more domestic stuff, sometimes taking off to the Lakes, or Somerset, or Wales, or the North Norfolk coast as money and the mood took her.

Robert loved Wales, and during the time they'd been together they'd rented a cottage in Snowdonia in all kinds of weathers, for a week or just a weekend so he could break out his walking boots and head off into the hills with a trusty rucksack that belonged to some elderly uncle or other, while she stayed closer to home to take photographs or sketch. They had had a lot of long weekends together.

She would miss that, all that companionable travel. Tucking her chin down, Susie sniffed back the tears – cross with herself for still feeling so sad. Thank god that the grief and the regrets came in waves and not all at once or they might sweep her away and drown her. Sometimes in the holidays, besides concentrating on her own work, Susie taught classes or did some private workshops, and now, as she walked back with the wind in her face, Susie realised that she hadn't made any plans at all for this summer because part of her had been waiting to see what Robert was going to do.

She had imagined that they would be making plans for their future together, maybe organising a wedding, maybe looking at houses. She bit her lip, realising how big a chunk of her future had been invested in Robert. Susie quickened her pace and headed back towards the main road that ran along the top of the sea defences towards the town. What she really needed were new plans.

By the time she got to the quayside Susie could have eaten a donkey in a bap. Fortunately she didn't have to. The fish and chips were superb; she and Milo went fifty-fifty on a large portion of cod, Susie ate all the chips, and while Milo had a bowl of water she sat on the low wall that skirted the car park and quayside and watched the boats bobbing at their moorings. One of the things she had always prided herself on was having a full life, with lots of good friends, and a good social life. She loved her job and did enough to pay the bills and still have time to do her own work. She loved her cottage and Milo, but there was a sense that at the moment it was all a little stale. A little too predictable and comfortable. Maybe that was why she had got involved with Simon, although it was disconcerting to think that he was the closest thing she could get to an adventure at short notice.

There had to be something else. She needed something to look forward to, some big adventure to turn things around, to make her think less about what might have been, and more about what was still to come.

Still deep in thought, she drove home, while Milo snored contentedly on the back seat.

Monday was a blur of activity; there was no time to think about anything other than getting the last-minute stuff done for the exhibition. It struck Susie, as she and Nina were wheeling various boxes and oddments down to the foyer, that it really didn't matter how well-organised you thought you were, there was always something else to do, some last-minute thing that threw everyone and all those carefully made plans into confusion. And it was something different every year.

This year the caterers had no glasses; and the printers had a problem with the machine they'd planned to use, but were hoping to get it fixed by lunchtime. One of the artists had broken a sculpture, another had shown up with three pieces that were listed in the catalogue but they had no space for, and a man called Rex from the management wanted to come round to do a risk assessment, while Saskia's troops were in watering the plants. There was a slight lighting problem that might mean the whole lighting rack had to come down to do the adjustment, although Susie was hoping they'd leave that until after the water was mopped up from some overzealous misting. All this and a girl from the local paper wanted to pop by and do a couple of interviews. Nothing heavy – oh, and maybe some photos with some of the students and their work. She was hoping to do a feature. Five or six would be good.

Despite feeling tired and frazzled, Susie also had a sense of elation as she helped one of the final-year students hang a series of exquisitely printed and embroidered banners. Glancing round she could see the way in which all the students' work had developed, grown – and took a sense of personal pride in how far they had come in the time that she'd been working with them. Across the way, the Head of Ceramics lifted a hand in greeting, salute and relief – it was going to be a really good show.

By mid-afternoon everything, at least in principle, was done and dusted. 'Fancy a glass of warm chardonnay?' said Nina, appearing from the refreshment area with two plastic wine goblets.

'I didn't think the bar went live until tomorrow night.'

'It doesn't, but the joy of using students is that they had no idea how far apart the shelves should be in the wine cooler, so they brought down a couple of bottles to measure. *Et voilà* – seems a shame for them to have to carry them all the way back to the catering kitchen.'

'And the glasses?'

'The real ones are on their way, these were some free samples someone dropped off.'

'We can't stand around here drinking.'

Nina grinned. 'I've found the perfect spot round the back in there in the jungle. A little hidey-hole where the gardeners have stashed their kit – follow me.'

'I've got to drive home.'

'In that case just have half a glass and I'll help you out with the rest. So what are you going to wear tomorrow night?'

'Something comfortable. How about you?'

'Well, you know the outfit I said I'd got on lay away?'

'For my wedding?'

'Uh-huh, well, it was only eight quid from the charity shop, seemed a shame to let it go really.'

'So –'

'Well, I won't wear the hat, obviously.'

'That's a relief.'

Nina looked Susie up and down. 'You've lost weight.'

'It's probably the worry.'

Nina snorted. 'Whatever, you're looking good. I think you should wear something really sexy, something wriggly.'

Susie laughed. 'Something wriggly? And why would I want to do that?'

'Well, for a start Simon is going to be here and the Ice Queen will be bringing ol' big ears – if it was me I'd want to show the miserable little toad what he was missing.'

'Really?'

'Oh yes, I'd go the full Ulrika if I were you.'

Which was why, when she got home, Susie found herself standing in front of the wardrobe in her bra and pants trying things on. Milo watched in bemused silence from the threshold as she discarded one thing after another, while muttering to herself as things got re-hung, put to one side or thrown onto the bedroom chair to be put into bags for the charity shop.

One thing Nina was right about, she had lost weight. Why hadn't she thought about what she was going to wear before? She'd known the exhibition was coming up for weeks now. It was too late to go out and buy something new, but Nina was right – she needed something with pizzazz that would out-Audrey Saskia and make Robert look twice. She didn't want him back, but she did want to make an impression, make him realise just what he'd lost. Although, she thought, glancing into the full-length mirror, the impression she had the last time they spoke was that he knew exactly what he'd thrown away.

She picked up a little blue silk top and posed, turning left and then right. She wasn't that worried about impressing Simon, he was so self-obsessed she doubted he would notice what she was wearing, but she did need to look good. So – back to the wardrobe.

Susie pulled out one thing after another, holding things up against herself and looking into the long mirror mounted on the bedroom wall, making snap judgements as she went. Trinny and Susannah-ing yourself was tricky, but she decided to give it a shot.

'Too old, makes me look too old or ill or as if I'm trying too hard. Too tight, too loose, wrong colour, wrong season, wrong size . . . Why in god's name did I ever buy *that*? – oh, for god's sake.' It was exhausting.

By mid-evening she was down to three outfits: brown linen trousers, a cream scoop-neck sleeveless top and a little shaped chocolate-brown jacket with lots of chunky ethnic jewellery; or a cream linen dress with a bias-cut skirt and a long crushed strawberry cardigan that had a tendency to slip sexily off one shoulder, worn with more feminine jewellery; or an olive-green crinkled silk V-neck long-sleeved top over cream linen trousers. She tried them on one after the other – the main thing was not only did they have to have some kind of zing factor but they also needed to be comfortable, as she would be running about in them for hours. And also, they didn't need to be too fussy as she would have about an hour to get home, get showered, grab a sandwich, let the dog out and then hurry back into work.

Eventually Susie ironed all three outfits and decided

she would choose when she walked in the door the next evening. They were all a little on the safe side, attractive, stylish but not wildly daring – which, thought Susie, with a wry smile, probably just about summed her up nicely. Maybe it was time to break out, be more adventurous.

For a change, no one phoned, so she Delia-ed herself a huge bowl of tuna and pasta with mayonnaise, added tiny baby tomatoes, fresh basil and spring onions, and sat outside in the last of the sunshine to enjoy it, and for the first time in days felt totally at peace.

On Tuesday morning Susie drove into work before eight. It felt like the whole of the art department were there, and all caught in the eye of the storm. There was still a lot of last-minute tinkering going on. The catalogues had turned up. The plants were watered. Students from Hotel and Catering were being briefed on front-of-house duties and having a last-minute run-through on serving drinks and how not to trip with a tray of canapés.

Susie and Nina spent the morning clearing up the studios as it was inevitable that people – parents, friends, all kinds of people – wanted to come in and see where the students had been working all year. There were also a few little last-minute repairs on a couple of things, a coat of varnish to apply to a driftwood goat, and a whole rake of posters, numbers and information boards to hang up, stick on and position. There was also a really nice, happy buzz too – most of the donkey work was done and dusted, today it was mostly cosmetic. Saskia's horticultural team came in and polished the leaves of the big plants, misting and wiping and making the whole place glow with verdant green.

'You know you could have come and got ready at my place this evening, saved yourself the drive home,' said Nina as she slid a pile of art boards back into the stockroom.

'I know, but then you'd tell me my outfit was far too dull and I'd end up wearing something of yours and feeling horrible all night.'

'Well, thanks for that,' sniffed Nina. 'You saying my clothes are horrible?'

'No, not at all, and not on you – it's just that I'm more –'

'More boring?'

Susie laughed. 'Could be. And besides, I haven't made up my mind what I'm wearing.'

'So what are you planning? A last-minute lunge into the wardrobe with your eyes closed?'

'Not quite.'

'So who have you got coming to cheer you on?'

'Simon said he was coming.'

'Good choice – still keen, is he?'

Susie smiled. 'Who knows? And then there's Matt.'

'The gay guy?'

'Uh-huh – how about you?'

'The usual crew, my kids, oh, and a couple of guys from that gallery I had stuff in, in the spring.'

Susie nodded. Nina's *usual crew* quite often included reps and staff from galleries all over the country who showed up on her say-so.

'And what are you planning on wearing?' asked Susie. The art room was now unnaturally tidy and smelt of a subtle combination of old wood, paint and furniture polish.

'I've already told you – your wedding outfit.'

'Oh yes, that's right, which reminds me, I told you that Saskia and Robert will probably be here too?'

'You did, about half a dozen times.' Nina back-heeled the stockroom door shut. 'You know that man deserves everything he gets.'

Susie lifted her eyebrows.

'Okay, okay,' said Nina, holding her hands up in surrender. 'I won't say another word. But I can't understand why he –'

'Stop,' said Susie. 'I don't want to talk about Robert, not today.'

Nina looked her up and down. 'Because?'

'Because I'm beginning to feel better, because today I need to be on top form, and the last thing I want is to burst into tears over something I can't have and can't control. I'm really looking forward to tonight.'

'Fair enough, so are you going off somewhere with Simon afterwards? A little supper maybe, in a European capital of your choice?'

Susie laughed. 'You really are a complete cow, and I have no idea what his plans are, if any. But yes, he did suggest we might go on somewhere else.'

She didn't mention the phone call from the crazed woman because she didn't want it raked over word by word in the way friends do when trying to help you sort something out. Not that Nina was likely to warn her off.

'So what time is he planning to show up?'

'No idea,' said Susie, gathering her things together.

'Did he say he'd meet you at your place?'

'No, he didn't,' said Susie. 'What is this, the Spanish Inquisition? And before you break out the Monty Python jokes, unless we need to do something else I'm heading home. I'll be back around six.'

'Fair enough,' said Nina. 'I'll be here. I'm going to go home and change into my party frock.' She paused, and then did a quick twirl, catching her reflection in the studio windows. 'You know I really wish I'd bought the hat now.'

Susie laughed and headed out to the car park. A minute or two later she slid into her car and turned on the radio. It was going to be a long night, although realistically it went with the territory – the great and good gathering, sipping chardonnay, all dolled-up to the nines while engaged in some heavy-duty mingling and networking, college politics to the fore. That side of it was always hard work, but this year there was the added bonus of Simon, Saskia, Robert and possibly Matt. And if previous years were anything to go by there was a good chance her father would turn up, never being one to miss free booze and platefuls of party food.

Back at the cottage, Susie stepped under the shower, turned it up to full and let the water cascade down over her, hammering the tension out of her neck and shoulders. She had locked all the doors, windows and the back gate to make sure that she wasn't disturbed. She washed her hair, soaping and massaging her scalp, trying to ease the kinks out of her soul.

Another two weeks or so and the term would be over and done with, she could relax, do whatever it was that took her fancy, get up early, get up late, not have to worry about pleasing anyone but herself, least of all pleasing Robert, who had always been envious of her long summer break.

She was free – and for a split second Susie got a glimpse of how good that felt. She remembered the sense of elation and delight she'd had when she was first on her own with the children, after years and years inside a failing marriage that was neither good nor bad but certainly wasn't healthy, and the sense of relief she felt when it was all over. It had been tremendous, and even though she had been nervous about the future there had been a real sense of finally being free – and for an instant Susie tasted it again and knew that whatever happened, eventually, everything would turn out right.

She didn't need Robert, or anyone else come to that, to give her peace of mind or a sense of wellbeing. How was it that when in relationships it was so easy to forget that emotional stability was an internal, personal thing and not something doled out like sweeties by the man you were with?

She let the water carry on washing the knots and twists and aggravations of the last few days away, then finally, feeling scrubbed and shiny clean, climbed out and wrapped herself in a big fluffy bathrobe.

Supper was a quick sandwich and then she sat at her dressing table and very carefully did her hair and her face, slipped on the brown linen trouser ensemble and then looked in the full-length mirror at the results.

Funny how fifteen minutes in the shower and a little bit of self-help could make you look so very, very good. She grinned at her reflection, doing a few fashion-model poses to see how the outfit hung together. The jewellery made her neck look long and slender, the neat little sandals with a kitten heel made her legs look longer, and if she was going to give herself marks out of ten for that instant she would have gone the whole ten – possibly eleven. Adding a cloud of her favourite perfume, Susie picked up her bag and headed downstairs, singing as she went.

In the kitchen Milo had eaten the last of his supper and was curled up in his basket. After years of experience he recognised going-out gear when he saw it and closed his eyes, a study in happy indolence. Before she went out of the door Susie checked her phone.

There was a message from her dad and Adele, who it seemed, were having a great time. 'Sorry we won't be there tonight, we've seen a couple of places we really like. Food is great – lovely walks –'And then in the background Susie could pick out Adele's voice. 'She said I should have rung you earlier on in the week. My fault, you know what I'm like with bloody dates.' And then obviously over his shoulder he continued, 'I would have but she's never bloody there and I hate answering mac—' and then he got cut off. Susie smiled. He sounded happy as Larry.

She had been hoping that Simon would ring to let her know what time he was arriving – she'd got no idea whether he planned to meet her at the cottage or the college. Ah well, he'd have to take his chances because having had a quick update on her dad she needed to be gone.

Chapter 19

Someone had put a red carpet down outside the main entrance to the college, which was a nice touch. Obviously they're expecting me, Susie thought with a wry smile.

'Would you like a programme, Mrs Reed?'

'They're catalogues,' said Susie, taking one from the tall gingery girl who had pulled the short straw and was doing the early-bird shift on front of house.

The girl nodded and then giggled self-consciously. 'Sorry.' She glanced back over her shoulder into the interior of the foyer. 'There's some great stuff in there. I really like them lizards.'

Susie had to agree with her. There really was some great stuff in this year's show. She had deliberately come in through the punters' entrance to try and gauge what their experience would be like – and on the whole it was impressive. The way in was flanked by tropical plants and the tall, tumbling, bubbling, stainless-steel water features, and then beyond the main door the eye was led, thanks to a lot of tinkering with plants, light and boards, to a life-sized sculpture of a satyr. Beyond, you were drawn into a beautifully lit, curving labyrinth of stands, bays and wall-mounted art, which, god willing and a fair wind, should lead the guests round through all the different exhibits – although Susie's and Nina's experience was that however well you planned it, the first port of call and sometimes only port of call for a lot of the guests was the bar and buffet area. Nevertheless, this year was an exceptionally beautiful layout, greatly enhanced by Saskia's extraordinary jungle planting – which was what they planned to say in the end-of-event report.

'Well, looky, looky, don't you look the cat's pyjamas?' giggled Nina.

Susie swung round and took in Nina's outfit. 'You don't look so bad yourself,' she said.

Nina took a little bow. Once upon a time her outfit had probably been a perfectly respectable summer suit, but since then it had been heartily stripped down and souped up by a sartorial anarchist. The plum- and gold-coloured suit was worn with black tights, a broad leather belt, hand-painted combat boots, with cream biker socks folded neatly down over the boot tops. From somewhere a large piece of fabric in an almost identical colour to the suit, but a lot silkier – possibly the jacket lining – had been used to make a headpiece that Nina had tied around her dreadlocks, teased and twisted up like an African tribeswoman. The effect was extraordinary, very, very striking, and in an odd way it all came together beautifully to make it a stunning hippy-chick outfit not a ragbag of pieces. Susie was always slightly in awe of how Nina managed to pull off outfits like this.

'So,' Nina rolled her wrist and looked at her watch. 'We're in the final countdown, honey. Time for a glass of wine and something small and slimy in a pastry case, I think.'

Gamely, Susie followed Nina over to where the students were arranging glasses on trays and sorting out the food under the watchful eye of the staff from the Hotel and Catering department. One of the lecturers, dressed in full catering whites, big hat and checked trousers, grinned as they pushed open the doors to the impromptu prep area. 'Might have guessed it would be you pair.'

Nina made the effort to look offended while he poured her a glass of wine, and Susie – waving the wine away – took a glass of apple juice.

Susie looked around at the hum of last-minute activity. The sense of being in the calm before the storm had been with her all day. Realistically nobody was going to turn up fashionably late for tonight's do – quite the reverse if anything, proud parents turned up early to get a good look at what their child had been beavering away at all year, friends of the mature students stopped by on their way to somewhere else, not planning to stay for long unless the conversation and the canapés captured them. So it wasn't all that long before people began to congregate outside, around the main doors. Nina, meanwhile, was busy chatting away to the chef.

Susie looked around anxiously and checked her watch, keeping an eye out for Simon, just as Austin appeared.

'How much longer before we let people in?' Susie asked, as he took a glass of wine from the tray closest to him once the usual pleasantries had been exchanged.

'Another five minutes. Although it would be nice if we could keep them out of the main exhibition area until the principal comes down and tells us how clever he's been this year. I've asked the front-of-house people to put up some of that nice new rope-and-post stuff they were so keen to get their hands on at the last budgeting round, give him a bit of an arena.'

'And what time will his nibs be here?'

'Well he's promised bang on seven, so we'll see.' Austin's attention wandered to a tray in one of the coolers. 'Umm, what are those exactly?' he said, pointing enthusiastically.

Susie watched as the girl who had been loading it slipped the tray back out for him to select the one with the biggest prawn, and realised as he smiled at her that she was nervous.

It came as a complete surprise. Normally events like this didn't faze Susie at all. She had been involved in god knew how many shows, first nights and exhibitions over the years, but tonight she had butterflies. Great big butterflies. Taking a deep breath she tuned into the conversation Nina was having with the chef. It didn't help. Austin was preoccupied with the food and what time the principal was making his appearance, and whether his wife would mind driving home. As he chatted on, Susie's sense of anxiety grew. What the hell was that about?

'Okay, I think it's show-time, folks, don't you?' said

Austin, consulting his watch for the umpteenth time. Nina agreed, Susie nodded, and they, along with the rest of the department, made their way out into the foyer, and with a couple of words from Nina the front-of-house girls opened up the main doors.

There was a really nice little buzz of voices and laughter as the people made their way inside. Bang on seven the principal came down and gave a speech, although the sound system wasn't that brilliant so anyone more than six feet away had no idea what he was talking about, although everyone applauded rapturously when he finished.

Susie mingled. There was a lot of cheery hello-ing and 'how are you's from students and guests. Small talk bubbled and babbled all around her. And all the time Susie kept looking across the crowd trying to see if she could spot a familiar face amongst the others. It didn't take long.

Around half past seven, Saskia, clutching Robert's arm like she would keel over if she let go, teetered in through the main entrance on impossibly high heels. She looked amazing, lightly tanned and dressed in a chic little black number, her hair up, earrings, engagement ring and matching necklace glittering under the spotlights.

As she processed towards the start of the exhibition, Saskia looked left and right, smiling in an unfocused starry way. A tad overdressed, she really looked like she was there for a proper gallery opening night and deserved every inch of the red carpet. The principal, immediately assuming she was somebody important, was already heading her way with his hand out to greet her.

Spotting Susie, she waved. Susie waved back, feeling slightly sick, although she couldn't have looked any sicker than Robert, who wore the pasty-grey look of a condemned man.

'Well, don't they look the happy couple,' said Nina, heavy on the sarcasm as she handed Susie another glass of apple juice.

'Aren't we supposed to be mingling?'

Nina pulled a face. 'By the time we get this show up and running I'm always knackered, to be frank I'm all mingled out. Nice of Jack to come along and cheer you on, though.'

'Jack's here?'

'Yes, didn't you know? I saw him a couple of minutes ago over by the lizards. He scrubs up really well,' she purred.

'Hands off, he's my little boy. He said he wasn't coming.'

'Well, he lied,' said Nina. 'Oh look, there he is.'

Susie swung round to see not just Jack but Matt as well, making their way through the little outcrops of people towards her. Seeing the two of them really lifted her spirits.

Jack hugged her enthusiastically. 'You're right, it looks really good this year. Love the plants. And you look fab.'

'I didn't think you were coming,' she said.

Jack lifted a glass in salute. 'What, and miss your moment of glory?' He paused, Susie waiting. 'Actually, Adam is back home tonight and there is only so much billing and cooing and tears of joy I can cope with without throwing up.'

'They're sorting it out?'

'Oh god, and then some, last thing I heard was that Alice asked him to move back.'

'Oh that's wonderful – but what about Adam's new job in Manchester?'

'What job in Manchester?' asked Jack.

'Adam just took a job up there –' Susie began, although something about Jack's expression stopped her short. 'What?' she said. 'What am I missing here?'

'There never was a job in Manchester,' said Jack with a wink.

Susie stared at him. 'What do you mean there wasn't one?'

'It was my idea. It was ripping the two of them to bits, all this bloody TA stuff – and Alice can be such a stubborn cow. I knew if she thought Adam was really going away it would make her realise that actually she adored him and she can't manage without him. Those two are made for each other.'

Susie smiled. 'You are a devious little bugger.'

Jack grinned. 'Why, thank you, ma'am.'

Susie turned to Matt.

'Don't look at me,' he said, holding his hands up in surrender. 'Golden boy here came up with that one all on his own.' He closed in to give her a hug.

'Uh-huh, that's true,' said Jack. 'Matt just rang up and asked for Adam at home and said how excited he was that Adam was going to join us – him – them – the new company.'

Matt shrugged. 'What can I say? It seems to have worked.'

He was dressed in a crisp white shirt under a long dark jacket with a Nehru collar and jeans, hair brushed back. He looked gorgeous.

'I don't know what to say about that – but thank you so much for coming this evening and lying to my daughter, I'm really pleased to see you,' Susie said.

'Thanks for inviting me.' He grinned. 'You look fabulous.'

Susie blushed. 'You too,' she said, delighted that he'd noticed. 'How are things going?'

'Not bad, actually – you know that we've got the dig on up north?'

'How's it coming along?'

'Okay, another couple of weeks – we've more or less got a team together – should be fun if you like life in the great outdoors, driving rain, wind like razor blades and being dive-bombed by mosquitoes the size of corgis.'

'Sounds perfect.'

'You should try it sometime. As I said, we can always do with a good artist on site, and the dog can come along for the ride.' He paused. 'I was wondering if maybe we could have some supper once you've finished up here – I'm not sure how much time I'm going to have free between now and shipping off up north.'

Susie hesitated. The truth was she really wanted to accept, but there was Simon to consider. 'The thing is –' she began.

'Oh don't worry about me,' said Jack, pulling his hard-done-by puppy face. 'Leave me all on my tod. I'll go and get a burger somewhere, press my poor little face against the window, looking in at the rich folks. And you realise of course now that Adam's moving back in with Alice I'm homeless again.'

Susie stared at him. 'What about Ellie?'

He sighed and shook his head.

'Oh Jack,' Susie began, but before she could think of anything to say Jack continued, 'So it looks like I'm going to have to shack up with Matt and his hideous carpet after all.'

Susie looked at Matt. 'But I thought Alex was moving back in?'

Matt shook his head. 'No – no, it didn't take either of us long to realise it was a complete mistake. We've both come a long way since we split up. So – no going back.'

'I'm so sorry,' she said.

Jack grinned. 'Alex's loss, my gain.'

Matt shrugged. 'Alex and I had been together a long time. Realistically it was over and done with years ago. We just didn't recognise it.'

Susie smiled and touched his arm. 'I'm still sorry, breaking up is never easy, whenever it happens.'

He smiled. 'No – so, about supper?'

Susie looked up into his gentle big brown eyes. 'I'd really love to, b—'

Jack groaned, cutting her off. 'God, I'm going to have to sit in the high chair, aren't I, and pick from the little person's menu?'

'What's this about menus?' asked Nina, all ears.

'Me, Mum and Matt are going on to eat afterwards. You want to come too?' said Jack brightly.

Nina looked questioningly at Susie. 'Sure, would you mind if I brought Ralph and Eddie along – they're the guys from the gallery I was telling you about? Oh, and Electric Mickey and his wife are around here somewhere.'

Matt looked at Susie. 'What do you reckon, the more the merrier?'

Susie nodded. He was smiling. 'Fine by me,' she said. 'Now, if you'll excuse me I have to go and mingle a bit more and check up to make sure everything's running smoothly. I won't be long.'

'I thought you were supposed to be having supper with Simon,' hissed Nina as they headed across the room.

'I was, but you know what? I really can't be bothered. Having supper with you lot will be so much more fun. Matt is a nice man, he's great company, and I'd rather be with friends I trust than some good-looking sleaze who is going to string me along. I don't know what Simon's game is but my spider senses tell me I don't know the half of it. Something's not right. And my feeling is it's not going to end well.'

Nina nodded. 'Can't argue with that. So what are you going to tell Simon when he turns up?'

Susie grinned, taking a drink from a passing tray. '*If* he turns up? I'm going to tell him that I've had a better offer.'

Nina laughed.

'Susie? There you are. I've been trying to catch up with you all evening.' Susie turned at the sound of her name to come face to face with Robert. He looked haunted and nervous. It struck her that she wasn't the only one who had lost weight.

'How nice to see you,' she said. Her voice sounded flat and formal. 'Glad you could make it.'

Like Matt, she'd come a long way too.

'I didn't feel I'd got much choice really. Saskia said that we had to come.'

'Well she has worked very hard,' Susie said, casting an eye around the profusion of greenery. 'The plants have really added something this year, don't you think?'

Robert pulled a peculiar face. 'If you say so. I can't stay long. She gets –'

Susie took a sip of apple juice. 'You told me.'

'The thing is, Susie, I don't know what I'm going to do. I think she's –'

Susie cut him off. 'Robert, you know I really don't care what she is. This has absolutely nothing to do with me. *Capisce?*'

He looked at her. 'But I was depending on you. When we talked the other day, I thought you understood – I need you, Susie, can't you see that? I can't talk to Saskia like I talk to you. I thought you were my friend.'

Susie looked at him. She didn't know whether to be angry or just plain sad. In the end, holding his gaze, she said, 'Go away, Robert.'

He looked hurt. 'Please, Susie.' He hesitated. 'I've made the most awful mistake – I love you.'

The words hit her like a body blow but she didn't let it show.

'*Now*,' said Susie. Still he hesitated. 'For god's sake, Robert. Grow up. You made your choice and now you have to live with it. I've got better things to do with my time than stand around listening to you whine.'

She saw his jaw drop, saw him take a breath to speak, but didn't hang around long enough to hear what else he planned to say. The sense of elation and power as she made her way across the room made her head spin.

The pain of missing Robert was still there, but it had almost faded. She couldn't reconcile the man with her memory of him. Knowing that Saskia wasn't quite the compliant fertile fairy princess Robert had hoped for was a great second prize but fell way short of what she now knew. Over the last few weeks she had been trying to convince herself that Robert wasn't what she wanted or needed, but now she knew, without a shadow of a doubt, that it was absolutely true.

Robert wasn't the man her imagination had him cracked up to be and never had been. She really had moved on.

Once Susie had done the rounds, chatting to parents and students, staff and guests, she made her way back to Matt who was talking to Nina and Jack, who was flirting outrageously with a couple of the girls in one of Susie's classes.

Matt handed Susie a drink as she stepped into the group.

'Thanks,' she said, moving in alongside him. 'Having a good time?'

'Not bad. Simon not here yet, then?'

Susie looked up at him in surprise. 'No, I'm not sure what time he'll show up.'

'If he turns up at all,' added Jack. 'You know what he's like. Would you lot excuse me, only Lily and her friend over here were just going to show me their work.'

Susie smiled; there was definitely more than a little chemical attraction going on between Jack and the girls. Matt lifted his glass in salute as they headed off through the crowd laughing.

'It's nice to see him looking happier, it's been hard for him too. The whole Ellie thing.'

Susie nodded. 'Relationships are such a bloody nightmare, sometimes it makes you wonder why we bother.'

Matt looked at her, eyes sparkling with amusement. 'Oh, my, my, cynical or what.'

Susie pulled a face. 'Come on, nothing hurts quite like it.'

'True, but when it's going well there is nothing on earth that feels like being in love, being loved, caring for someone.' As he spoke his eyes didn't leave hers. 'I miss that.'

'If you can find the right person,' she said, and as she did Susie got an odd feeling inside, that fuzzy, heady feeling you get when you fancy someone. She took a long pull on her apple juice. 'I'm sure you'll find someone, Matt,' she said. 'You deserve to find someone nice – you're a great guy.'

The mischievous look stayed firmly in Matt's eyes. 'Well, thanks,' he said.

Susie looked away, feeling her colour rise. God, her

radar really needed recalibrating. He leant closer. Unexpectedly Susie felt her stomach flutter; god, he was gorgeous. This was so crazy. She could hear Nina talking behind her but found herself in that odd vacuum that cuts out every sight, every sound except for the person you are focused on. Her brain tried the idea out again – *the person you fancy*. Susie sighed. No doubt about it, she really was on a hiding to nothing if she fancied Matt Peters.

And then a very odd thing happened. Just as Susie was thinking that she should really get out more, Matt slipped his arm very gently around her waist and pulled her closer, and very, very slowly he kissed her. The touch of his lips on hers made Susie go weak at the knees.

She pulled back, breathless, heart beating furiously, totally bemused. This was even crazier. Life was complicated enough already.

'Why on earth did you do that? I can't do this,' she spluttered, hands on Matt's chest, pushing him away. 'I'm really sorry, but you know – there's the whole Alex thing. I mean, it's not that I'm not attracted to you because I am –' which, said aloud, came as a bit of a surprise to Susie if not Matt '– but – and, trust me, I am broad-minded, but I – well, I wouldn't be comfortable knowing that – well. I'm not . . .' The words came out as a jumble, a great self-conscious embarrassed muddle. Meanwhile it was Matt's turn to look bemused and slightly uncomfortable.

'I'm so sorry,' he said. 'I didn't mean to upset you – I thought it was okay. I thought it was what you wanted. What we both wanted.'

Susie felt her colour deepen. 'Well, it is. I mean it was, just then, at that particular moment, but what about Alex?'

Matt looked even more confused. 'I thought I just explained. It's over between me and Alex. Since we've been talking recently it's become more and more obvious that she had someone else lined up even before she moved out. To be honest I'm not sure why she wanted to give it another go. I've got a horrible suspicion she was trying to work out which of us was the best option.'

Out of all those words, Susie only heard one thing. *She.*

'Alex is a woman,' she said, almost to herself.

'Yes, of course she's a woman.' Matt stared at her and there was a funny little pause and then she saw comprehension dawn and then he smiled, and then he laughed. 'You thought Alex was a man, didn't you?'

Susie cringed. How could she possibly deny it? 'I didn't have a problem with it,' she said quickly. 'It was kind of a relief really. I thought that we could be friends – and that there wouldn't be any pressure. You know – with you being gay.' Her voice trailed off. 'Sorry.'

'No need to be sorry,' Matt laughed. 'It certainly explains a lot, I thought I'd lost my touch.' And with that he kissed her again and this time Susie kissed him back.

'Mmmm, you know I've been waiting for ages to do that, I just wanted the right moment,' he said.

At which point Nina turned up and looked from one to the other. Susie could see her considering what to say, and finally she settled on, 'Just thought I'd let you know, Simon's arrived.'

'Oh, okay,' said Susie, feeling no conflict of interest, feeling no real anything about Simon.

'He's brought someone with him,' said Nina.

'Fair enough,' said Susie. The only someone she could think of was Ellie or Simon's ex-wife. Neither presented any problem, except perhaps to Jack, who, by the look of it, was busy playing chase me, chase me with one of her final-year students.

However, Nina lingered pointedly.

'I better go and find them, then,' Susie said to Matt. 'I won't be long.'

He looked at her, an electric charge arcing between them. 'You're not going to change your mind, are you?'

'About what?' she asked.

'Supper, me, you, the whole possible us thing – I've got a table booked at this great place down by the river. Actually, thinking about it I'd better see if they can do one for –'

He looked at Nina. 'Eight, so far,' she said.

'Eight,' said Matt to Susie.

Susie grinned. 'With that many people you won't notice if I'm not there.'

'Oh, believe me, I will,' said Matt.

'Okay, well in that case, I promise I'm not going to change my mind. I'll be back in five –'

'With Simon?'

'Possibly. We're the only people he knows here, but don't worry, I won't be inviting him to supper.'

Nina fell into step beside Susie as they made their

way across the hall. 'Was it my imagination or were you just snogging him?'

'I was,' said Susie. She felt warm and smiley, and full of bubbly possibilities. It was almost like having a head full of pink champagne.

'So what are we saying here? That he plays at home *and away*? I mean, I'm as broad-minded as the next woman but –'

'Alex is a woman.'

'What?'

'*Alex is a woman.*'

'Who the hell is Alex?'

'Matt's ex, her name is Alex. I put two and two together –'

'And came up with Julian Clary?'

Susie nodded. 'God, yes. More or less. Where did you say Simon was?'

Nina pointed over towards the buffet. Standing under one of Saskia's beautiful palm trees, Simon looked every inch the off-duty rock star. Open-neck shirt, blond hair swept back off his perma-tanned face to reveal those carefully preserved features and perfectly veneered smile. He carried himself with the air of a man who was somebody. And next to him was somebody else. A very tall, Junoesque, Latino woman, with a mass of shiny black hair. She was wearing a short cerise dress that left only the barest of essentials to the imagination. She had lots of jewellery on, some matching, some toning, some just out-and-out loud – and all of it with lots and lots of bling. She was wearing equally large amounts of make-up and the highest heels

369

that Susie had ever seen outside of a cartoon, accentuating her long, heavily set legs. How she walked in them was beyond Susie, who nevertheless made her way over to them.

'Simon,' Susie said as she drew level with him. 'How nice to see you.' Her tone was deliberately neutral. His companion meanwhile swung round and eyed Susie up like the range-finder on a Chieftain tank.

'Susie, lovely to see you,' Simon said. She could hear the appeal in his tone and see the sheer panic in his eyes. He caught hold of her hand and clasped it firmly in a presidential handshake, pulling her closer and air-kissing each cheek. 'Call me,' he hissed in a whisper.

Susie hastily stepped away.

'Thank you for coming. Aren't you going to introduce me to your friend?' she said, smiling in the direction of his Amazonian companion.

'You got that wrong, honey, I ain't no friend of his,' said the woman proprietorially in a voice Susie recognised from their recent phone conversation. 'My name is Romeen – and I'm Simon's wife.'

Susie stared at the woman for an instant. She had been anticipating all kinds of explanations and excuses for the phone call, but she hadn't been expecting this one.

'Well, delighted to meet you, I'm sure,' she said briskly, sounding like a young Joyce Grenfell. 'I hope that you both enjoy the exhibition. Now if you'll excuse me –'

She could see an expression of panic in Simon's eyes.

God only knew what was going on but she didn't plan to be party to any of it. With a pleasant smile she turned on her heel and made her way back towards Matt.

'Susie, Susie,' Simon called after her. 'I was rather hoping that we could talk.'

'I'm awfully sorry,' she said, the words spoken over her shoulder, 'but I'm busy at the moment.' And as Susie walked away it felt as if a great weight had been lifted off her shoulders.

When she got back to Matt, he was smiling. 'So we're still okay for supper?'

Susie nodded. 'Yes – I'm sorry about, you know.'

He laughed. 'Alex?'

Susie nodded. 'You must think I'm a complete idiot – I really thought – well, if it's any consolation I thought it would be great to have you as a friend, someone to talk to – someone to rescue me.' She grinned. 'Sounds like a bit of a one-way street but you know what I'm saying. Whoever you were dating I thought we could be friends.' Susie paused. 'Have I dug myself a big enough hole yet? Okay – what can I tell you? My intuition is completely crap. Every time I got a little flutter about you I kept telling myself I was being stupid.'

Matt grinned as she squirmed. 'A little flutter – so you fancied me from the start, did you?' he said mischievously.

Susie reddened. 'Might have – how about you?'

He topped up her glass. 'From the minute I first saw you.'

Susie smiled.

'You okay?' he asked.

'You know, I really think that I am. Were you serious about needing an artist on the Scottish dig?'

He nodded, eyes twinkling. 'Absolutely. Were you thinking of applying?'

She took the glass he offered her. 'I might be. I've been thinking, I could really use an adventure.'

He grinned. 'It'll be adventure all right, if you like life in the great outdoors, driving rain, wind like razor blades and being dive-bombed by mosquitoes the size of corgis. Be the perfect way to test your theory about whether or not we could be friends.'

'And the whole me, you, possible us thing,' Susie said.

Matt nodded.

She grinned. 'Sounds absolutely perfect.'

And with that Matt kissed her again.

Read on for an exclusive extract of Kate Lawson's
new book, coming in 2009

Chapter 1

'Blonde wig, sunglasses –' Cass looked herself up and down in the rococo mirror leaning up against the wall in the spare room, turning left and right to gauge the full effect and then shook her head. As a makeover, it wasn't exactly a roaring success.

'Fiona, I can't go out dressed in this. I look like a hooker.'

'No, you don't. Of course you don't,' Fee said briskly, tugging Cass's wig down at the back. 'You look –' she hesitated, making it painfully obvious she was struggling to find the right words.

'Conspicuous and very dodgy?' suggested Cass. 'Let's be honest, it's the last thing you want from a spy.'

Fee's expression hardened. 'Spy is a very emotive word,' she snapped, handing her a trench coat and a rolled black umbrella.

'And these are meant to help me blend in, are they? I really don't think this is a very good idea, Fiona,' Cass laughed, dropping the umbrella onto the bed. 'I barely know Andy.'

'Exactly.'

'What do you mean, *exactly*?'

'Well, if you knew him well you could hardly spy on him, could you? He'd get suspicious, but this is fine. You know Andy just well enough to recognise him in a crowd, or pick him out in a bar, but not well enough for him to come rushing over, or worse still, go rushing off.' As she spoke, Fiona flicked Cass's collar up and fluffed the wig so it looked a little more tousled. 'There we are,' she said. 'That's perfect.'

From a large overstuffed chair on the landing, Mungo, the resident ginger tom, and Buster, Cass's matching mongrel, watched proceedings with interest.

'I mean, it's not like I'm asking you to bug him. All you have to do is watch, take a few photos – and possibly notes – and let me know exactly what he is up to. I know he's up to something.' Fiona paused; there were no two ways about it, she definitely did look stressed. 'I wouldn't ask but I can't afford a private detective and I don't know what else to do.' She sounded upset or maybe angry or possibly both; it was hard to tell which.

'Does your mobile phone have a camera with a zoom lens?' Fiona asked as she buttoned Cass into the trench coat.

This wasn't exactly how Cass had imagined the evening going at all. She'd been thinking more in terms of a DVD, maybe a bottle of wine, possibly a take-away.

She'd known Fiona for the last three or four years since they started singing together in Mrs Althorpe's Community All Stars – the local choir, which was a lot sexier and loads more fun than it sounded.

As lady basses and occasional tenors, they did a lot of well synchronised *do-be-do-be-doos, dms,* and finger snapping that made up the heartbeat of the doo-wop and blues numbers the band was famous for knocking out at carnivals, festivals and community gatherings of all kinds and colours. Fiona usually stood next to her, in front of the male basses.

Originally Cass had joined the choir because she hated her aerobics lessons and wanted an opportunity to sing and meet men. While she had met men, most of them were well over fifty, and all were mad as a haddock.

Fiona had joined a couple of terms later because she was bored with conversational Spanish.

For performances the All Stars always wore full evening dress, men in black tie and occasionally tails, the women shimmying and swaying in every colour under the sun, all glitzy and glamorous and very over the top with lots of diamante, ecru feathers, tiaras and an ocean of bugle beads. It certainly beat workout Lycra.

After their Tuesday evening rehearsal, the choir traditionally went on to the pub and although there was some cross-pollination between the various groups, for the most part people did tend to stay in their sections. This was how Cass and Fiona came to find themselves squeezed into the end of a pew, behind a long table in the snug bar of the Old Grey Whippet, alongside Ray, Phil and Welsh Alf whose voice came straight from the heart of the Rhonda – which didn't quite compensate for the fact that he often forgot the tune and occasionally the words – and Norman who only came because his wife had an evening class across the road on Tuesday nights and didn't drive.

While they weren't exactly friends, they did often chat between songs, agonise over learning new words and try to help each other to find the right starting note. And they giggled a lot.

Their only real gripe was that while the sopranos got the tune and the altos had the harmony, the tenors grabbed the twiddly bits, so nine times out of ten all the basses got were the notes left over and they didn't always make much sense musically. There certainly wasn't much in the way of a catchy little tune to hum to while making toast. When Cass joined there had only been one man, Welsh Alf, so, Alan – their musical director – had suggested that some of the female altos sing the bass parts, an octave higher (which at that point meant nothing to Cass, who hadn't sung a note anywhere other than in the bath since leaving Callaby County Primary aged eleven). Four years on, there were half a dozen men and around the same number of women in the bass section, with a sprinkling of men in the tenors and of course Gordon in the sopranos, who sang falsetto, plucked his eyebrows and occasionally wore eyeliner.

So, after choir on Tuesday evening everyone was just finishing a blow-by-blow dissection of how the evening's rehearsal had gone and Gordon was at the bar halfway down his second Babycham, when Fiona, who was sipping a bitter lemon said, 'I was wondering if you could do me a favour?'

Cass looked round. Fiona said it casually, in a way

that suggested she wanted Cass to pick up a few bits from Tesco on her way home from work or maybe pop round to let the gas man in, and so halfway down a glass of house red, Cass nodded, 'sure. What would you like me to do?'

But before she could answer, Bert, the big chunky tenor, an ex-rugby player who sang like an angel, drank like a fish and was tight as new elastic, said, 'Anyone fancy a top up, only it's m'birthday, so I'm in the chair.' And Fiona's reply was lost in the furore.

'Maybe it would be easier if I popped round some time?' Fiona shouted above the general hullabaloo, as people fought their way to the bar to put their orders in.

'Good idea,' said Cass, easing her way to the front.

Which was why they were now standing in Cass's spare room with a suitcase full of props and the remains of a bottle of Archers, which Fiona had brought round as a liquid inducement. It had slipped down a treat. Unlike Fiona's little favour.

It had taken Fee a couple of glasses, a lot of idle chit-chat and much admiring of Cass's cottage before she managed to get around to what she had in mind. What Fiona wanted, it seemed, was a little light surveillance. More specifically she wanted Cass to follow her live-in boyfriend, Andy, and find out what he was up to, where, when and with whom, although so far the reasons behind it were a little hazy.

'So what exactly has brought this on?' asked Cass. 'If I'm going to go the full Mata Hari at least I should know what I'm getting myself into.'

'I'm convinced that Andy's seeing someone,' said Fiona, gazing past her into the mirror trying, presumably, to gauge the effectiveness of Cass's disguise.

'Because?'

'He's been acting strangely. First of all he's changed the password on his email account.'

'And you know this *because*?'

'Well, when I was on his computer I couldn't get into his email,' replied Fiona, casually.

'You read his email?'

At least Fiona had the decency to look a bit sheepish. 'Of course I do, doesn't everyone? I mean we're practically married . . .'

'And that makes it all right?'

'What on earth has right got to do with it?'

'So presumably Andy's got your password too?' asked Cass, helping herself to a hand full of nachos from a bowl she had brought through and put on the dressing table. Shame she hadn't had the forethought to bring the Archers as well, really.

Fiona looked outraged. 'No, of course not, but that's different – I mean I'm not up to anything.'

'Having another email account is hardly any proof of being up to anything though, is it?'

'He keeps getting texts.'

'Oh for goodness sake, Fee, we all get texts.'

'Which he erases,' Fiona countered. 'I know because I've looked while he's in the shower.'

Cass wasn't sure there was any sane answer to that. The trouble was that if you think someone is up to something, then experience told her that your mind was only too happy to fill in the gaps, invent the evidence, and everything they did only conspired to make them look more suspicious. And that while it sounded crazy from this side of the fence, no doubt inside Fiona's head it sounded just fine. Cass's ex husband had been just the same. This was the man who had gone through all their old phone bills to see who she'd been calling, monitored her car's mileage and accused her of making a pass at the postman. What some might consider to be jealousy, insecurity and uncertainty could be an all-engulfing madness.

'How long have you two been together?' asked Cass, adjusting the wig and adding a bit more lipstick. She had always wondered how she'd look as a blonde; maybe she needed something a little less Barbie.

'Seven years. And you know what they say about the seven-year itch. If he's got nothing to hide then why does he keep wiping the inbox on his phone, why does he have a new email account and why does he sneak about? Did I tell you he's been sneaking about?'

'Have you thought it might be because you're trying to break into his email account, read his phone messages and are currently setting someone up to stalk him?'

Fiona considered the possibility for a few seconds and then shook her head. 'Don't be ridiculous. Andy's got no idea he's going to be stalked. He's up to something, I know he is, and I want you to find out exactly what it is.'

'Because?'

'Well, because we're friends. I'd do the same for you.'

Cass stared at her. 'Really?'

'Oh God, yes,' said Fiona, the woman who the previous term had refused point blank to lend Cass a tenner when they were out on a gig and she found she'd left her handbag backstage. 'Neither a lender or a borrower be,' had been Fiona's sage advice as she'd headed off towards the cafeteria.

'Fee, my handbag is locked in the green room; I only want to get a coffee and a sandwich. You can have the money back before we go home.'

At which point Fiona had smiled a funny vague little smile and said, 'My mother always used to say "don't ask for credit, a refusal may offend".'

Cass considered for a moment. 'Did your mum run a corner shop?'

'No, she was on the game,' said Welsh Alf, who had been standing behind them, straightening his bow tie and obviously earwigging while checking his reflection in a window. 'Here,' he pulled a wad of notes out of his back pocket. 'How much do you need?'

'A tenner,' said Cass.

He peeled a note off and handed it to her.

'Thank you – that's great. You can have it back once Dudley Do-right in janitorial services unlocks the dressing-room door,' Cass said.

Alf waved the words away. 'Whenever, I trust you,' he said and turned his attentions to combing what was left of his hair into a rock and roll quiff, patting any bootblack well-greased stragglers carefully into place with his fingertips.

*   *   *

'I don't think blonde's really my colour, do you?' asked Cass, narrowing her eyes – not that it improved things much. 'Maybe something with a bit more caramel?'

'Can we please concentrate?' snapped Fiona. 'Andy's going to be at Sam's Place, Saturday night, around eight. I've brought my camera with me just in case yours didn't have a zoom.'

Cass looked at her. 'Sam's Place?'

'Uhuh you know, the trendy new place not long opened – by the old cinema.'

Cass shook her head.

'Oh come on, you must have seen it. It's been all over the local papers. They did a double-page spread in the *Argos*, and a thing on local TV. Some guy off the telly is one of the business partners in it; he used to be in *The Bill*. There's a cocktail bar and restaurant, all retro Casablanca and with a nightclub upstairs. I've been trying to persuade Andy to take me for weeks.' Fiona paused. 'You know what he said?'

Cass decided it would probably be wiser not to make any suggestions, so made an *I have no idea face* instead.

'He said, "Fee, darling, you're nearly 40, I'm even older so what in God's name do we want to go there for? Clubbing at our age? It's ridiculous." That's what he said, Cass, "*ridiculous*". It was horrible. It made me sound like some sort of desperate pensioner.'

Fiona was wearing a skirt that was bang on trend if you happened to be 18, a pair of Christian Louboutin knock offs and a haircut that cost more than Cass's sofa; maybe 'pensioner' was a bit cruel but 'desperate' wasn't far short of the mark.

'So you haven't been?'

Fiona shook her head. 'No, of course I haven't been, but now it looks as if he's going to be going without me. There was a message on the pad in his office – 'Sam's Place, 8 o'clock, and what looks like next Saturday's date. I was going to bring it with me.'

'Did you ask Andy about it? I mean surely if he left a note on his desk he meant for you to see it,' asked Cass cautiously.

'He would think I was mad.'

Cass decided not to comment. 'Maybe he's planning to surprise you?'

Fiona didn't look convinced.

'Why don't you just ask him? He left you a note – in plain sight –'

'The thing is,' Fiona answered, after a few seconds. 'It wasn't actually the note I saw, and Andy didn't leave it out on the desk for me to see. It was more an impression on the pad underneath. I could see that it had something written on it, but I couldn't really make it out.'

'Right,' murmured Cass in an undertone. This was getting weirder by the second.

'Anyway I saw this thing on a film once, you get a soft pencil and then very lightly shade over the indentations,' Fiona mimed the action.

Cass had heard enough. 'Ok, I think that is about enough, Fiona – this is nuts. You need to talk to Andy about all this stuff. It's crazy and I'm not doing it.' She pulled off the wig and dropped it onto the bed. 'I'm sorry but I really don't think this is a good idea. Do you want to be with Andy?'

Fiona stared at Cass as if the question hadn't crossed her mind. 'Well of course I do,' she snapped. 'Why on earth would I go to all this trouble if I didn't want to be with him? Have you got any idea how hard it is to get a decent blonde wig?'

'Well in that case you need to talk to Andy, not go creeping about spying on him'. Cass slipped off the trench coat. 'I'm really sorry, Fee. I'd be glad to help but not like this.'

Fiona looked as if she was about to speak, and then she hesitated, and then she bit her lip, and then her eyes filled up with tears, and then she started stuffing things into her holdall, the wig, the brolly –

Cass sighed, feeling guilty. 'Fee –' she began.

'I thought you'd understand,' Fiona said, between sobs, rolling the coat into a ball.

'I do,' said Cass. 'Really, I do, but this isn't going to achieve anything.'

'How do you know unless we try?' cried Fiona. 'I thought you were my friend. I don't know what else to do.' As she spoke, Fiona carried on gathering things up.

'Fee, let's talk about this,' said Cass, but it was too late. The last thing Cass saw was Fiona heading out of the door with not so much as a backward glance.

'Oh bugger,' cried Cass in frustration.

The Chinese takeaway they'd ordered arrived half an hour later. Mungo and Buster waited by the kitchen door on standby; there was no way Cass was going to manage all those chicken balls on her own.

Chapter 2

'Excuse me, Miss, Miss?'

Cass glanced up from her book and looked at the man framed in the shop doorway.

'I was wondering if you could help me? Is that computer desk out the front Chippendale?'

The guy was six two, maybe six three, tanned, with great teeth and an Armani jacket dressed down over good jeans and a black tee shirt. He had subtle high-lights in his thick-swept back, blonde hair, and there was just the hint of a transatlantic twang in that voice somewhere, making his accent hard to pin down. He had shoulders broad enough to make a grown woman weep and the biggest, brownest eyes. If he were a spaniel, women would arm-wrestle each other to take him home.

Cass closed her book and nodded. 'Uhuh, it most certainly is, and you see that TV cabinet in the back there? The black ash one, with the stainless steel knobs?' She pointed off into the shadows, down between a bentwood hat stand and the little painted pine chiffonier that she'd sold earlier in the day.

The man looked around. 'Which? Oh right – oh yes, that's very nice.'

'Hepplewhite. Genuine George III,' she said.

'No?' said the man, extending the *oooo* sound to express his incredulity. 'My God, really? I'd imagine they are just so hard to find.'

'In that kind of condition.' Cass said. 'Rare as hen's teeth.'

'Oh my God, this is just too wonderful. I've got just the place for them – do you take cards? Do you think we can maybe do a deal on the two pieces?'

'Maybe, but there's been a lot of interest in them.'

'I'd imagine there has been. What's your best price?'

Cass considered for a few moments. 'Give me your best shot –'

'You're a hard woman, Cass.'

Cass broke into a broad grin. 'So, how's life treating you, Rocco?'

He didn't answer, instead he made a lunge for her desk, which initially she mistook for an attempt at hugging.

'Oh my God, are those Fox's Cream Crunch?' he asked.

Cass whisked the biscuits away before he could grab them. 'Still not quite fast enough, eh? Never mind, maybe another time. What are you doing out here in the boondocks anyway?'

'Come on, you're a legend, baby. Cass's place – great gear, reasonable prices – and you always have such good stuff. You've got a great eye. Nice *chaise* by the way –' he tipped a nod towards the dark green brocade number she had recently finished re-upholstering, which was currently sitting in the shop's bay window. 'That won't be there long.'

Cass smiled. 'I've already had a couple of decent offers.'

Rocco grinned mischievously. 'Really? And you're still here selling tat – I'd have been long gone by now, honey.'

'What, and leave all this behind?' she said, heavy on irony. 'Besides one man's tat is another man's design classic. Talking of which, what is it you're looking for?'

'Peace on earth, goodwill to all men,' Rocco suggested.

'And besides that?'

Rocco shrugged. 'Couple of bedside cabinets, art deco, 1930's. Walnut veneer would be good, but to be honest, after the day I've had I'd settle for a half decent tea and some sympathy.'

Cass smiled. 'I can probably do you a good deal on all three.'

'You've got bedside cabinets?'

'Might have.'

Rocco's eyes lit up. Cass grinned. 'Darling, you'd never make a poker player.'

'What are they like?'

'Quite nice actually, cylindrical, still got both shelves. You mind the shop, I'll go and put the kettle on.'

'Have you got the cabinets here?' Rocco shouted after her, as Cass made her way into the back of the shop.

'No, but I think there are some pictures on the computer. Take a look. They should be in the file marked, stock, warehouse. Under bedside cabinets.'

'Bit obvious, darling, oh mind you, I think I'd rather look in the one marked "this year's diary."'

Cass laughed. 'Knock yourself out, Rocco, all you're

likely to find in there at the moment are my dental appointments, haircuts and choir stuff.'

'Oh pul'ease,' he whined. 'Don't say that – I was hoping for a few stars in the margin and marks out of ten.'

Cass went back to making the tea. She could hear him fiddling about, tapping on the keyboard and then he said, 'Isn't technology wonderful. Oh they're nice. Are those the original handles?'

'Yup, and they're not bad, few nicks and dents and there's been some repair to the veneer, just general wear and tear really, overall they're not bad for their age.'

'We are still talking about bedside cabinets here, are we?' he asked. Cass could hear the smile in his voice.

Rocco and Cass went back a long, long way, to the dim, distant days when Cass had been Katherine, and Rocco had been Richard, and Katherine had been married to Neil, and Richard had been dating girls.

She brought in a tray of tea and the biscuits. 'So what are you up to?'

'At the moment? Job wise we've got a complete makeover for some media type, art deco mad, she's bought one of the apartments in Vancouver House.'

'On the old wharf?'

'S'right. Cold Harbour. You'd have thought the marketing guys would have come up with something a little cheerier –'

Cass grinned. 'Very nice conversion though. I remember the days when it was full of junkies and rats down there.'

'Cynics might say it still is, they're just driving

Porsches and Beamers these days.' He looked at the photos on the computer screen. 'Presumably "very nice" means you'll be doubling the price of these if I say I'm really interested?'

Cass grinned. 'Not necessarily. I'm sure we can do a deal – how's your love life?'

Rocco took the mug of tea she handed him. 'Same ole, same ole, Nicky is still trying to persuade me that we should sell up and buy a fucking barge. Anyway I've told him I get seasick in the bath, but he won't have it. Anyway we're going over to Amsterdam to look at a Tjalk next week. And before you ask it's some kind of huge bloody canal boat. He's arranged for us to go sailing with the guys who own it. He's thinking party. I'm thinking Quells. How about you?'

'Nothing so exciting. Choir trip in three weeks, which should be fun – we're going to Majorca. Oh, and we've got a concert-come-dress rehearsal before we leave – can I put you down for a couple of tickets?'

'Don't see why not. And how's what's-his-name?'

'Gone but not forgotten.'

'What was *his* name, help me out here?'

Cass shrugged. 'No idea, he came, he went – you know what men are like.'

'You're making it up,' said Rocco, helping himself to the biscuit tin. 'Oh – oh, wait – it's on the tip of my tongue. Jack, Sam –'

'Gareth.'

'That's it. I remember now. Bit little boy lost, big soulful eyes. I thought you were quite keen?'

Cass dunked a custard cream. 'Which just confirms

what kind of judge of character *I* am. Bottom line? Once the initial lust had cooled down to a rolling boil, it took me about two days to work out that we had nothing in common. Worse, he was kind of picky and undermining. It's hard to describe but he was always making little jokes about my weight, or my hair and stuff and then when we were out, spent most of his time ogling other women. Oh and then he got blind drunk at Lucy's wedding – you know Lucy, runs the shop across the road? – and then tried to pick a fight with the best man. And he kept calling his ex-wife a brainless muppet, and I just knew that one day that brainless muppet would be me.'

'So you jumped ship?'

Cass nodded. 'I most certainly did. Best thing I ever did. It felt great when it was done and dusted.'

'And how did he take it?'

'Well, he was hurt, and then he was weepy, and then he was angry. And then a couple of weeks later, I was talking to a mutual acquaintance and sure enough, I'm the muppet now.'

Rocco pulled a sympathetic face. 'Not in my book, honey. Anyone else on the horizon?'

Cass laughed. 'What is this, *Mastermind*? No, there is no one on the horizon at this particular moment. I was thinking of maybe joining an online dating agency or putting an ad in the *Argos* and *Echo*, but to be honest at the moment I'm not that fussed.'

Rocco looked horrified. 'What do you mean *not that fussed*? You're fit, you're gorgeous, talented, great company –' he grinned. 'How am I doing?'

'So far, so good. Maybe I should get you to write my

lonely hearts ad. The thing is, Rocco, I keep picking idiots.'

'Oh God, is that all?' said Rocco. 'We all do that, baby, but realistically if you kiss enough frogs, one of them is just bound to turn into a prince. It's purely a numbers thing.'

Cass sighed. 'You want the truth, Rocco? To be perfectly honest I'm all frogged out.'

Rocco looked pained. 'Tell you what, how about coming to Amsterdam with us?' he said. 'There's plenty of room, according to Nicky. You'd be doing me a favour. Nicky can play the gay pirate prince, while you and me could go shopping or do the markets and the galleries. It'd be fun.'

Cass laughed. 'The only straight woman on a boat full of buff, tanned good-looking gay guys with perfect teeth and pecs to die for? My ego would most probably set itself to self-destruct.'

Rocco paused. 'Ummm, hadn't thought about it like that – tell you what, how about coming round to supper instead? You know how Nick likes to cook, he'd love to see you and we'll go through our too-tough-to-turn list, and see if we can't fit you up with someone. And we can take you on a guided tour of the new kitchen – did I tell you we've got to have the roof off the bloody house? Anyway he'll cook and while he's in there griddling and steaming away I'll show off, get horribly drunk and make a complete fool of myself. Remember last Christmas? It'll be just like that, only with less advocaat.'

Cass laughed. 'How could anyone possibly resist an invitation like that?'

Rocco grinned. 'How about Saturday night? Nicky's been threatening to drag me off to see some peculiar foreign film with subtitles, and bicycle baskets full of sardines. You'd be doing me a favour – honestly. Mind you we stick with the fish theme for supper. There is this great stall on the Saturday market we've just discovered, I could pick something up first thing – Nicky does this amazing thing with halibut and Gruyere?'

Cass pulled a face. 'Do I want to hear about this?'

'No really. It's absolute heaven. Oh and you could dig something or pull something up out of your allotment – something trendy and seasonal and Gordon Ramsay for the resident chef. It'll be just like *Ready Steady Cook*, only more stylish. Now, how about you go fish these cabinets out of storage and while you're gone I'll mind the shop and ring Nicky to let him know about Saturday?'

Sounded like a done deal.

*   *   *

Cass tried ringing Fiona when she finished work, in between feeding the cat and dog, but got the answer machine instead. She had a feeling that Fiona was probably there listening, screening the calls, and whether Fiona was right or wrong about Andy, Cass had to be careful about what she said in case he picked up the message. The last thing she wanted to do was add fuel to the fire. Cass sighed. It was making her feel guilty when really, none of it was her fault. So after the beep Cass made a real effort to sound warm and cheery and said, 'hi Fiona, hope you're well. Be great to hear from you if you've got a minute. See you on Tuesday if not before . . .'